I0773490

ARLAND: BOOK ONE

SECRET OF THE SANDSTORM SEA

AUSTIN PARENTI

I am grateful for the wise and caring community that supported me in writing this story.

To the faculty of the Frederick M. Supper Honors Program at Palm Beach Atlantic University, thank you for inspiring this tale with your lectures on Truth and Virtue.

To Daniel Grasso, Lillian Laitman, Nate Esbenshade, Tim DeMoss, Dave Doyle, Evan Berlanti, Stephen and Johnny Hedger, Mike and Diane Parenti, and Sarah Parenti, thank you for your advice, edits, and encouragement.

To my wife,
a truly loving and
courageous woman.

the pipyan mountains
galleran ruins
elos
onaga
the yellow sea
frek
the blue sea
yavyu highlands
the last forest
fallengard
lemuk
jayma
the mystic mountains
N
SOUTHERN ARLAND

CONTENTS

Chapter I

A STOWAWAY

Jay dunked his mop into a pail of greyberry juice and swabbed the crew quarters. Why greyberry juice? At that time, water was still the stuff of legend. Jay hated swabbing the deck. *Why swab it at all?* he thought. *It will only get sandy again!* But Jay needed the coin, and being a deckhand paid.

Frustrated, he stabbed the deck with his mop, lapping the dirt and debris, shifting the sand, and slaying barnacles. Jay's mind wandered to tasks he would rather do at home, like fixing the wheels on his chimney or painting the floors green. He was completely lost in thought when a sour growl rang in his ears and startled him back to reality. The poor boy slipped on his greyberry juice and fell to the deck.

"Rise, you dog!"

Jay sprang to his feet and wiped his sticky hands on his pants. He sloppily saluted the young woman who barked him to attention. She was Sakona, the first mate.

Slouching over, he asked "Yes, ma'am?"

"Captain wants to see you."

"Yes, ma'am."

"Quickly, dog!"

"Yes, ma'am!" Jay ran out of the crew quarters and into the

engine bay—and you would have, too. The captain had called upon him; it could mean anything! Perhaps he wanted to promote Jay. Or, perhaps he found out about Jay's true identity. Jay's body jittered with a nervous energy.

He zipped through the room, the air thick with greyberry steam. He dodged mammoth, churning gears and rugged engineers. A handsome harpoon mounted on the far wall caught Jay's eye. It distracted his stride as he passed the largest gear in the room (about five meters tall). Jay's right boot caught on the iron machine, and his foot slipped out as the boot rose higher and higher up the gear.

Jay tried climbing for the boot. When that failed, Jay snatched the harpoon and tried swatting at the boot.

Sakona entered the room and gasped: "What are you doing? You're going to break the gear!"

But Jay hurled the weapon at the gear to dislodge his boot. The harpoon missed its mark, sailed past the gear, across the room, and struck centimeters from Sakona, barely missing her head.

Now she was huffy, even nastier than before! Sakona marched up to Jay, grabbed his collar, and dragged him to the top deck and into the captain's quarters. One foot with boot and one foot without, Jay braced himself for the captain's rage.

"So, you want to be a sailor?" The captain's voice sounded surprisingly gentle.

Jay relaxed his stance. Maps and odd trinkets lie on a weathered, solid oak desk. Tall, crowded bookshelves stuffed with more maps and a few flags lined the room's sides. The captain himself stood before his desk, sporting a sparkling, sapphire coat with a black tricorn hat. A scraggly, golden-brown beard cloaked his bronze face, tanned from a lifetime of sailing.

"Um, yes Captain—aye Captain." Jay tried to seem relaxed.

He leaned against the bookshelf as his hands slipped into his pockets.

"What's your name?" His old eyes studied the boy.

"Stu." This, of course, was a lie.

"How old are you, Stu?"

"Fifteen, sir." Another lie, and a smooth one at that. Jay didn't mind this sort of lying—no one would let a 13-year-old hunt yavyu. Or so he thought.

"Hunting yavyu is dangerous," said the captain. He probed the boy's physique with his eyes, fixating on his arms and stature. No doubt the big, bearded man found the boy small and weak, which made Jay a little angry, so he stepped off the bookshelf.

"I've hunted 'em before and I'm tougher than I look." This time, only one of his statements was a lie.

Sakona, who stood silently next to her captain, chimed in, "I ought to throw you overboard for disrespecting Captain Zye like that!" Grabbing Jay by the arm, she nearly tore it off when she tried yanking him out of the room. Jay fought back, thrashing this way and that.

"Sakona, enough!" commanded the captain.

The scuffle ceased but the two locked eyes on each other, like wild rolfs. At last, Jay found the courage to look Sakona directly in her eyes, and, only then did he realize how young she was. Why, she was about Jay's age, maybe a year older at most!

A bell rang and ended their heated contest. A voice howled from the crow's nest: "Yavyu spotted off the starboard bow!"

Jay and Sakona's focus turned to their captain. Zye licked his lips as he pondered whether or not to accept Jay. He knew the boy was too young (Zye wasn't so easy to trick). Though he didn't believe Jay, he did believe *in* Jay—as he did most people. The captain nodded his head and smiled at the boy.

"Ready the longboat, Stu. You're up."

Jay smirked and nodded back at Zye. Jay was happier than he showed; he wanted to play it cool. He took one look at Sakona's sour face, smirked at her, and marched out of the cabin. He went to the bow of the ship and gazed at the horizon.

Now the ocean of this world was quite different from that of your world. This ocean was not made of water but sand. An endless sandstorm sea raged across the land. Sandwaves tossed to and fro, slashing at the ship—or rather, airship. Small grains of sand scraped Jay's bald cheeks.

The sailor in the crow's nest called, "Rise, ten meters!" A few moments later, a dainty steam whistle sounded from the engine room. The airship's propellers spun faster, and the vessel rose higher, just above the sandwaves.

The white sun beamed in the pale blue sky, heating the world like a furnace. New sailors soon learned that sweat and burns were unavoidable. Jay had read of these things in books, but only then, standing at the bow of the vessel, did he realize how uncomfortable sailing could be.

He bit his bottom lip to keep focus. Squinting his eyes, he searched the horizon for any sign of the yavyu.

"Stu!"

Jay, forgetting his fake name, didn't budge.

"Stu!" Sakona yelled, smacking Jay in the back of his head, "Longboat. *Now*."

"I'm going, I'm going!" Jay rolled his eyes and moved toward the longboat, sauntering to spite her. He climbed into the craft, followed by Groff the quartermaster, who was a short, chubby male of about forty years. He wore a brown sailor's coat, a yellowed top, dirty black pants, and boots so grand they looked of steel.

Groff was followed by a tall, muscular woman with blonde hair and burnt skin. She wore a wide, round hat, a faded-blue top and navy shorts. She was followed by a fierce-looking man with grey hair and weathered skin. He had a black outfit, a wooden pegleg, and a devilish grin. Jay tried in vain to hide his bootless foot from his esteemed crewmates.

The craft was small. It had one propeller, a rudder, a long line, and a score of harpoons. But best of all, it had a harpoon swivel-gun. Jay, like most boys his age, drooled at the sight of such a weapon. He desperately wanted to shoot that gun.

Groff yanked at a rope and plunged the longboat into the sea. The main vessel shrank into the distance as they drifted farther and farther into the endless ocean of sand. The rickety boat swayed and rolled with the waves. A breeze blew over the dingy, but that did little to chill the arid heat of the sea and sky.

The two men sharpened harpoons while the woman angled the rudder. A real adventure had begun, and Jay couldn't be more pleased. He felt his nerves tingle, but that was a good thing. All adventures need a little risk. Suddenly, the man with the pegleg tossed him a harpoon and line.

"Tie it, boy," the man ordered.

Jay searched the harpoon and found a wide hole at the far end of the shaft. He looped the rope through the hole and, tying the best knot he could, gave it back to the peglegged man, who seemed content. Jay watched as the man loaded the harpoon into the swivel-gun: First, he coiled the rope by the cannon. Next, he stuffed the spear down the long, tarry barrel. Lastly, he added black powder.

The tall woman in blue inspected Jay closely, "You ready for this, kid?"

"Sure, sure. I've hunted 'em before," said Jay.

The woman rolled her eyes, "Guess you don't need any tips."

"Well," Jay scratched his chin in thought, acting the part. "A few tips couldn't hurt. It's been a while since I fought one."

"Right," she said in disbelief. "We shoot a roped harpoon from that cannon. The line stays attached to the longboat, so we can reel it in. It's like fishing, but deadlier. We aim for the skull or the heart. The faster we kill it, the better."

"The longer it's out there," added the man, "the angrier it gets. And the angrier it gets, the deader we get."

"But you've killed them before, right?"

"Aye," said the man. "Six."

"Ten," said the woman. "What about you, Groff?"

"I only work the longboat. I don't kill 'em."

"But how many have you helped with?" she clarified.

"Fifteen or so."

"We'll be alright," said the man. He read Jay like a book. "As long as it's not an alpha, we'll be fine."

Looking out at the waves, Jay saw no signs of the yavyu. For a moment, he thought that perhaps the spotter was wrong. But as if to spite him, an immense tail fin rose out of the ocean. It was dark red and tall as the main ship's foremast.

"It's an alpha!" shouted Groff.

Jay regretted everything he had ever said or done to this point: lying to the captain, signing up for the voyage, being born, and so on. The peglegged man aimed the swivel-gun, lit the starter fuse, and shot his spear at the great fish. The harpoon struck! A deep moan bellowed from the beast. In anger, the fin slashed down, sending a rogue sandwave into the longboat.

Jay held on for his life. Sand splashed in his face and coursed down his shirt, but he held on tighter. After a few more moments of pain, the sand cleared. The peglegged man and the woman were gone—only Jay and Groff remained. For a moment, all was still. The waves settled and the line lay loose on the deck. Had the beast snapped the line?

Jay and Groff looked at one another, then to the sea. There

was no sign of the beast. Neither one spoke, both out of respect for their fellow sailors and for fear of the fish.

Suddenly, Jay heard another moan. The rope tightened, dragging the longboat forward. Jay moved to untie the cord and set the longboat free, but Groff stopped him.

"We can kill it." Groff rose to his feet and heaved on the rope with amazing power. He unlatched the line from the boat and with his bare hands, held the beast like a pet on a leash. To Jay, Groff somehow appeared larger than before, like a true hunter. With every tug, he drew the beast closer and closer. The yavyu roared and the surf replied with violent waves.

"Grab a harpoon!" said Groff.

But Jay was frozen. You must excuse his flub. If you've ever been as terrified as he, you know what it's like to hear and not understand. Groff, holding the rope in one hand, grabbed Jay and tossed him at the harpoon stash. Jay returned with a spear and held it up for Groff.

"No, not me. You! Get ready."

The yavyu breached the waves with another wail. Slowly, surely, it turned toward the longboat, flapping its tail fin, speeding toward its prey. Jay gulped. He rammed the spear into the cannon—as the peglegged man had—but Jay blanked on what to do next. The beast swam closer and closer. Groff pulled hard on the line, keeping the longboat steady amid the wild waves.

"Stu, light it!"

At last, Jay remembered the black powder and lighter. He dashed across the deck, looking for both, dreading they washed overboard. Miraculously, he found both items wedged between the guard rails. He sped back to the cannon, poured in a heap of black powder, and lit the fuse.

The cannon fired, launching the harpoon into the air, but it missed the beast entirely. Groff wailed, flung Jay aside, and snatched two harpoons for himself. The yavyu was upon them with its right fin raised, ready to smash the boat to bits. With eyes fixed on the yavyu, Groff aimed and hurled the first spear, then the second. Both harpoons struck the creature's chest.

The terrible fish leaned away from the longboat, wailing and groaning. It frantically slapped its tailfin against the sea. Then, at once, the yavyu ceased and floated still. Jay and Groff exhaled as the longboat settled with the waves.

Like all fish of the sandstorm ocean, yavyu are bizarre creatures. Though they are strikingly strong and large, their bones are hollow, which makes them light enough to sail through the windy air. As such, hunters could drag their carcasses by a single rope.

Groff and Jay easily dragged their prize back to the vessel. The crew hauled up the fish. It was no more than a pod with fins and a tail. Jay found it far friendlier now that it was dead.

When Jay and Groff hoisted the long boat out of the sand sea and stepped on deck, shipmates gathered around them. Jay thought they had come to celebrate, and perhaps they had, but when they saw that only two of the four sailors returned, they kept silent and still.

Sakona carved her way to the front of the company, staring at Jay and Groff. "Where are the other two?"

Groff sighed and took Sakona to the helm, where Captain Zye stood. Jay watched Groff's gestures—counting, pointing, and shaping. Apparently, he was describing the tail-fin slap, the loss of the sailors, Jay's failed shot, and the final catch. When he finished his tale, Sakona chuckled and crossed her arms.

"Liar!" she hollered, turning back to Jay. "You've got no hunting experience at all. I bet if you hadn't lied, we wouldn't have lost two sailors."

"Well, it wasn't quite his fault," started Groff.

"Sakona, silence!" said Captain Zye. "Show some respect for our fallen members."

But the damage was already done. Jay felt a sudden knot in his stomach. It was a grave thing to consider; two people were gone, and it might have been his fault.

He tried to speak but he found that he had lost the strength in his throat. The best he could muster was an awkward shrug and hair-scratch. He felt and looked pathetic, missing a boot and hair full of sand. The embarrassed stowaway showed himself below deck.

Chapter II

SCHEMES OF THE GREEN-CAPPED GIRL

Long days passed, and Jay seldom left the crew quarters. He tried to act natural, but he didn't fool anyone. He swabbed the deck and dusted the hammocks, but he spent most of his time drowning in a sea of guilt. He often thought of the man and woman from the longboat who fell to the yavyu and wondered, *Was their fate really my fault?*

He only left the cabin twice a day, once to grab a meal and once to try and spy his home on the horizon. The latter he only did when Sakona and the captain weren't around.

One good thing happened to Jay in those days: he found a new boot—bright and brown—though it didn't fit quite as snug, nor match with his black one, but Jay didn't mind. He thought the mismatched style might catch on.

By the first evening, his shipmates had cleaned out the entire yavyu—separating its meat and oil into barrels—and tossed its carcass overboard. The meat was especially tender and therefore, pricy. But even more costly was the oil, which had many uses: it burned in grand lighthouses on many islands; it greased the gears of airships; in some lands, they used it to make deadly weapons.

Days later, Jay saw his homeland: the twin mountains of

Onaga. It was a humbling sight. Jay's entire world was but a grain in an endless ocean. When the airship docked on the western mountain, Jay spied out the gangplank. He wanted to leave quickly, thinking Sakona or Captain Zye would scold him, and he wasn't in the mood for that. Of course, that meant he would leave without any coin, but he wouldn't dare to ask for his wage.

Sakona was nowhere to be seen, but Captain Zye stood by the bow with his back to the gangplank. Jay took a breath and strode quietly across the deck. As he neared the gangplank, the captain spotted him.

"Stu! Stu!" he called. But Jay was already off the brig. He slipped away, down the fishing town's muddy streets.

He climbed to a point overlooking the docks. Stopping to catch his breath, he gazed back at the ship. The Noble Rogue was her name, and she was the most beautiful craft Jay had ever seen. She had a rich, oak hull and royal blue sails. Her curves were seamless, like silk robes on a queen. Her golden propellers shined and bent with ease.

After a moment or two more, Jay started toward his house, located at the top of the mountain. He left the fishing town behind and prepared for the long climb home.

But on the outskirts of the town, he bumped into a guard of six sluggish men. Five wore rusty knight's armor and pointy helmets. The sixth, the leader, was portlier than the rest and wore a long, maroon cape patterned with muddy splotches. His head was dotted with a graceful, silver crown. The town called him 'the Colonel,' and he was as proud as he was dumb.

When the guards saw Jay, they seized him at once. The Colonel waddled up to Jay, spitting as he spoke in his usual singsongy, mountainous accent.

"Jay, ye feisty rodent. Ye haven't paid your dues!"

"Well, I was out… earning them for you, Colonel," said Jay,

wiping the spit from his forehead. He put on the most charming face he could. "I was fishing. In fact, I left my whole pay cut with the captain. If you'd like your dues, you can chat with *him*." Jay started to walk away, but the Colonel pulled him back.

"You know what I like more than a boring story? Dues. Pay 'em."

The Colonel's guards laughed and that ticked Jay off, but he took a breath and said, "I'm sorry, did I use big words? Let me try again: 'Me no have money. Go talk to boat boss.'" Jay shot the Colonel a cheeky grin.

But the Colonel wasn't amused. His forehead wrinkled with frowny lines and his nostrils flared as he shouted for his guards to grab Jay. "Come along boy! Ye can sweat out your dues in the tower."

Jay fought with the guards, trying to break free. "Oh c'mon! I didn't mean it! Look, I've got your money, it's just not here, it's down by the docks."

A loud voice suddenly pierced through the air. "Colonel, stop that!" A little girl marched toward the Colonel. She was pale, having spent much time indoors, reading books. Above her braided black hair, she sported a green cap. The rest of her wardrobe was predictable for Onagans: sand-goggles, stained clothes, and muddied boots.

"Perl!" said Jay with relief.

But she ignored Jay and stormed right up to the Colonel, pressing her index-finger against his armor and trying to push him, though, of course, the portly Colonel wouldn't budge.

"Let him go," Perl said.

She stood fearless before the massive man. The Colonel held a stern gaze on her for a moment, then licked his lips and smiled.

"Ye know what it'll cost ye."

Perl knew he was proud and dumb. She knew exactly how to

use that against him. She growled, "You're on."

The Colonel's guard circled around the two and cheered on their leader. Perl and her enemy locked eyes and paced back and forth.

"If I win" spoke the Colonel, "Ye and the boy stay with me—the boy as my pet and ye as my squire. If I lose, he goes free."

"Deal."

The Colonel stopped and heaved in a breath of air. In a commanding voice, he declared, "I run in fields yet try to prove why ye shall never see me move."

For a moment, Perl's face was plain in thought. Then she smirked. "A fence."

The Colonel stomped on the ground and his guard roared in wrath. Perl spoke her riddle. "The more you leave, the more you take. I'll leave you hoping for a break."

A hearty chuckle escaped the Colonel. He spat out the answer, "Footsteps. We've heard that one before!"

His gang cheered. He stepped toward Perl, towering over her. "My tongue cannot speak, my soul cannot shriek, I'm too heavy to sneak, no pits, yet I reek."

Perl was stumped. She never heard this one before. She tried to look calm, but her eyes darted to and fro, searching for a hint. Jay, on the other hand, grew a bit anxious. He knew the answer as soon as the Colonel spoke the last phrase. But he dared not speak up. Instead, he twitched his left foot back and forth, tapping on the ground.

Perl noticed his foot and his mismatched boots. "A boot!"

The Colonel's face went bland. His eyes stayed on Perl. "Your turn."

Perl, wishing to prolong the game and prove her smarts, spoke an easy riddle: "It's shorter than the rest, but when you're happy, you raise it up like it's the best."

The Colonel paced in deep thought. He hushed his gang and clogged his ears with his fingers to better concentrate. After an absurd amount of time, he chirped: "Me thumb! Ha!"

Perl gave Jay a proud look—the kind one makes before trying a dangerous feat. But Jay didn't like the risk she was taking.

"When needed," said the Colonel, "I'm tossed away. When task is done, I'm brought back to stay."

Perl smiled. She paced and thought carefully. She imagined farms and fields, foods and creatures, homes and shops—none satisfied the riddle. She thought of more abstract things, like time, light, histories, and truths—still nothing fit. She worried.

"Come along, Perly," said the Colonel, "I've won."

Perl's mind flew over everything she had ever learned. She thought of every nook and cranny on Onaga. Nothing fit the Colonel's riddle. She looked to Jay who shrugged his shoulders in anger. She tried to think of places outside of Onaga—though she never left the island herself. She imagined herself on a boat, raising the anchor and pulling away from the harbor. Then it hit her.

"An anchor!" cried Perl.

Jay breathed in relief. Perl thought hard before posing her next riddle. She posed the hardest one she knew.

"I have as many sisters as brothers, but each brother has only half as many brothers as sisters. How many of us are there?"

The Colonel clenched his fists, "That didn't even rhyme! And ye know I can't do math."

"You didn't say it had to rhyme," snapped Perl. "Do you forfeit?"

The Colonel frowned and gathered his guards around him. They huddled up and tried hard to answer the riddle. Their debate grew louder. One guard howled at another. Someone threw a punch and a brawl ensued.

"Enough!" roared the Colonel, but his command went un-heard.

In the chaos, Perl grabbed Jay's hand and slipped off the path, into a rocky forest, and away from the town. Once a good distance away from the Colonel's guard, they slowed their pace to a walk. Though he didn't want to admit it, Jay choked out a thank you.

"You're welcome. I love embarrassing the Colonel."

"You almost lost though… the one about the boot."

"Almost. But as always, I turned out to be the smarter."

Jay rolled his eyes and kept quiet. He didn't like to argue with Perl, even when he knew it was what she needed.

"How was the yavyu hunt?"

"Fine, fine." He tried not to think of the fallen sailors. "Caught a pretty big fish."

Perl knew something was off, but she didn't pry. "So, you *did* earn some coins. Good move, hiding them from the Colonel."

"Well, no. That's the thing, they didn't exactly pay me."

"What! Why? Did they figure out your age and all?"

"Something like that."

"Great. That's great," said Perl sarcastically. She paced back and forth. "How are we going to pay the Colonel's dues?"

Jay pondered for a moment. He was out of ideas except for one old idea, maybe the oldest one he'd ever had. "We could leave."

"Not this again."

"C'mon, think about it! There's a whole world out there to see. There's bound to be a better place than this."

Perl nodded along, having heard it all before. "Stop with that. We need a real plan. Let's go; I'll take some coins from the mansion."

"Stealing's wrong."

"Says the stowaway. Come on!"

The duo walked up the mountain, staying off the main road. Climbing higher, they left behind the docks, the village, and the rocky forest. They crossed grand farms, rolling green hills, and lush woodlands. But this beautiful land was not for play. Fences selfishly hogged every field and wood.

They came to a fork in the road. Jay turned toward home, but Perl pulled him the other way.

"C'mon, Jay. I told you—we've got to stop by the mansion!"

"Now?"

"Yes! The Colonel knows where we live. He's probably on his way up now."

"Fine, but make it quick. I don't like this."

"When he comes," said Perl, "We either pay his dues, or we go to the tower." She yanked Jay right and they continued down the path.

By and by, they came to a magnificent, wooden gate. The name 'Mikil' was carved along the top. Two grand oak trees stood tall before the gate, like sentinels. Perl and Jay glanced up and down the path. Seeing and hearing nothing, they moved toward the fence, which Jay promptly boosted Perl over.

"Whistle if you see the Colonel!" and with that, Perl dashed away.

Jay paced about the path, peering this way and that. After a few minutes, Jay began to worry. Over the fence rolled acres of hills. A long way off there stood a mansion (anything with more than one chimney was a mansion to Jay, and this home had seven). Suddenly, he saw Perl sprinting away from the house over the farthest hill.

A woman who appeared at the front door of the mansion yelled. Shortly after, three men piled out of the home and chased after Perl. She was halfway to the gate when Jay heard footsteps down the road. The Colonel and his guards strode toward the gate.

He thought about running and saving himself. He nearly did, but a small twinge in his chest held him back. He couldn't leave Perl. He leaned over the fence and blew a warning whistle. With moments to spare, Jay latched onto the oak tree before him. He pulled and tugged and shimmied. Jay was a poor climber on a normal day, but panic gave him the push he needed. He reached the tree's crown just in time and settled himself among the leaves.

He tried to view the field and see Perl, but the leaves and branches were too thick. He could only hope for her safety. Jay watched as the Colonel and his guard marched underneath the tree and through the gate. He lost sight of them. He heard yelling and running and drawing of swords. Thuds and clashes rang throughout the field.

At last Perl flopped over the fence. "Jay?" whispered she, looking around in a panic. Jay slid down the tree, grabbed Perl's hand, and dashed up the path.

Chapter III

UNEXPECTED GUESTS

Jay and Perl ran all the way to their home nestled near the mountain's peak. Onaga was like a rock sandwich: the top and bottom were stony and plain, but the middle was rich and grassy. Jay and Perl made the best of their arid, windy land.

The house was more of a shack than a home, slanting a bit more than usual today. It was made of fallen trees, cobblestone, clay, and mud. There were no glass windows—only holes poked in the wood or gaps in the stone. But it was still home. They had lived there for a few years, ever since they ran away together. Over time, they grew close, but in the way that a brother and sister do. Jay had no feelings of romance toward Perl.

They loved the sand-ocean view and the clean air. Only a year or two earlier, Jay enjoyed playing make-believe (for one knows it is much easier to imagine your home a castle when it is set high on a mountain).

Although they both enjoyed reading, it was mostly Perl's hobby. She collected books from all over the island. Some she even found in old ruins and deep caves. Most people didn't have books anymore, but Jay and Perl's home was filled with them. Perl loved history books, maps, and old letters while Jay read story books and logic lessons.

With all the running and chasing of the day, the two looked forward to food and rest. They strolled toward their home's front door.

"So," started Jay. "Did you get any coins?"

"No. She was awake."

"Who?"

"My mom. She usually sleeps all day. But when I snuck into her bedroom this time, she wasn't there. I looked for loose coins, but she must have heard me. In a flash, she and her servants came through the door. She screamed, and they tried to grab me, so I sprinted out of the mansion. They were still chasing me when I heard your whistle, so I ran straight for the gate."

"Why would you do that? I whistled because the Colonel was coming!"

"I know. So when the Colonel opened the gate, he saw a mob of servants running toward him. He thought they were going to attack him, so he and his guard drew their swords."

"Oh," Jay nodded, impressed. "Did anyone die?"

"Nah." Perl sighed, "I think they figured it out pretty fast. But by then I had lobbed myself over the fence and found you."

"Not bad, kiddo." Jay smiled at Perl which made her blush. At last, the two arrived at their front door and entered. But to their great surprise, they found a visitor.

A Woman rose from her seat at the round dinner table, moving to greet Jay and Perl. Her skin was fair, her hair was blonde, and her pale blue eyes were captivating. She carried herself with elegance and strength. She wore a finely woven white blouse, a red satin sash, black trousers, and glossy brown boots. It was the finest and cleanest outfit Jay and Perl had ever seen. She looked about twenty years old.

"You must be Jay," said she, her sweet voice fluttering across the room.

You or I would have questioned the unexpected Woman at once, because it's an odd—an alarming—thing to find a stranger in our home. But to Jay, it seemed quite alright. This wasn't the first time they happened upon an unexpected guest. Jay would often chase vagabonds out of their home with a stick (since they couldn't afford a lock and key to the front door). But there was something different about this guest. She seemed safe and delightful.

Jay stared at the beautiful Woman and grinned, "That's me. Though I would've said so no matter whose name you called." That made the Woman giggle, so Jay followed it up by leaning against the doorframe and asking, "What can I do for you?" He was absolutely smitten with their guest.

"And what are you doing in our home?!" demanded Perl. She was absolutely *not* smitten with their guest.

"Is that any way to treat a visitor?" returned the Woman. "In fact, I'm rather parched. It was a long hike from the village. Perhaps, Jay, your friend might fetch us some tea?" Her eyes never left Jay's and he found it hard to take his from hers.

"Great idea. Perl, do you mind?"

Perl, annoyed by his command, bit her tongue and excused herself without a word. The Woman returned to her seat, and Jay followed suit. They sat in silence for a moment. Jay nervously tapped his fingers on the table. She was just so alluring. He tried to think of a clever line, but nothing came to mind. She, on the other hand, seemed lost in thought. She studied Jay, then her surroundings.

Jay and Perl's home was small but quaint. They built most of their furniture and, honestly, it showed. But it was all designed for comfort or fun—like the table that spun like a top. This was handy when Jay and Perl wished to trade dishes. Or the rolling-fireplace that they could move to the coldest parts of the house. In a normal home, smoke would be an issue, but they popped holes in their ceiling to remedy the fact.

At last, she broke the silence.

"How old are you, Jay?"

"Thirteen."

"And are you happy?" The Woman glanced about the disheveled home.

Jay chuckled at this, as if the question was a waste of breath. "I could be happier, if that's what you're getting at."

"Yes—and I think I know why. Jay, it seems to me that you have so much potential and it's all wasted here."

"Is that so?"

"Yes. Look around: your home is falling apart, and your best friend is a thief. You can be so much more. You can have so much more."

"I suppose you can help me with that." Jay crossed his arms. A little doubt seeped in as he wondered if the Woman was only a merchant, trying to sell him something.

"I know you, Jay. You're the kind of boy who stares at the horizon. You watch ships sail away every morning, wondering when it's going to be your turn, isn't that right?"

At this, Jay became somber, even worried. How did she know that about him?

"Well now, it's your turn," she continued. "I want you to come with me. You can serve on my crew. We'll sail the seas and explore the farthest lands together."

He felt his heart leap in his chest, but he kept his cool. Why, only an hour earlier he was longing for the chance to leave. Fate, it seemed, was at work. He scratched his chin to hide his smile. But that silly twinge in his chest came back. "Can Perl come?"

"Well, no. There's only so much room on my sloop, and I need the strongest people I can get."

Jay leaned back. "I'll think about it."

"Jay, you're stronger than you know. There is something so unique and special about you, you just don't know it yet. You have a gift, and if you come with me, we'll discover it together."

Though it sounded too good to be true, Jay couldn't help but dream. Her words startled his heart, playing on old desires.

Perl barreled back into the room, "What did I miss?"

She slid cups of tea across the table and sat herself down. Jay slurped at his drink and found it was cold (Perl had grown impatient waiting for the greyberry juice to boil—wanting to hear what was being said).

The Woman answered, "I was telling your friend how special he is, and how he ought to believe it himself."

Perl, distrusting the Woman, wanted to argue. She searched for a flaw in her words but found none.

The Woman turned back to Jay and said, "Take the night to think about it. My sloop leaves from the dock tomorrow morning. You'll find me there."

The guest rose and bid her hosts farewell. She gracefully walked out the door. She hadn't tried the tea. Perl's squinting eyes lingered on the door.

"Who was she? What did she say?"

"I don't know, but she wants me to come on an adventure with her."

"You said no, right?"

"I said I'd think about it."

"Think about it? Are you crazy?"

"Since when was thinking crazy?"

"Jay, she's a total stranger, you don't even know her name!"

"I forgot to ask is all, I'm sure she would've told me."

"And how did she know your name? Isn't that at all suspicious?"

"C'mon, she probably just asked around about me."

"Why are you defending her?"

"I'm not! I'm…" Jay stood and paced across his home's torn floors and leaned on a rickety wall, beneath the cracked ceiling. "Look around! Do you want to spend the rest of your life on Onaga?"

"Why not? Why do you want to leave so badly?"

"I don't know," he walked over to a window and gazed through it. Golden sandwaves rippled on and on, shimmering under a dim red sky. A few airships sailed toward a slim, thin horizon, where a thick fog wrapped the towering Pipyan Mountains in a silver blanket. More than anything, Jay wanted to be out there, riding the glittering waves into the unknown. "Ken and Hera left last year and Skuppo left years before that. They're out there, seeing the world, but they didn't want to leave half as bad as I do. It's not fair. When's it going to be my turn?"

"I guess we're meant to be the ones who stay."

"That's stupid."

"No, it's not! We get to have a home and some friends, right? We know almost everyone in town. We can't have friends if we're always leaving, always going."

"Yeah? Well, we can't have friends if they keep leaving us, either."

This all had more to do with Jay's heart than mind (though the two are not completely separate, of course). No matter how much Perl reasoned, it wouldn't move Jay's will. He wanted adventure and he couldn't explain why.

"Well I'm not going with you. Are you okay with leaving me here? You know my mom's crazy. She kicked me out! I can't ever go home. I'm all alone." Tears welled in her eyes. She took a deep breath. "I get it. You can't be stuck here your whole life because of me. If you want to leave, that's fine. But I'm not going with you. Not with her."

Seeing Perl cry made Jay feel guilty. His guilt turned to anger, and his anger turned to words.

"You want me here because you need me to work and pay for everything. That's why you saved me from the guard."

"I saved you because you're my friend!" bawled Perl. "Jay, don't you dare go with that woman."

"What's wrong with her? Why do you hate her?"

"I don't know. I have a bad feeling about her." Perl searched for reasons, but she found none. She knew there was more to her feelings, but she lacked the words to express them. She stormed off to her bedroom, shutting the curtain behind her.

Jay sighed as he drifted to the hammock in his bedroom. He stared at the ceiling, tossing, turning, and swinging. No matter which way his thoughts turned, they each led back to his oldest wish: to sail the seas.

There was no logic to it, no deep rationale. In fact, it felt out of his control, as if someone else had put it there. And what better time to follow the call? When might he ever get this chance again? But fate was at work: as he thought over these very things, he heard a knock on the door.

Jay slipped out of hammock and into the living room to find Perl already opening the door—she had shrugged off her anger in favor of curiosity. In rushed a young man with a desperate look on his face.

He slammed the door behind him. Lunging for the window, he looked out, and shut the blinds. He clutched his stomach in pain.

"Food!" he pled in a hoarse voice.

Perl raised her eyebrows: "What?"

"Food!"

Perl rolled her eyes at the madness of the day and left for

the kitchen. Jay brought the man to the dinner table and sat him down. He was tall, lanky, and pale with dusty hair. He had kind, earthy-green eyes, round as portholes. Sweat covered a fledgling handsome face. He was a few adventures and years short of full maturity.

His clothes were quite silly to Jay and Perl. Some parts appeared like armor, but were wooden, not metal, and vines and ivy held it together in place of leather straps.

The man's eyes darted all over the room as he tried to calm down. He smiled and wiped the sweat from his face. But every few moments, the man looked over his shoulder, out the window.

Perl returned with a few biscuits. She barely laid the platter on the table when the man snatched it from her hands. He scarfed down the biscuits one by one, gobbling them whole. Not knowing what to say or do, Jay stared at the all-consuming man. When he finished his meal, the man swallowed hard.

"Water!"

"Sure, and I'll get you a few fairies and elves while I'm at it," said Perl, sarcastically.

"Drink!"

This time, Jay ran to the kitchen and brought him a glass of greyberry juice. The man downed it in a single gulp and handed it back to Jay, suggesting he go fetch more. Three trips later, the guest was quenched. He eased back into his chair and closed his eyes.

A few moments passed and the guest's eyes remained shut.

"Is he dead?" whispered Perl.

Then the man let out a loud snore. You must forgive the man's bad manners. A hefty meal after a desperate run always puts me to sleep, too.

Jay had quite enough of this nonsense. He stormed over to

the guest and kicked his chair, waking him at once. Startled, the man awoke and resumed his paranoid stance. He ran to the window again and glanced cautiously outside. Perl could not contain her curiosity. She joined him at the window but saw nothing out of the ordinary.

"What are you looking for? I don't see anything!"

"I'll believe it if *he* says so." The man's voice was less hoarse now. He pointed to Jay and gestured to the window.

"My eyesight is fine, you know!" growled Perl."

"We're not doing that kind of looking, little missy. Go on now!"

Jay drew near the window. He leaned two hands on the ledge and took a long look outside. Nothing and silence.

"Nothing," said Jay.

"Excellent, excellent!" the guest said. He clapped his hands with joy. "Now come here. Closer. We don't have much time." Jay and Perl drew near to the guest. He put his hand on Jay's shoulder. "I'm Bobo. I've been sent here to find you. We need to get you off this island and sail south. There's a haven there. It's not safe here. You can come too, little missy. It's probably not safe for you, either."

But Jay was frustrated and tired. "What are you talking about?! How do you know me? What's this all about?"

"Sorry, sorry," Bobo smacked his head, "of course, of course. This is all probably a lot for you to take in. Plain and simple: there's a war going on. A secret war. No one knows about it because they don't want you to know. The world as you think you know it is a lie."

Perl gasped and Jay doubted.

"You're special, Jay. You have a gift. The others—the enemy—they want to use you as a weapon. But I've been sent to bring you to our sanctuary to be trained. Your gift can be used for good."

"What gift?!" laughed Jay at how ridiculous it all sounded. "You clearly don't know me at all, you or the other woman."

"Woman? So, she's been here. And you're still here?"

"She tried to convince Jay to go on some adventure," said Perl (with a great deal of attitude).

"You need to trust me," said Bobo. "I can explain everything later, but we have to get off this island."

"No," said Jay with a firmness that even rattled Perl. "I'm not going with you." You see, deep down, Jay was afraid—very afraid. While his first guest invited him on a safe and lavish trip, his second guest invited him on a daring, dangerous one. Had he then known the nature of adventure, Jay might have made a wiser choice.

Bobo, a silly man, became rather sober. His eyes locked on Perl's bookshelves. He walked toward them and glanced over the titles.

"You've read these?"

"Yes!" declared Perl.

"A few," said Jay.

Bobo breathed deeply and said, "These stories you've read, they tell the same story, the only story. Good and evil. Good: the virtues—freedom, joy, truth, and love—the enemy vomits at the thought of them. I stand here and confess that I am a servant of the Good, that I love the Good."

Perl's eyes stayed on Bobo; his words enchanted her. But Jay set his eyes on the ground.

"Jay," Bobo held out his hand, "you can trust me."

"I'll think about it," said Jay, walking toward his bedroom.

"Jay," said Perl, "we need to think about this now!"

"Good night." Jay entered his room and closed the curtain behind him. Sitting on the hard, wooden floor with his back to a creaking wall, he held his head in thought. The Woman looked strong and wealthy. Bobo looked weak and pathetic. But if he chose to follow the Woman, he'd have to leave behind Perl. Was that something he could do?

Chapter IV

FLIGHT FROM ONAGA

Jay awoke early the next morning—as he did every day. He climbed through one of the many holes in his ceiling and sat on the roof. From there he watched the black sky change from purple to red to blue. He gazed down the mountain at the early-bird boats, floating away from Onaga, sails full of wind. Jay imagined himself standing at the bow of the farthest brig, his face bathed in the growing light with a cool breeze blowing down his shirt, biting him awake. What undiscovered lands lay just beyond that horizon? What unseen wonders awaited his gaze?

He knew that today was the day to leave, either with Bobo or the mysterious Woman, and he struggled to make the choice. In the end, he reasoned the following: Bobo wanted to take Jay to some sort of haven, and that didn't sound adventurous at all. It sounded more like hiding. The Woman, however, wasn't running from anyone. She wanted to explore the world, and she wanted Jay by her side.

But what of Perl? Even though she was only twelve, she was a strong girl. Perhaps she would be okay. Perhaps she would join Bobo on his adventure. One day, she and Jay might meet again and swap tales. But as he thought about these things, Jay felt a sharp twinge in his chest. So he forced himself to stop thinking and start doing.

Quiet as a wookapod, he gathered his belongings into a satchel (two sets of clothes, a rusty dagger, and a few books). As he crept through his home, he snuck past Bobo, who was fast asleep on the spinning dinner table, slowly turning round and round. Jay felt grateful for Bobo's loud snores; they covered his creaking footsteps. He left his home, and feeling quite victorious, slammed the door shut. Bobo's snoring stopped. Worried Bobo woke, Jay ran down the mountain as dim sunlight dripped over the world.

He blitzed through the fishing town. Sailors, by the dozens, lugged supplies from shops to ships. Jay followed the parade to the docks where he found a score of airships preparing for liftoff. Some were small, fishing sloops. Others were grand galleons—once used for war, now altered to hunt yavyu. Jay kept his head down as he walked by the Noble Rogue and her crew. He remembered his failure on the longboat and the loss of those sailors. Jay had nearly passed by the Rogue when her captain spotted him.

"Stu!" he said with joy.

Jay sank with shame as Captain Zye approached.

"Where'd you go yesterday?" asked the captain, "I never paid you." He held out his hand and dropped a few coins into Jay's.

"Sir?" was the best he could muster—Jay was shocked.

"Stu, listen to me very carefully. What happened to my sailors is not your fault. Groff made that clear. That was an alpha yavyu. Had we known, we wouldn't have sent anyone out there. Don't waste your time feeling guilty for something that's not your fault."

Jay felt halfway better, but there was still another matter. "But I lied to you. I had never hunted before."

Captain Zye scratched his chin and squinted his eyes. "Well, then I want you take these coins with a promise: be honest. I think if you told me the truth, I still would have let you stay. If you want a second chance, you're welcome to it."

Normally, Jay wasn't a fan of promises. He thought they were for kids, but this was a special case. He shook the captain's hand. "Thanks. But I'm not sure your first mate would be happy about that."

Captain Zye nodded, "That's true. But I'm her captain and her father."

"Oh! Well, I guess she gets her personality from her mother."

The captain bellowed a mighty laugh. "Now that's the truth. But you know, I think she could use a friend like you." He eased back and thought for a moment. "One more thing. Why did you lie in the first place?"

Jay spoke the truth, "Well, I wanted to be out there… in the action. I can't explain it."

"I know exactly what you mean." The captain smiled; his eyes full of good memories. His expression stirred, remembering a painful one. "Remember not to leave anyone important behind. That's the hardest thing for men like us." He stepped back and turned toward his brig. "See you soon, Stu."

"Jay. My real name's Jay."

Captain Zye smiled and replied, "Mine's Carack."

While Carack Zye left for the Noble Rogue, Jay stood still, touched by the captain's grace. He thought about his eerie last words—to not leave anyone important behind. And he thought of the promise he made: to be honest.

He realized he had not been honest with Perl and Bobo. He should have told Perl everything the Woman said—that she would not allow Perl to come on the adventure. With Bobo, he should have confessed his fears. He should have confessed those fears to himself, first. He realized that the Woman had not been honest with him—she didn't tell her name, nor anything of the secret war.

Jay stuffed the coins in his pocket and made ready to dash home when he heard a cool voice, calling "Jay! You decided to come after all."

Jay turned around and found the enchanting Woman standing before him. She took his hand and walked him down the docks. Jay was terrified. He didn't know what to do. He wanted to run, but as soon as the thought crossed his mind, the Woman's grip tightened.

"I'm so happy you're here, Jay. My crew has heard all about you."

They marched toward the end of the dock, where a small, angular sloop made ready for takeoff. It had a pale, birch hull with metal plating. Crimson-red sails cast out from a slim, white mast. The sailors were thin, weathered, and blue as they loaded supply barrels and angled the sails.

Jay's eyes locked on the hollow sloop. His heart beat wildly in his chest.

"You know what," said Jay, "I think I've changed my mind. I'll be going now." Jay stopped walking and tried to pull his hand away, but the Woman gripped harder. She smiled and set her gentle eyes on Jay's.

"Are you sure?"

Jay nodded. Suddenly, he felt something hit him. His vision went black.

*   *   *

When Jay woke up, everything looked fuzzy. He had a splitting headache and reached on the back of his head, feeling a bump. As he tried to get up, he noticed the floor was rough and scratchy. He heard a course wind and fast thumping like a drum.

His vision came into focus, and he noticed a small, white spot before him—a window! It was barred with no glass. Jay stumbled over to it. At first, it was too bright to see, and wind blew in his face. He squinted his eyes and saw the rolling sandstorm ocean. Jay was on the Woman's airship.

The thumping came from the boat's razor-sharp, red propellers that sliced through the air. The sloop sailed fast over the sea below. In the distance, Jay saw his home islands shrinking farther and farther away. He felt empty. Hope slipped out, over the horizon as Onaga vanished completely. He realized he might never see his home again. He thought of its grassy fields, tall woods, and rocky peaks; he thought of his cozy home and broken fireplace. He thought of Perl. He cursed himself, thinking of her, all alone. Who would take care of her now?

Then despair joined his anger. Where was the ship going? What was the Woman going to do with him? His mind filled with all sorts of scary thoughts, horrid thoughts! He might be fed to a giant beast, or crushed by a mammoth stone, or chained in a cold, dark dungeon forever.

He resolved to escape. He searched the dark floorboards for anything that could help him, but he found nothing. He scurried back to the window and tried to pry out the bars, but they wouldn't budge. He noticed something—in the distance, a small dark item grew larger and larger. It was a brig! As it sailed closer, Jay saw the dark oak hull and royal-blue sails. It was the Noble Rogue, armed with cannons and sailing straight for him. Jay rejoiced, wondering, *Had they seen the Woman kidnap me?*

Jay knew he ought to keep trying to free himself. It would do his saviors no good if they destroyed the Woman's sloop with him still on board. He studied his prison. The room was bare, save for a large metal door opposite the window—locked, of course. But dangling from the ceiling was an unlit lantern.

Jay heard the Woman's sailors scurry about, drawing blades and loading cannon balls. The fighting began. The thumping of the Noble Rogue's propellers beat loud against the Woman's sloop. Then Jay heard a score of cannon blasts. A short whistle came after, followed by the crunching of wood and metal. Jay fell on his face as the Woman's sloop rocked to and fro. The Noble Rogue struck first.

Moving faster than his thoughts, Jay unhooked the lantern from the ceiling. He checked it for loose oil and, finding some, dripped it on the wooden wall's planks to loosen the nails. He used the lantern as a crowbar, digging its sharpest corner into a gap. He wedged and pulled with all his might. Bit by bit, the plank loosened. He took the lantern and bashed it against the plank until it popped out of the wall.

With no time to lose, Jay shimmied through the opening, taking a few nasty splinters with him. He had no idea which way to go, so he ran straight—it felt like a good choice. All around him, a fierce battle raged. Cannon fire exploded on both ships. Sailors dashed about the cabin in a frenzy. Many of the Woman's crew lay on the floor, cold.

Her voice called from somewhere above deck: "Prepare to be boarded!"

In the heat of the battle, it was easy for Jay to pass unnoticed, as sailors focused on their own lives, or the lives of their enemy. He crossed the cargo hold, found a rope ladder, and climbed. Once on deck, he saw the Noble Rogue close in-line to the Woman's sloop, on the starboard side. The Rogue's grappling hooks tugged them closer.

The shipmates of the Rogue heroically swung over the gap between the vessels, landing a few meters before Jay. Captain Carack Zye led his crew as they drew their swords and fearlessly charged the enemy. Then three others swung from the Noble

Rogue: Sakona, Bobo, and Perl.

"Perl!" shouted Jay.

He ran toward his friend, but the mysterious Woman stepped between them. She faced Bobo but left her twin swords sheathed at her belt. Bobo stepped in front of Perl and Sakona, to protect them.

"Elska!" he spat in hate.

"Bobo," said Elska (for that was the Woman's name).

Then something supernatural occurred. With clenched fists, Elska lifted her index and middle fingers on both hands, drawing them to her chest. Once there, she snapped them forward, pointing at Bobo. Out of her being flowed glistening, white orbs, somewhat like morning dew—perfectly round and beautiful. The orbs coursed together down her arms and wrists until they formed a beam, a ray that elegantly pierced the air toward her foe.

Bobo replied with a similar ritual, but instead of drawing his fingers to his chest, he drew them to his wooden armor. He held his palms up. Out of the wood sparked golden flakes, warm and mysterious. Some of Bobo's armor faded and turned to dust. The gold energy bound together as a shield before Elska's blasts. The white and gold forces clashed. Energy, wind, and colors exploded everywhere. All this happened in a matter of seconds.

The blast knocked Bobo, Sakona, Perl, and even Jay off their feet. Bobo's golden flakes faded, but Elska's white orbs survived and returned to her chest. Jumping to his feet, Bobo drew more energy from his armor. Forming it into spheres like cannon balls, he cast his power at Elska, who used her white energy like a whip, slashing Bobo's blasts away.

Meanwhile, Jay crawled around the duel to Sakona and Perl. There was no time to marvel or question. Perl gave Jay a quick embrace and pointed to a rope.

"Go!"

"What?" Jay faltered. "You mean, swing?"

"Yes," cut in Sakona. She sarcastically added, "I'm sure you have plenty of experience."

Jay took the line in his hands, stood on the guard rail, and gazed at the gorge before him. He gulped and made ready to swing, but he was too late: Bobo's armor—the source of his power—was gone. To make matters worse, another volley of cannon fire crippled the starboard propeller of Elska's sloop. The vessel began to sink. Desperate, Elska drew her fingers to her chest, ready to fire a deadly strike.

But then, Captain Zye dashed at Elska with his cutlass drawn. He slashed with a roar, but she dodged the attack, lunging to her side. She drew her swords and the two locked blades.

"He's stalling for us," said Bobo, "we have to leave now!"

"No!" called Sakona as she ran toward her father.

Now Jay didn't understand much of what was happening, but he did know that if Sakona stayed, she would surely die. He dropped the rope, leapt from the guard rail, and grabbed her hand.

"Sakona, go!" yelled Captain Zye, "Take her, Jay!"

Jay pulled—he felt he owed it to Zye, who had risked everything to save him. Sakona shrieked and wailed at Jay. She even hit him, but he held on tight and pulled her toward the sloop's edge.

"C'mon, you two!" called Bobo. He turned to Perl, "Go, little missy!"

Perl swung away and landed safely on the Rogue. She sent the line back to Bobo, who gave it to Jay and Sakona. Across the deck, Captain Zye and Elska's duel raged. Elska gained the upper hand and pressed Zye toward the port-side railing. With an elegant spin, Elska slashed Zye's chest and thrust her blades into him. Sakona screamed.

"Hold on tight!" called Bobo as he shoved Jay and Sakona off the ship. Together, they clutched the rope and swung to safety. They sent the line back for Bobo and he quickly swung across the gorge. On board the Noble Rogue, they found Groff (the sailor who killed the yavyu), waiting for them.

"That witch's boat is going down," he said to Sakona, "and she's taking us with her! What should we do? Where's Captain Zye?"

Sakona mustered all her strength to hold back her tears. "He's gone." She looked Groff dead in the eye and ordered, "Cut the lines and pull away."

Groff closed his eyes and frowned. "Aye, Sakona—aye, Captain."

Sailors cut the ropes and the Noble Rogue sailed away from Elska's sloop. All watched as Captain Zye, Elska, and her dreadful airship eased beneath the yellow sandstorm sea.

*   *   *

For a long time, no one spoke. A deep sadness lay over the crew. Jay leaned against the guard rail and laid his eyes on the rolling sand waves. Perl joined him and the two stood together in silence. After a while, Jay spoke in a hushed voice.

"What happened?"

"After you went to bed, Bobo told me all about Elska. He said she had an evil power, and if you didn't go with her willingly, she'd kidnap you. He stayed the night to protect us, but no one came. In the morning, you slammed the door—it woke us, so we followed you."

"The whole way down the mountain?"

"Yup," said Perl with a small grin. "We saw you talk to that captain, then we watched Elska take you away." Suddenly, Perl became frightened—the memory of losing Jay rattled her. She threw her arms around him and hugged him tight. "Why did you leave this morning? Were you going to join her?"

Jay didn't want to lie; he was fresh off his promise. But he didn't want to tell the truth either. So he was thankful when Bobo approached to continue the story.

"Elska's too powerful for me," he said. "When she took you, I knew we needed help. We told the captain you were kidnapped. Without a second thought, he took us onboard and we set out to save you. He was a good man."

Jay felt sad and angry, but most of all, he felt confused— he didn't know whether to cry, or yell, or speak, or be still. He put his hands in his pockets and felt coins. He remembered his promise.

"Bobo, what exactly is going on?" asked Jay. "Who was that woman, and what's this secret war really about?"

"Yeah!" pouted Perl, "And were you using magic?!"

"I'll tell you all I can."

Chapter V

THE SECRET OF THE SANDSTORM SEA

"Gather, gather," said Bobo, drawing Jay and Perl near. "Evil monsters from another world have conquered this one. They're called the Kan'zi—hideous, lizard-like beasts. Ugly and evil to their core."

Perl cast her eyes upward in thought. "If they've taken over our world, why haven't I heard of them?"

"Because they're a secretive bunch. They work from the shadows. Think about it. It should be easy to conquer people who don't know they're being conquered, right? The people wouldn't fight back! And that's just what the Kan'zi did."

"But what exactly did they do?" asked Jay. "Besides being kidnapped, the world seems fine to me."

"That's the biggest problem," said Bobo. "You think the world is as it should be, but it isn't. Come over here." He brought them to the edge of the brig and pointed to the sandy ocean. "See that? Did you know the sandstorm sea wasn't always there?"

Perl leaned out for a better view, "Really?"

"Before the Kan'zi came, the world was full of flowering green trees, bigger than you've ever seen, and oceans, not of sand, but of *water.*"

"I've read of big forests and water oceans in my books," said

Perl, "but I always thought they were myths, not history. Why did they create a sandstorm sea? What's the point of that?"

"To hide the history of our world. Their best tools are lies and deceit, and those only work when the truth is hidden."

At hearing this, Jay felt a bit uneasy. He thought of how he lied to Captain Zye. If the Kan'zi were real, Jay wanted to be as different from them as possible.

"For example," continued Bobo, "do you know the name of our world? Our country?"

That stumped Jay and Perl (much to Perl's displeasure).

"See? That's something else they've hidden from us! This world's real name is *Arland*."

Jay and Perl shivered. Though they had never before heard that name, it somehow felt both scandalous and heavenly.

Jay took a moment to think. It all seemed unlikely but possible. Besides, Bobo and Elska had blasted magical nonsense from their fingertips. And that led to another question.

"Is Elska a Kan'zi? She didn't look like a monster, she looked like us."

"No, Elska is one of us, an Arlish. But she, like others, have joined the Kan'zi. She's a traitor."

"So, what do you need Jay for?" said Perl. "You said last night he had a gift?"

"Yes, yes. Excellent, excellent," Bobo clasped his hands at their progress. "My Master told me you have a gift to see and understand the Kan'zi. It will help us find them and fight them. He said you have 'special eyes.' He didn't say much more than that. If you help us, we can defeat the Kan'zi, draw back the sandstorm sea, and save Arland.

Jay thought of Bobo's golden magic, "Is my power like yours?"

"No, my power's called Vitex, but my master, Metrarch, will

teach you all about that. You and Perl can both learn to use that, too! But your 'special eyes' are something else."

"Well, if I did decide to help you," said Jay, "what would I have to do?"

"You two would come with me and meet Metrarch. He'll know what comes next. Jay, I can't force you to join me. If you want to go home, I'll see you there myself. But if it's in your heart, I'll take you to Metrarch."

Jay paced away to think it over. There was much to consider. Perl trailed behind and forced her way into the debate. With her help, he weighed the facts: Elska was evil (having kidnapped him) and Bobo was good (having risked his life to save him). But monsters from another world, who had the power to spawn oceans of sand? It seemed silly, and I think you can understand why. But Jay and Perl recalled Elska and Bobo's powers again. Perhaps it was possible.

But Jay still doubted—or rather, he acted as if he doubted. In reality, he was only disappointed. He thought adventure was supposed to be all fun, but this was turning out to be serious business. And while magic powers and airship battles excited Jay, they also scared him. He had spent his whole life wishing for adventure, but now he wanted to be home and safe.

He jolted upright. He felt appalled with himself. How could he give up his dream now? Why—he'd regret it for the rest of his life! Come to think of it, the best adventure stories always had struggle, risk, and sometimes pain. Suddenly, Jay wanted magic and battles and thrills and fears, too. So, in honor of Captain Zye, Jay told the truth.

"I'm, uh… I'm afraid. But I'm in."

Perl smiled at Jay, admiringly. Bobo clapped his hands together.

"Excellent, excellent. We'll need a ship to take you to Metrarch." He glanced around the Rogue, studying the battle damage, seeing if it would last the trip. Jay studied the crew; they were battered and bruised. The new captain, Sakona, stood by the helm and kept a firm gaze on the horizon.

"This'll do, this'll do," said Bobo, despite the brig's many holes, fractures, and tears. "It's a fast ship, too—having caught up to Elska's so quickly."

"You sure the crew would be okay with it?" asked Jay, obviously thinking they wouldn't be.

"Sure, sure they would. Go ask Sakona. After what Elska did to Captain Zye, she'll want to help us."

So Jay slowly climbed the stairs to the helm and approached Sakona.

"Hey. I'm sorry about your Father." It was all he could think to say.

"I never want to see you again," replied Sakona. Her gaze never left the horizon. "When we dock, I want you and your friends off my brig."

Jay nodded. He found her words reasonable, given her father would still be alive if Jay hadn't been kidnapped. He turned to leave, but stopped, daring to ask one thing:

"And where are we docking?"

"The Blue Eye."

Jay had never heard of it, and neither had Bobo. Thankfully, Perl read of it in her books.

"It's a legendary, secret, pirate outpost," she said, very matter-of-factly, "somewhere in the Pipyan Mountains."

Jay squinted his eyes, "Why would we go there? This is a yavyu ship."

"A yavyu ship with cannons, swords, and a battle-ready crew," said Bobo, suspiciously squinting his eyes. "We may not be out of harm's way, yet."

Staying focused, Jay reasoned out a plan: "We can find another captain and boat when we reach the Blue Eye. And we can barter for a trip." He thought of his coins.

"Or we can steal a boat," suggested Perl.

"Stealing's wrong," replied Bobo. Jay smirked, knowing Perl would have her way.

"But they probably stole it in the first place," she reasoned. "They're pirates!"

"Little Missy," said Bobo, "it's never right to steal, even from a thief. We'll find a boat the right way. We'll search for an honorable sailor, and if we're so lucky to find one in such a place, we'll barter for passage, like Jay said." Perl frowned, having no reply to make.

A few days passed, and the Noble Rogue neared the Pipyan Mountains. The sun dimmed, the dinner bell rang, and sailors rambled to the kitchen. Groff sent Jay to fetch a barrel of soontaplum wine below deck. As he searched the gloomy cargo hold, he heard a voice nearby.

"Start without me!" It was Sakona.

Jay hid in the shadows of the room, wanting to see what she was up to. He watched as she lifted the lid off a crate and dropped some food inside. Then she did something rather unusual: she made silly faces into the box—the kind a mother makes to her baby. She even smiled.

She had the prettiest smile Jay had ever seen. In the dim rugged room, Sakona's joy shone brighter than the lantern's light. Jay blushed. How had he not noticed her before? She was beautiful, but in a genuine way. She had long auburn hair, sun-kissed skin, and vast, brown eyes. Jay was so struck, he forgot that he was hiding.

"What's in there?" he asked gently.

Suddenly, Sakona drew her cutlass, tackled Jay to the floor, and held the blade to his throat. Jay tried to wiggle free, but Sakona pinned his arms with her legs.

"You didn't see anything," she growled.

"Yes, I did. Tough luck," said Jay, annoyed. Sakona's blade pricked his chin.

"No, you didn't."

"Yes, I did. You were making stupid faces in a box!"

Then, out of the box, leapt the most ugly, smelly, dumb-looking creature Jay had ever seen. It was a fat, floppy amphibian with deep purple scales. Its tongue drooped eternally out of its mouth. Altogether, it was no wider than Jay's chest and no taller than his knees.

The ball-like blob flopped at Jay's foot and gnawed on his boot (the bright, brown, brand-new one, of course). Its crossed eyes rambled about Jay's body in utter euphoria. It croak-barked, or *croarked* (I say this because the sound was neither a croak, nor a bark. It was, well, a croark). Sakona rolled off of Jay and crawled toward the pathetic creature.

"Here, girl. Come here, Loosha!"

But the creature, Loosha, leapt away. Sakona sprang to her feet and yanked Jay to his own.

"Help me catch her. Now."

"No."

"What?"

Jay folded his arms and smiled, "Take back what you said."

"What did I say?"

"That you never want to see me again."

"As if I could help that! What does it matter, anyway?"

Jay sat on a crate and shrugged his shoulders, still smiling. "I think you've got the wrong idea about me."

But Sakona wasn't in a playful mood. She shot back, "What idea? That you're a cocky liar who got himself kidnapped?"

"Well, besides that."

Suddenly, Loosha jumped toward the cargo hold's exit. Sakona ran after her and shut the door just before she could escape—though other cracks and windows lay open around the room.

"I'm your captain," Sakona snapped at Jay. "You'll do as I say."

But Jay called her bluff. He knew, for whatever reason, she was hiding Loosha.

"No," he said again as Loosha waddled toward a window.

"Fine!" said Sakona. "I take it back. Now help me!"

The two chased Loosha all around the room, but the creature was swift and slippery. She crawled up the hull and over crates and barrels. At last, she came to a stop—her sticky webbed feet clung to the ceiling. Hanging upside down, she croarked at Jay and smiled with her tongue sticking out. She looked—how should I put this?—stupid.

"It's useless," said Jay. "She's not going in that crate unless she wants to."

"Your boot," said Sakona.

Reluctantly, Jay slipped off his bright, brown, brand-new boot and held it up like a platter. Loosha wagged her stump tail and leapt at Jay's boot. He flung it into the crate—Loosha followed—and Sakona slammed the lid shut.

"At some point, I'm going to need that back," said Jay. They both laughed. Sakona smiled at him, so Jay turned away to hide his blushing cheeks.

"Loosha's a froad," she said, "a very, very rare animal. I found her in the mountains. My father wouldn't let me keep her. He said the crew would try and sell her on Lemuk or some other terrible island. 'Best let her go,' he said. But I couldn't... she's just so cute! Right?"

"Yes." Jay thought it best to keep his true thoughts to himself. Even Captain Zye would have forgiven him for this lie.

"So you're real name is Jay, right? Not Stu?"

"Yeah—" Jay was going to keep talking, but he was afraid of saying something stupid, so he nodded. This was among his wisest choices.

"That fits you better." Her mind went back to Loosha. "Promise me, you won't tell anyone about her."

"Sure." Apparently, this was a day for promises. "But since you're captain now, can't you tell the crew she's staying?"

"I don't know." Sakona looked away. "I don't trust them. They loved my father, but they don't like me."

"Well, I'm sorry to hear that. And again, I'm sorry about your father."

"Don't be. What he did was foolish."

"Whoa, alright. Never mind, then."

"Look, I know what you're thinking; he died to save me. Yeah, sure. He loved doing what was right, but look where that left him. And me. Is it right to leave your daughter without a father so you can look noble?"

Jay raised an eyebrow in doubt. Zye didn't strike him as vain, but Sakona knew her father best. Maybe she was right. After a few silent moments, Sakona left the room without saying a word.

Jay was alone. Once more, he had one foot with boot and one foot without. He knew better than to try and save his boot from Loosha. So, he left the lid closed and found another boot in the cargo hold. It was a mustard yellow. It fit and matched even worse than the one before. Jay didn't mind, thinking again that his mismatched style might catch on.

The last days of the voyage dragged. Jay and Bobo asked Perl many questions about the Blue Eye, and she, of course, loved sharing all her knowledge. Unfortunately, most everything she said came from rumors in letters. Perl herself was surprised to hear that the Blue Eye was real.

But everything she said made it sound like the worst place in the world—complete anarchy, a den of thieves and bandits. Though it did raise a question: why were they heading there in the first place?

So Jay searched for a sailor to question. Luckily, he found a friend in the crow's nest.

"Groff, why are we going to the Blue Eye?"

Groff was lowering and untying the vessel's colors (a blue merchant flag from Onaga) and folding it tight. "Well, boy, we need repairs, don't we?"

"Yes, but surely there are safer ports, aye?"

Groff laughed, "Why, you've gone soft! You lily-livered child. Ha!"

"I have not! It's my friend Perl, she's a bit nervous." She wasn't, of course, but Jay had to save face.

"Aye. She should be. But we've got some friends there so that's where we'll go." Groff packed the flag away in a crate and drew a new one. It was black with white crossed swords. It was a pirate flag.

Without a word, Jay climbed down the mast. His heart was beating fast with fear, but even so, he smiled. It was all so exciting, Jay couldn't contain it. He rushed to share his findings with his friends. Bobo somehow turned paler than usual while Perl rolled her eyes and said, "Yeah, I pretty much figured that out already."

But what interested Jay more than pirates and their hidden coves was Sakona. Whenever he tried to speak with her, she ignored him; she hadn't once acknowledged him since they spoke in the cargo hold. But that didn't discourage Jay—if anything, he saw it as a challenge.

At last, the Noble Rogue arrived at the base of the Pipyan Mountains. From afar, the mountains appeared about the size of Onaga's peaks, but now they towered far above the Rogue, stretching higher than the clouds, like a wall that marked the end of the world.

The little ship began its climb. No sight in all of Arland compared to these marvelous mountains. Glossy granite patches painted the white stone, obeying cracks and crevices, reflecting the pink sky.

After an hour, the Rogue reached the summit of the southern-most mountain and drifted to a stop above its peak. The air was bitter, and the wind tore the sails in every direction. Jay rubbed his bare arms, wondering if he had ever felt so cold. All the crew leaned and peered over the port-side railing. They saw a hole in the mountain's peak and a pale, blue light glowing from within.

"A volcano," said Bobo.

"I know," said Perl, who tried to look unimpressed.

Jay, however, stared in wonder. With its white-rock summit and gentle inner light, the volcano looked like a solitary blue eye.

Chapter VI

THE BLUE EYE

Jay's stomach stirred as the Noble Rogue began its descent. It slowly sank through the volcano's crest. The wind stopped and warm air cradled the brig—but there was no smoke nor stench of sulfur, for the blue magma had frozen long ago. The sun peeked through the volcano, shining light against the crystal blue rocks, drenching the grotto in an aquatic glimmer.

Jay and Perl gazed with wide eyes. They felt smaller than ever, for within this one mountain, Jay and Perl thought they could fit a hundred Onagas. The Rogue sailed deeper and deeper until the sunlight faded. But all was not dark, for ahead there stood the feint orb of an orange lamp. The brig drew nearer to the light—which was not one light, but several—no, a whole city of lights!

It was a pirate cove. The city webbed through three blue spires and a score of deep gorges. The spires looked like skeletal claws, gripping the cove in a boney-blue palm. As the Rogue soared over the streets, Jay saw hundreds of flags, airships, peoples, and creatures he had never seen before. Golden lights glistened on curious fabrics and metals. The chatter and clatter of a thousand barters echoed throughout the city.

The Rogue sailed to a shipyard on top the city's center spire, making ready to dock. When airships land in Arland, sailors pull a series of levers that deploy landing gears: small feet-like brackets that drop out of the ship's hull and help it stand on solid ground. In this way, the Rogue landed in the cove's shipyard, which stood like a fort, with battlements and cannons surrounding the inner dock.

Many sailors stopped and stared at the Rogue and her crew, whispering to one another. A few dashed away, down to the dark city, as if to report something urgent.

Tired from the long flight, Jay, Perl, and Bobo left first. Some of their shipmates said farewell, but most ignored them. Sakona was nowhere to be seen, which left Jay with the slightest hint of sadness. He wanted to see her one last time, but Bobo rushed him along.

Together they stumbled down the pale spire's narrow road. It widened as it sloped down the spire and landed in the city. Once there, the trio came to a crooked street. Outlandish, creepy figures with dark eyes lurked in windows and around corners. They made the Colonel and his guard seem like a rather silly bunch.

The buildings matched the people: crooked, unkept, and hollow. But soon they came to an old house—a tavern called 'The Hickelberry Pie.' Smoke puffed out of two chimneys and playful music pattered within. Jay, Perl, and Bobo soon found refuge in the warm, cozy lodge.

Two musicians stood in the room's center, singing about love and plucking their stringed instruments. Jay usually hated love songs, finding them dull and overplayed, but he listened to the lyrics with new interest.

They sat down near one of the fireplaces. A moment later, a large fellow with a radiant, red beard toured their table.

"Welcome! My name's Creyg. I'm this 'ere owner of this 'ere

tavern. Might I be interesting you in our famous Hickelberry Pie?"

"Pleased to meet you, Creyg," replied Bobo. "My name's—"

"We need a ship," interrupted Perl, banging her fists on the table. "Can you help us?"

"With a good captain," said Jay, "a good person."

"A good person in this 'ere Blue Eye? Well that's hard to come by. Save for the good captain himself, Carack Zye—but that man there be gone-goodbye." His rhymes impressed Perl.

Bobo gulped, "How do you know that?"

"Yeah, who's the rat?" added Perl, rhyming with Bobo. But no one noticed.

"His brig's come back but he ain't there. Saddens me heart, that I swear! He wasn't picky, nor shrewd, he simply loved this 'ere food. Speaking of that, why, would you like our famous Hickelberry Pie?"

Instead of praising her skilled waiter-poet, Perl soured her face in jealousy. "This *'ere* customer is going," she mocked. Standing to leave, Jay tugged her back down.

"Forgive us, Master Creyg," said Bobo, most agreeably. "My friends *'ere* are in a hurry. Can you think of anyone else, anyone good as Captain Zye?"

"The only thing as good as Captain Zye be this 'ere tavern's Hickelberry Pie. Would ye like some to try?"

You may be thinking that there is more to Master Creyg's famous Hickelberry Pie than he admits. Perhaps it is poisoned and Master Creyg is an agent of the enemy. Or perhaps "Hickelberry" is code for something else—something good, and Master Creyg is truly a friend of Metrarch sent to save them! In truth, Master Creyg—having spent most of his life trying to sell Hickelberry Pies—had forgotten how to speak about anything else.

"No!" said Perl.

"Well, well, no need to yell," sighed Creyg.

He backed away from their table and went to seat a new guest, who was cloaked under a hooded blue robe. Bobo and Perl argued of what to do next, but Jay watched the new guest. Slowly, the guest's head tilted to Jay and nodded toward its table—inviting him over. Jay slipped away from Perl and Bobo unnoticed and approached the cloaked figure. When close enough, he saw that under the hood was Sakona.

"I'm in trouble. I need your help."

"So, you've finally got the right idea about me," said Jay.

"Don't get ahead of yourself," she said hiding a smile. "But look, this is serious—"

Suddenly, Creyg bumbled up to their table, with the words Hickelberry Pie clearly on the tip of his tongue, but Sakona held up one finger and commanded: "Don't."

Without a word, Creyg turned and walked away (though he kept his chin up).

Jay leaned in. "So what's going on? What's with the disguise?"

"It's my crew. They're calling a mutiny against me—I overheard Groff saying so. I snuck off the brig before they could get me."

Jay pitied Sakona. Sure, she was mean to him at first, but she was in real trouble. She lost her father and now her ship.

"Stick with us. Bobo's got magic… or something like it. And once your crew leaves, we'll find a new ship—"

"No! That's my father's brig. And Loosha's still on board. I'm not leaving without either one." Jay had forgotten about Sakona's pathetic pet.

"Well, let's tell Perl and Bobo and think of a plan."

"No," growled Sakona. "I don't trust them."

That flattered Jay, for it implied that she trusted him.

"Well, you trust me," he liked how that sounded, "and I trust them. So, you actually do trust them. It's just logical. I can't help you without them, anyway."

Sakona agreed, so he brought her back to Perl and Bobo's table. Sakona told them everything about the mutiny and her pet froad, Loosha.

"You have a froad!?" said Perl. She nearly fell out of her chair.

"Yes," said Sakona, "but don't get any ideas. She's mine, and so is the Rogue. Both are guarded by my crew. They'll be making repairs, waiting for me to return so they can mutiny. We'll have to fight our way through."

"Why should we help you? What do we get out of it?" said Perl, who was hoping to exchange her help for Loosha.

"Help me get my brig and froad, and I'll take you anywhere in the world. One free ride."

"You think we could take the Rogue back?" asked Jay. "With only us four?"

"Sure we can. Like you said, Bobo's got magic!"

"Whoa, whoa," said Bobo. "First, it's not magic, it's Vitex. Second, even if I had fuel, my powers couldn't stop *all* our old shipmates."

Sakona thought hard. "My father told me that the Rogue is the fastest ship in the world. It's also very, very valuable; he said it once belonged to a princess. All the pirates here know it. I bet other captains would love to steal her. In the past, they wouldn't dare—not with my father in the way. But now, they might try."

"Yeah, dummy, so how does that help us?" As you may have guessed from Perl's informal reply, she did not like Sakona one bit.

"Because, if we can persuade other pirates to try and take the Rogue, they'll fight with my crew and we can sneak aboard while they're distracted."

"That could work," said Jay.

"But it's wrong," said Bobo. "People would die in the fight. That's something we can't cause."

"Killing isn't always wrong," said Sakona.

"Well not when you're defending yourself," said Perl, "or someone else. But this is different."

"No, it's not!" said Sakona, "I *am* defending myself. My crew is trying to kill me."

Bobo leaned in, "They said that?"

"Yes. That's what mutiny means."

"In that case," said Bobo, "we'll need weapons, and I'll need fuel."

"I saw a market before we docked," said Jay. "Let's pick up supplies then split up and spread the news: 'The Rogue has no captain. She's ripe for the taking.'"

So Jay took them to a cluttered market. Using some of Captain Zye's coins, they bought cutlasses for Jay and Perl, and fuel for Bobo—magma pebbles that teemed with life.

"I didn't know stones could hold life, but I feel the Vitex within them!" said Bobo in awe.

"Now let's split up and spread the rumor," said Sakona.

"Wait," said Bobo, "that might not be safe. Maybe Jay and Perl should stick together, at least."

"Yeah," said Jay, "Perl, would you be more comfortable with that?"

"No, I'm fine by myself!" she said, folding her arms.

"Alright, we'll meet at the Spire's base in an hour," said Jay.

The group split up. Of all their separate journeys, Perl's was the most eventful:

Perl left the market and found a dim, narrow street. The road was long with no end in sight, and many alleys splintered off toward other roads. But the dark was only half as scary as the sounds: steady creaking and dripping sounds. It was like a cold, black cave. Places like that are not so bad when you have company, but Perl had insisted on going alone.

At first, she marched down the alley in confidence, but after a few steps, she nervously stopped. Odd smells oozed in the air, and whispers echoed through the buildings. Perl made the best decision she could. She ran.

Not knowing where to go, Perl searched for any place brighter than the alley. *Why didn't I stay with Jay?* she thought to herself in anger.

She heard a faint noise growing; the sound of a party. She followed the noise and came to an opening in the road. Before her was a crashed airship, a frigate, which was altered into a saloon. The entrance was a hole on the frigate's port side—likely made by a fiery cannon blast. Carved above the "doorway" was the name 'The Watering Hole.' Pirates dizzily stumbled in and out. Music echoed from within—but it sounded unlike the Hickelberry Pie's tunes. These songs were sharp and loud.

Perl, wanting nothing more than to escape the darkness of the street, stepped into the Watering Hole. The scene was chaotic, to say the least. Sailors danced on tabletops. Little furry animals—Pithians—hung by their tails from the ceiling, screeching and wailing at patrons. Waiters dashed all about the room, throwing goblets and tankards to every man and woman. And the music! Such wretched music! It's the sort that young people love.

But Perl was not easily overwhelmed. To tell you the truth, she was rather ashamed of her frightful run down the street, and she hoped to reclaim her dignity. She climbed up on a table and screamed.

"Hey!!!"

The room fell silent. Every pirate—even the dizzy ones—

stared at the odd-looking girl.

"Carack Zye is dead. The Rogue is ripe for the taking!"

The pirates eyed the girl and each other. At once, they sped out of the saloon, flipping tables and smashing bottles. Even some of the waiters and musicians left. The room settled down and Perl noticed a bulky man with a feather hat, sitting at a table nearby. He watched Perl while nursing his drink.

"Young lady, ye know much about that Noble Rogue?"

"Yes, sir. I was on her when she arrived."

"Then you can help my shipmates and me steal her."

Chapter VII

BATTLE FOR THE NOBLE ROGUE

At the same time, Jay, Sakona, and Bobo came to the spire's base. They gazed up at the harbor, trying to plan their summit. The spire was like a mountain within a mountain.

It was tall and too steep to climb except for one spot; a slim slope that stretched from top to bottom. On the spire's peak sat the harbor, which was less like a dock and more like a fort. It had high wooden palisades and towers lined with cannons. If Perl had been there, she would have explained that the harbor was built to defend the cove from invaders.

And where was Perl? A few minutes had gone by and she still hadn't arrived. Try as he might, Jay couldn't hide his worry; he kept scratching behind his ear and pacing around.

"We may have to go find Perl."

"We don't have time," said Sakona, gazing up the tall spire.

"We'll make time," snapped Jay.

Sakona crossed her arms—either out of impatience or jealousy or both. But just then, a terrifying explosion sounded above. The battle for the Noble Rogue began.

Two crews assaulted the spire, both hoping to defeat the Rogue's sailors and claim the legendary craft. First was Captain Noran of 'The Wrathful Krusk.' His galley bombarded the harbor from the sky and circled the spire. Second was Captain Taylune and her metal-clad crew. They marched up the spire's slope with long swords and shields drawn. Other pirates came to the spire's base, but most fled after sighting Taylune.

Groff and the Rogue's sailors defended their brig with tremendous bravery. Some manned the harbor's cannons and returned fire on the Wrathful Krusk. Others barricaded the slope and flung crates and rolled barrels at the invaders.

All the Blue Eye cheered and sneered as the sky boomed with cannon fire and cried of a hundred warring sailors. Though brawls were a common sight in the cove, a battle of this scale hadn't been seen in years. Chaos filled the streets as pirates rioted in the market, taverns, and homes.

"We need to get up there," said Sakona. "Now."

Jay would have snapped at her again, but he saw she was worried. He knew the cause.

"Loosha and the Rogue will be okay... and so will Perl," hoped Jay.

And he was right. Perl arrived, leading an entire posse of pirates, though smaller than the others, with ten sailors totals. They held rock picks and wore sharp metal boots.

"Meet my new friends!" said Perl.

But Jay grabbed and hugged her tight. "You scared us, kiddo!"

"I'm fine! Of course, I'm fine!" said Perl, but she enjoyed the hug. Perl introduced her kooky, bulky friend with the feather hat. "This is Captain Mackie Slook."

"Pleased to meet ye. And it's President Mackie, not captain. No captains on me democratic crew."

"They let me join—they're nice," said Perl, "and Mackie's smart. He wants to scale the spire on the side using these." She held up a pair of rock picks. "Catch 'em by surprise! I told him where the ship was and which side to climb."

Sakona grinned. "Mackie, I used to serve on the Rogue—I know how she flies."

"What are ye proposing, young lady?"

"This is the girl I told you about," said Perl. "You won't have to fight the other crews. Get her on that ship, and we can steal it right out from under them. She can get the Rogue in the air. Fast."

Sakona looked down. A few moments before, she tried to abandon Perl.

"And what be ye wanting in return, Miss Perl?"

"A ride—my friends and I need to leave here. Our business is our own."

Mackie studied Perl's weird-looking friends. They weren't pirates—that was clear enough. There was likely little risk to himself. But to Sakona's surprise, Mackie didn't make his decision alone.

"What do ye all think? Okay with these tagalongs?"

The pirates gathered in a round. Out of their coats and pants and boots, they pulled out slips of paper and feather pens. They cast their votes on the slips and tossed them in Mackie's hat. Unbelievably, he took the time to tally them!

"We don't have time for this!" cried Sakona. "Mackie, make your choice."

"No! That's how tyranny starts: it's a wild beast, prowling around every corner, ready to seize man, woman, and child!" Sakona rolled her eyes as Mackie tallied the votes. He nodded to his sailors. "Nine to one. Looks like they'll be joining us!"

"Who voted 'no'?" asked Perl, greatly offended.

"A secret ballot is the cornerstone of democracy!" said Mackie, and his crew cheered. "So, we're climbing the back side of the spire. The harbor's palisade only surrounds the front. From here, we'll summit on the inside. Keep up." Mackie slammed his pick into the rock and began to climb.

"We can't climb that whole thing freehand!" said Sakona.

"Sorry," shrugged Perl, with her rockpicks in-hand, "I guess he only had one pair to spare."

But Jay had an idea. He sent Perl to climb with Mackie's crew while he, Sakona, and Bobo returned to the market. Zooming through riots and brawls, Jay found his way to a yavyu-hunting vendor whose stand was surprisingly still open, and they found out why: The vendor was completely deaf and partially blind—I don't think she knew about the horribly exciting things happening all around her. After a hard bargain, Jay used the rest of Zye's coins to buy a harpoon swivel gun with rope. Together, the three heaved the cannon to the base of the mountain.

The battle waged on the path to the spire. The Rogue's crew shot down Captain Noran's galley. It crashed onto the sloped road, blocking the path. Scaling the scorching remains of the boat, Groff and his sailors fired a volley of arrows at the invading pirates. But survivors from the galley's wreckage crawled out of their would-be coffin and flanked the Rogue's crew—forcing them to retreat higher up the spire.

Down below, Jay tied the line to a harpoon, stuffed it in the swivel gun, and chased it with black powder. He aimed at the top of the spire. But Sakona grew nervous, with all the shouting and explosions.

"Jay," she said, "let me shoot it. You'll miss again."

"Gee, thanks," said Jay without looking up from his work. He kept angling the gun in defiance.

"Jay! C'mon!"

"Shush!" He lit the fuse and fired the gun. The harpoon sped out of the cannon and cut through the air; it passed Mackie's crew, and lodged in the rock just short of the harbor.

Jay tugged on the cord. "There," he said, proud of himself. "Now we hold on tight and walk up the spire."

And so, they did. The three hiked the steep rock while holding the rope for support. Sakona went first, eager to reach her brig and pet. Jay went second, thinking he could gallantly catch Sakona if she slipped. Bobo went third, knowing he could catch them both if they slipped. They soon caught up to Perl, who preferred her method of climbing to the line. She likened the rope to cheating.

The steep climb took all of Jay's strength. His hands burned as the coarse rope chewed his skin. His feet ached as the jagged slope twisted his legs in weird ways. He was glad that Sakona was in front of him so she wouldn't see how stupid he looked.

The sound of battle intensified. Cannon fire beat like a ticking clock. Jay's arms wobbled. Sweat dripped off his back and splashed on Bobo's face. Those moments of pain seemed to last for hours, but at last, the spire plateaued. They reached the shipyard.

They quietly crawled over the edge and into the harbor. Jay was an aching sweaty mess, but he had no time to rest. To his left stood the palisade and burning tower. Ahead, the Rogue's crew ran toward the wall, ready to make a final stand. To his right, the Noble Rogue sat silent and still on the dark, smoky cliffside.

"Stay low and make for the ship," whispered Mackie. "Them sailors are distracted—we might take her without a fight."

They shuffled on, toward their prize. But when they were halfway to the brig, a cannon blast shattered the palisade. Pirates poured in with swords and bows drawn. The Rogue's crew charged their enemy shouting fierce words and war cries.

The battle was explosive: sparks, dirt, metal, and splatters of blood flashed through the air. Some pirates slashed at each other with rusty cutlasses in fierce, yet elegant duels. Others found cover and fired sharp arrows from afar.

But the resistance didn't last long. The Rogue's crew could not stand the onslaught of two pirate troops. Mackie ordered his sailors to sprint for the empty brig. Jay, Perl, Sakona, and Bobo followed close behind them.

They reached the Rogue and boarded the gangplank, but once on deck, they found a short, vigorous sailor, with four others waiting for them. It was Groff.

Mackie and his crew drew their swords and readied for a duel, "Stand down, ye gizzards."

"Let her go, Slook!" said Groff, pointing to Sakona.

Sakona stepped forward, "Don't pretend to care about me now, Groff. Give me my ship."

Groff lowered his blade, confused. "Huh? Wait, did you cause all of this!?" he said, gesturing to the battle.

"No, that was me," said Perl, wanting all the credit.

"I did what I had to," said Sakona. "You were going to mutiny me!"

"For your own good, Sakona. You're not ready to be captain. In time, maybe, but not now."

"Hold on," said Jay. "You mean you weren't going to kill Sakona?"

"Kill her? She's practically my niece! Sakona, you worked the crew too hard; you didn't earn their respect. And you're too young. I was going to take over and teach you how to captain so one day you could have the Rogue back. It's what your father would have wanted."

For a moment, this all shocked Jay. He thought Groff might be bluffing, but he took one look at Sakona and everything made sense. Sakona had known this all along. She lied to Jay.

With hands outstretched like a wise, old sage, Bobo walked between Groff and Mackie. "Everyone, everyone," he called in his friendly, raspy voice, "I'm sure we can settle this peacefully. Put down the swords."

But Mackie took the hilt of his blade and bashed Bobo in the head, knocking him out.

"I care not for this drama," said the bulky man. "Remove yourself from this brig, or I remove you from the land of the living."

Groff and his sailors met his challenge; they drew their sabers and lunged at Mackie, but before they struck, a thick, sloppy tongue stretched from the main mast and slapped the sailors in the neck. Groff and his sailors fell to the deck, stiff. Loosha the froad withdrew her tongue and leapt off the mast, landing on top of Groff.

"Loosha's a murderer!" gasped Perl.

"He's not dead… I think he's paralyzed." said Jay, crouching over Groff's body.

"I didn't know she could do that!" said Sakona, smiling wide. "What a good girl!" She tried to give her pet a hug, but Loosha sprang away, leaping about the deck.

"Crew, kill them," said Mackie, pointing to the paralyzed sailors.

"Whoa, Mackie. Wait a minute," said Jay. "You can't kill 'em, they've done nothing wrong." Though they may not seem it, Jay's words were bold. For all he knew, Mackie might have killed *him* for disagreeing. But deep down, beneath that big belly of his, Mackie was a man of heart.

"Fine. Throw them overboard."

Jay sighed in relief as Mackie's pirates carried Groff and his sailors down the gangplank and off the ship.

"Mackie," said Sakona, "send six men to the engine room, one to the foremast, two to the main, and one to the aft." Mackie echoed her orders, splattering his spit all over the deck. His crew scurried to their places as Sakona dashed up the stairs to the Rogue's helm. "Jay and Perl, on the cannons."

Jay and Perl obeyed, manning the port-side cannons which faced the battle. Looking over the ship's edge, they saw the Rogue's crew retreat, running straight for them!

Steam whistled from below deck. The brig's propellers began to spin as Mackie's pirates set the Rogue's royal-blue sails.

"Jay and Perl," said Sakona, "you need to buy us time—fire on those pirates!"

"Aye, aye!" said Jay, but he pulled Perl aside and whispered, "We can't kill them. It's not right. But we've got to escape somehow."

"We need to slow 'em down. Let's shoot in front of them and knock 'em on their butts!" laughed Perl.

Jay smiled. He quickly showed Perl how to load her cannon. They angled their guns and lit the fuses. As the pirates neared the Rogue, Jay and Perl fired!

Their rounds smashed into the dirt, just in front of the pirates, blasting them backwards. Then they heard Sakona call, "We have lift off!" The Noble Rogue took flight once more, gently lifting off the spire, floating over the pirate cove.

The crew cheered—they danced and pranced about the deck. Jay and Perl high-fived and chuckled at their good fortune. Already the air seemed lighter and cooler. Their daring plan had actually worked.

Mackie peered below deck, "More steam! Higher, higher!"

The Rogue sailed up toward the volcano's summit, ready to complete her escape. She neared the top and daylight poured over the mountain's crater, onto the Rogue.

Mackie yelled, "Another ship—off our starboard! A ship with green sails!"

Sakona's eyes widened. Jay and Perl dashed to the starboard

side to spy out the craft. It was a machine of death, huge and angular, with dark green canvas and a pitch-black hull. Sporting three decks of deadly cannons and four mighty sails, she was a Man O' War.

She flew behind and below the Rogue, a few hundred meters away. Jay would have loaded a cannon and fired right away, but the green-sailed Man O' War was too low and out of range. This, however, did not stop the enemy vessel. Chase-cannons on her bow flashed and boomed. The first rounds missed, but they would surely fix their aim and land their next shots. To make matters worse, she seemed to be gaining speed.

"Jay, look!" Perl pointed at the roof of the volcano, the edge of the crater. Squinting, Jay saw hundreds of sharp rocks which seemed to drip over the volcano's lip. "Maybe we can loosen them with a cannon blast—send them down to crush that ship!"

"Perl, you're brilliant."

Perl blushed.

"Sakona," called Jay, "tell us when that ship is directly under that edge!"

Sakona smiled when she realized their plan. She left the helm and stood on the starboard rail for a better view. Jay and Perl loaded their cannons and aimed high. A cannon ball from the Man O' War ripped through the bow railing, meters from Jay.

Daylight had barely touched the galleon when Sakona cried, "Now!"

Jay and Perl fired. Their shots exploded against the cavern's roof. Chunks of rock fell from the sky and pounded on the grand vessel.

"Direct hit!" cheered Sakona.

The Man O' War wobbled to her port side and spiraled down until it faded into darkness.

After a few minutes, the Noble Rogue emerged from the

volcano and sailed away from the Blue Eye. With the battle won, Jay's focus changed. He knew he had to confront Sakona.

Chapter VIII

A NEW CAPTAIN

The Noble Rogue drifted down the volcano's side, heading south with full sails. The ancient ship shined amid the dull sandstorm sea. Rolling and lapping, the yellow sand spread far over each horizon. Behind the Rogue, the Pipyan Mountains shrank until a gray haze swallowed them whole.

Jay made a list of things to do. First on his list was to recover his bright, brown, brand-new boot. That proved simple enough: it was still in Loosha's crate, though covered in saliva. He slipped it on without cleaning it.

Second (and not so simple) was to confront Sakona about her lie. What she did was wrong, there was no doubt about it. Sakona had used Jay to take back her boat. This embarrassed Jay. He couldn't let himself be pushed around so easily! So, he planned to confront her. But he couldn't catch her. She busily bustled around the craft, rigging and trimming the sails.

To pass the time, Jay and Perl sat with Bobo's unconscious body. Mackie assured them that Bobo would awake within the hour. Mackie was, apparently, an expert in knocking people out, having practiced many times before. So, they sat with Bobo, Jay rubbing his own sore arms and Perl playing drums on Bobo's belly. And the two were quiet; for silence can be a nice thing after a loud day.

Once she trimmed the sails, Sakona scooped Loosha in her arms and joined Jay and Perl. "You two did so well. Things couldn't have gone better. Now we need to get rid of Mackie and his pirates."

And here was Jay's chance to confront her, but he hadn't thought it through. What words should he use? What words shouldn't he use? Lacking a plan, he chose an immature path: he gave her the cold shoulder. He gave a slight nod, frowned, and looked away dramatically.

"What? What's wrong?"

"Oh, I don't know. Nothing."

But Perl had a battle plan: "You lied. You said Groff was going to kill you."

"That's not what I said—"

"No, stop," said Perl, "and think about what you did. A lot of people got hurt today, maybe even died, because you couldn't wait to be captain."

Her honesty had a bit of spite in it, which only made Sakona more defensive. "This is my brig. He had no right to take it."

"Maybe that's true," said Jay, gently, "but is a brig worth someone's life?"

Sakona felt a sting in her heart and a dryness in her mouth. She wasn't used to thinking backwards, reviewing her actions. It left her feeling stale. Not knowing what to do, she dropped Loosha and stormed away.

Loosha bounced on the deck with a frown, but, upon spotting Jay, she hopped onto the boy's leg and gave his boot a good gnaw.

A while later, as a flaming-red sky settled over the ocean, Bobo woke rubbing his head and belly. "Did we... Did we make it?"

"Take a guess, genius," said Perl.

Bobo peered about the vessel. "What happened to Groff? And what happened to me?"

"They left Groff behind, alive. You got hit," said Jay.

"Mackie hit you," added Perl.

Bobo sighed and said, "I need to talk to Sakona about her lie."

"We already did," said Perl.

"She's pretty upset," said Jay.

Bobo squinted his eyes in thought. "Telling a friend when they've done something wrong is hard to speak and hear. But I think it's one of the most loving things you can do."

"Well, she's not our friend, anyway," said Perl.

"Yet," parried Jay, scratching his chin. Perl opened her mouth to object but Bobo, seeing this, cut her off.

"She'll have to apologize, that's her job. It will be our job to forgive her."

Mackie approached from the helm, eyeing Bobo. "Good, you're awake. Come here and give me a heading—you're the one who knows where to go, right?"

"Aye, to Metrarch. To the Hearth!" said Bobo, springing to his feet. "And by the way, I forgive you for hitting me."

Mackie stared with a face that read, 'I don't care.' The two walked toward the bow to figure the Rogue's course.

Wanting to check on Sakona, Jay crept below deck. Loosha trailed the boy as he searched the cabins, the kitchen, and the engine room.

At last, he found her in the gloomy belly of the brig, the cargo hold. She was sitting with her back to a crate and legs spread out. Her slim eyes were glued forward; they didn't even twitch when Jay entered.

Wanting to help, but not knowing what to do, Jay sat next

to her and said nothing (and this was, in fact, what she needed most). With his back to the same crate and legs spread out like hers, Jay sighed. He picked up Loosha and offered her to Sakona, like a tissue. Sakona received her pet with a polite, "Thank you."

After a long silence, Sakona shuffled, "Do you really think people died?"

Jay nodded. Her glossy, brown eyes broke his heart.

"I didn't think it through," said Sakona. "Why didn't I? I wanted the Rogue. It's all I have left of—"

Sakona cried. And her tears weren't slow and gentle; they were heavy with lots of heaving.

"It's alright, it's alright," said Jay. "Come here." He opened his arms to suggest a hug, which Sakona accepted, tightly wrapping her arms around him. As her tears dripped down his back, Jay felt a peculiar stir in his chest and stomach. It was a warmth; he wanted to care for her.

Through her tears, Sakona bawled, "Why did he have to die?"

Jay softly replied, "I don't know."

Sakona loosened her hands and sat against the crate. Her tears slowed. "I hate death. I want nothing to do with it anymore." She thought not only of her father, but of the sailors who died in the battle for her ship.

"Same," said Jay. "So what now? Are you going to stay with Mackie and the Rogue? You can come with us… if you want."

"I don't know. I want my ship back so badly, but I guess that's impossible." Sakona wiped her eyes. "Thank you, Jay. You're alright."

"See? You did have the wrong idea about me." The two laughed.

Then Sakona did something very mature, something I myself often neglect to do. She turned the conversation on Jay, asking "Do you have any parents?"

"No. I mean, I did at one point, I guess. I don't remember them."

"Really?"

"The earliest memory I have is working on Perl's family farm."

"Is that how you two met?"

"Yeah." Jay thought it best to not say more—the rest was Perl's story, not his.

"But even though you don't remember them, do you miss your parents?"

A sudden sadness overcame Jay. It was an old sadness, one he hadn't felt in years. He nodded and the two sat together for a while longer, enjoying each other's silent company.

For the rest of the day, Sakona stayed close to Jay—which he enjoyed very much. Even at dinner, she sat with Jay and Perl, sharing of her life on the high seas and asking questions about theirs on Onaga.

Perl, though she wouldn't admit it, was warming up to Sakona. She liked sharing about Onaga—and Sakona seemed to care.

In the dead of night, Jay woke to a harsh creaking sound and a violent gust of wind. The ship's planks moaned as though bent between a giant's fingers. He raced on deck to find most of the pirates already there. A few lanterns littered the brig, but past their glow was total darkness.

A savage wind swiped sand across the deck and slashed at Jay. A bolt of lightning splintered across the sky and shined its blue light on hideous black clouds. It was a storm.

Mackie rushed across the deck, "All hands, grab a sail."

Jay scurried to the aft sail on the port side. Sakona joined him and together, they grabbed the line, ready to raise or lower the sail at Mackie's command.

"Full sail!" he cried.

But while Jay tugged at the line, Sakona stayed still.

"What is it?" said Jay.

"I think Mackie wants to catch the wind and sail up, over the storm," said Sakona, "But the winds are too strong!"

Sakona's point proved true. The main sail had just reached full when a blast of air snapped the mast like a twig. It timbered down toward the helm and smashed onto the deck. Jay and Sakona rushed to see the damage and found Mackie pinned down, his legs crushed under the mast. He wailed in pain.

The brig rocked to her starboard. More sand poured on board, while the starboard propeller dunked beneath the waves. In a few moments, the Noble Rogue would sink.

Perl and Bobo joined Jay and Sakona. Bobo looked at Mackie, then at the empty helm, and then to Sakona. "We need a captain."

"Sakona, take the helm!" said Jay.

But Sakona addressed Mackie's sailors. "If anyone thinks they can captain this brig better than I, speak now."

None spoke.

"All in favor of myself taking command, say aye."

"Aye!" the crew roared from their chests. Sakona was captain again.

She took the helm. "Half sail and slow the propellers! Bobo, take Mackie below deck. Jay and Perl, pass out those goggles!" She pointed to a barrel beside the cabin door.

The sailors scurried to their places while Jay and Perl lifted the lid off the barrel. Inside, lay dozens of goggles designed to keep sand out of one's eyes. They took an armful each and tossed them to the crew.

As soon as the sailors followed her commands, the brig steadied. It still rocked and creaked, but by showing less resistance, the brig eased. While her crew stood by their posts, awaiting orders, Sakona battled the Rogue's helm. The wild waves whacked the wings and propellers back and forth. If Sakona let go of the helm, the brig would spin out of control.

As her strength failed, Sakona called for Jay and Perl to share her load. Together, they held the helm straight and survived the storm.

Chapter IX

BENEATH THE SEA

With Bobo's guidance, Sakona sailed her brig south by southeast toward Metrarch's haven, the Hearth. The storm passed, but left its mark on the ship and crew.

Mackie's broken legs kept him bound to his hammock. He was sick and spent most days sleeping or puking. Half of his sailors tended to his needs while the other half repaired the brig, hoisting the main mast and fixing it in place—though more crucial repairs were needed.

Since Sakona became captain again, Jay wondered if she might return to her old, mean ways. He approached her at the helm. But when he found her, he didn't know how to begin—as was his habit. So, he started to speak and hoped that what came out would be intelligent.

"You look good at the helm. I mean… you look good anywhere? I mean, as captain!"

Jay blushed and Sakona chuckled.

"Thanks, Jay. It's good to be back."

"Do you think they'll let you stay captain once Mackie's all better?"

"They voted on me, so it's settled." Sakona stood tall and tightly gripped the helm.

To get to the heart of the matter, Jay asked another question. "Have you decided if you're going to stay with us, or move on?"

Sakona stared at the horizon with a careless face. "I don't know yet. There's a lot of the world I'd still like to see."

"Got it." Jay tried in vain to hide his frown. His sadness moved Sakona—it showed that he cared for her. He turned to leave, but she grabbed his hand.

"Jay, I'm sorry. I don't know why I said that. Of course, I'll stay with you."

"Really?"

"Yes. You're the only friend I have."

That filled him with joy. And those feelings continued until the night before their arrival when Jay found Bobo on deck. He was smiling as he gazed at the night sky.

"Excited to be home?"

"More than that, Jay. My mission is almost complete. Metrarch sent me to find you and bring you here. That's what I've done, against all odds. He'll be so proud."

"What's Metrarch like?"

Bobo's smile disappeared. "He's magnificent." Bobo looked to the sky and tried with all his might to describe the indescribable. "He's powerful, yet beautiful. Strong, yet meek. In a word: perfect. So perfect that it makes me feel repulsive."

While that description might have excited some people, it did nothing of the sort for Jay. It startled his nerves. And the only way he knew to deal with that feeling was denial. He started thinking that Bobo is too easily impressed and Metrarch is likely a standard fellow.

As if aware of Jay's thoughts, Bobo said "It's scary, but it's also exciting! Tomorrow, you'll learn what your gift is, and with it, your destiny."

Tomorrow came, and after a long day of flying, as the sky

dimmed, Bobo told Sakona to stop the ship. As the Noble Rogue floated to a halt, Jay and Perl joined their friends at the helm.

"Excellent, excellent. We're here," said Bobo.

Jay searched every direction but only found the yellow ocean. He looked again, thinking that perhaps he missed something. "Are you sure?"

"Yeah," echoed Perl, "there's nothing here!"

"Yes, there is," replied Bobo with a grin. "Vast ruins and hidden civilizations lay beneath the sandstorm sea. The Hearth is here. Beneath us."

"What?!" said Sakona. "You want me to sink my brig? After everything we did to get her back?"

"Your brig will be fine. Trust me. Have the sailors equip their goggles and lower the vessel on my command."

Jay and Perl scurried about, handing out goggles while Bobo walked to the edge of the ship. He reached into his pockets and pulled out the magma stones from the Blue Eye.

Bobo breathed in and out, closing his hands around the orbs. Eyes shut, he lifted his hands away. The stones were gone—replaced with a small, but blazing flame of Vitex. Pushing his hands up and to his sides, the Vitex spread out, flickering around the Rogue.

Jay, Perl, and Sakona gazed at the wonderous energy. The Vitex danced and blinked in the sky until Bobo sent it down, between the brig and the sea. He shaped it into a net-like shield.

"Sakona!" squealed Bobo, sweat dripping down his red face. His powers clearly took much effort. "Lower the ship!"

Sakona obeyed. Slowing the speed of the brig's propellers, the Noble Rogue eased into the sandstorm sea. The world darkened as the vessel submerged beneath the waves, but the Vitex shield blazed like a campfire.

Bobo's shield protected the hull and propellers, but some

sand flew over top and slapped down on deck.

"Get below deck," called Sakona, "everyone!"

The crew obeyed, but Loosha stood by Sakona. You see, some creatures are so full of courage and loyalty, that even in great danger, they stand by their masters. Such talents are found too often in pets and too seldom in Arlish. Loosha perched herself on the helm's guard rail and stared at the ship with dramatic (yet crossed) eyes.

Jay and Perl were almost below deck when they saw Bobo, still at the bow with his hands raised. They rushed back to him.

"Bobo, come!" begged Perl.

"I can't move," he said—his face redder than before. "If I do, the Vitex will fade!"

But the winds and sand pressed on Bobo, trying to shove him off balance. Jay and Perl held onto his legs to anchor him.

A sudden shriek sounded across the ship. Wind swept under Sakona and raised her off the deck. She held tight to the helm as another burst of wind flapped her like a flag.

"Help! Loosha, help!"

But Loosha stood still. She kept staring forward, unaware of her master's dire status. Perhaps she wasn't so noble a creature as I just now suggested. Perhaps she was stupid and useless, as I much earlier suggested.

Jay ran to her aid. As Sakona's hands slipped off the helm, Jay caught her by the arm. He heaved with all his might but the winds were mightier. As his hands began to slip, a shimmering white and gold light flashed. The wind and sand vanished. Sakona fell out of the air and on top of Jay. All was silent and light again.

What they saw was something that changed their lives forever. It was so wonderful and so beautiful, not only to their eyes, but to all of their senses. It was a new world.

The ground was flat with a few hills, like ruffles in a shirt. Blanketing the land was fuzzy green grass. But the color took Jay, Perl, and Sakona's breath away. It's difficult for me to describe. The grass was so green, it made the grass from the upper world look almost yellow. This, Jay thought, was the real, true green.

In the land's center sat a brilliant blue circle. Its surface ebbed and flowed like the sandstorm ocean, but it was calmer and glassier. Could it really be water? Could Perl's books be true?

There stood by its side a peaceful town, with homes, a market, and a harbor of airships. Nearby was a dense forest with enormous trees, dripping with a thin, white mist. And in that forest stood a massive building, ruined by time.

And how did such a world exist, beneath the sand? A dome of gold and white energy stretched above and away in every direction, covering kilometers of land. The dome shielded the land from the sandy sea, holding it up like a ceiling.

Jay's heart raced with wild joy. He wanted to jump off the ship and scour this new land at once. Following Bobo was nothing like what he had imagined. This was a real adventure.

A breath of wind flowed up and over the brig. It carried the scent of the lake, the forest, the fields, and the town. It was fresh, clean air. It moved Jay and Perl and Sakona to tears of joy, there was simply no guarding against them. Imagine hearing only sad songs your entire life, and then to finally hear a joyful one. In a way, that is what our three friends felt.

As Jay wiped his eyes, he noticed another smell, but this one was rather unpleasant. It did not take him long to realize that *he* was the source of the smell. Perl and Sakona thought the same of themselves. Even Loosha noticed her own putrid stench. Turning their sights toward each other, they realized for the first time how smelly and dirty they were. Jay felt embarrassed, as if he were standing naked before a crowd.

"Don't worry," said Bobo, "I won't let you see Metrarch until you're spotless."

Eager to see this new world up close, Jay, Perl, and Sakona rushed to the helm. Sakona called for her crew to trim the sails and land the vessel. They obeyed, but slowly, for their eyes stayed on the land below. It enchanted them, too.

Soon, the Rogue landed in a meadow beside the town. At once, Jay and his friends raced down the gangplank and tumbled to the shaggy, green grass. They dug their hands into the ground, feeling every strand of life.

"This must feel amazing on your feet," said Perl.

"Try it, try it!" said Bobo, marching down the gangplank and slipping off his boots.

The others followed his lead, resting their bare feet on the cool, mossy earth. Jay thought he could walk on it for hours without needing to rest. Another breath of air flowed by, urging Jay to search out more wonders.

He led his friends toward the town, climbing a hill of twinkling blue flowers. From its top, they could see the entire village. It sat on a hill of its own. One large home sat on the hill's top while twenty or so dotted the sides. Jay thought the large home must belong to Metrarch.

Each home was crafted from wood and clay, but they weren't grey like the homes on Onaga. These were a rich brown. It was as if the wood still teemed with life.

Surrounding the town were farms and gardens—each masterfully tended. Wagons, pulled by wooly beasts, toured the fields, and farmers filled those wagons with colorful crops.

Jay heard a new sound, like the pitter-patter of a delicate drum. Searching for the sound, he found a smooth stone in the hill's side. Out of the stone poured a slim stream.

"Is that…" started Jay.

"Yes. That's water."

Jay's jaw dropped, Perl gasped, and Sakona smiled. They watched the water flow out of a stony sliver, bubble into the stream, and rush down the hill. It was lighter and cleaner than greyberry juice, but truly, the two could not be compared.

"Try some," urged Bobo, "Try some!"

Jay cupped his hands and dipped them into the cool, starry stream. He raised the water to his lips and drank. It flowed through his mouth, kissed down his throat and sparked life in his chest.

"Wow," was the only thing he could think to say, as he scooped and gulped more and more. "It's like I didn't know I was thirsty until now."

The others joined Jay and drank their fill, which—strangely enough—came sooner than they thought it would. The water worked so well that it quenched their unknown thirst in moments.

Jay chased after the stream and his friends followed close behind. It widened with every step. At last, they came to its end; the stream flowed into a long lake. Jay, Perl, Sakona, and Loosha beheld the glimmering body. The dome's light danced along the water's surface, flickering an ever-changing aurora.

Jay felt the urge to drop his mismatched boots and flop into the lake at once. But as he stepped toward the water, Bobo stopped him.

"We should get Metrarch's permission, first. This whole place is sacred, after all."

Bobo took the lead. He brought his beaming friends toward the town, passing a troop of warriors on their way. They wore wooden armor with vine straps, similar to what Bobo wore on Onaga. They punched and kicked in unison, slashing heaps of golden vitex through the air. It was an awesome and chilling sight.

Soon they came to the village, where many people smiled and waved at the newcomers. But Bobo wore the biggest smile of them all. He proudly marched through the streets, showing off his friends to his home and his home to his friends.

"Tell me something," he asked the group, "do you see any shadows?" Jay, Perl, and Sakona saw no shadows anywhere. "The dome is made of Vitex—Metrarch himself built it. It lights the Hearth from all sides. No shadows. Except when you're inside, or in the forest, of course."

Perl scanned the area, "Bobo, are there any children here?"

"Oh no, I'm afraid you're the only ones. This place is an army camp and we're at war. It'd be too dangerous for our families."

"Do you have a family?" said Jay.

"Oh yes, oh yes," said Bobo with a small frown.

"This doesn't seem like an army camp," said Sakona. "It's all too... peaceful."

"I know what you mean," said Bobo. "This war is unlike any you've seen in the upper world, but Metrarch will tell you more about that. This is a camp, but it's also our home. Some of us have been here for years."

They came to a long one-story building with a porch. Inside was a single hallway with many doors on both sides.

"This is one of our barracks," said Bobo, leading them down the hall. "The girls can have this room here, and Jay you can have the room across from them. Wait here. I'll fetch you some drinking and bathing water. Don't confuse the two."

When Bobo left, Perl spoke first.

"This place is amazing! Sakona, have you ever seen anywhere like this?"

"Never." Sakona was certainly as excited as Perl, but she

kept calm. "Sometimes, when flying high, it's sort of like this; clean and crisp. But not as much as here."

"All my books have come true!" Perl was so absorbed in this new world that she didn't notice Jay's silence. But Sakona did.

"Jay, are you okay?"

"I'm fine."

"You're not telling the truth."

That made Jay feel guilty, "Look, I'm... a little nervous is all."

"About what?" said Perl, finally noticing Jay.

"Well, look at this place! And look at us. Don't you feel like we don't fit in here? I've got to meet this Metrarch tomorrow and I look like a pithian."

"That's why Bobo's bringing us water," said Perl. "To clean us up."

"Sure, sure," said Jay, trying to frown it off. He nodded at Perl and went in his room, closing the door behind him. After a few confused moments, the girls went to their room with Loosha following behind them.

Perl's words seemed to discourage Jay. Maybe she missed something at the start of the conversation? Sakona was first to notice Jay's sadness, which made Perl angry with herself and jealous of Sakona. She wanted to be the one to help Jay, but Sakona beat her to it.

Across the hall, Jay struggled with a different matter. He felt anxious. Think: if you had to meet a great person like a King or Queen, wouldn't you be nervous? What should you say? How should you dress? And it wasn't only his outside that troubled him.

Jay tried to calm himself down, thinking again that Bobo is too easily impressed and Metrarch is likely a standard fellow. But deep down, Jay knew he was wrong.

Chapter X

THE LEAGUE MASTER

Bobo came to Jay's room with two pails of water, rags, and a set of clothes.

"Drink up, clean up, change up, and meet me in the hall."

Once Bobo left, Jay chose to clean himself first. But he had never done so before; he did not know where to start. First, he took the dry rags and wiped his face—but the cloth felt rough on his skin. So, he dropped the rags and dipped his hands in the water pail. He wiped his face with his hands, and though it felt better on his skin, it left his hands dirtier than before. Finally, he dipped the rags in the water pail and wiped himself down.

Jay smiled. Now cleaned, he felt ready to meet Metrarch. But he noticed one black spot on his arm. He scrubbed and scrubbed but the spot remained. This made Jay angry. He scrubbed with all the force he could, past the point of pain. It left a rash bigger than the spot itself.

But Jay found the shirt Bobo brought him—it had long sleeves that would cover the mark. He changed into his new clothes. His top was a fluffy white button-down and his bottoms were slim crimson trousers. They were soft as a blanket. His smile came back.

Someone knocked at the door. Before Jay could respond,

Perl let herself in, but at once she stopped and stared at Jay for a moment, his face clean and in new clothes. "Wow, you look handsome!"

"Thanks, kiddo," Jay blushed. "You don't look so bad yourself."

Perl was wearing a green blouse with black trousers and a new, wide-brimmed hat.

"Thank you, sir," she said with a curtsy. "How are you feeling now? About meeting Metrarch?"

"Fine. Still nervous, but better."

"Well if he doesn't like you, he's dumb."

"Thanks." Her words did not help, but her intentions did. It warmed Jay's heart.

They met Sakona and Loosha in the hallway. Loosha was wearing a lime-green bow and was as hideous as ever. Sakona wore a sky-blue blouse with dark pants. She looked so beautiful to Jay that he choked on his own saliva.

Sakona's eyes widened when she saw Jay, but before she could say anything, Bobo approached the group.

"Excellent, excellent, you all look fantastic. Now come along Jay, it's time we meet him."

"Wait," said Perl, "can't we come, too?"

"Oh no," said Bobo. "Metrarch's the Master of the League. He's a very busy man. He only has time to meet with the most important people."

Sakona rolled her eyes and Perl furrowed her brows.

"Are you saying I'm not," started Perl, but she corrected herself, "I mean—we're not important?"

"No, no, I didn't mean it like that. It's just that Metrarch is like a King here and I'm—"

"Whoa, a King?" quoted Jay, "And you want me to meet him by myself?"

"Look girls," said Bobo, "I must take Jay now. You are free to explore the town, but don't go in the lake—it's sacred. League members only."

The girls folded their arms, and even Loosha frowned, while Bobo brought Jay out of the barracks and through the streets. Instead of heading up the hill, like Jay expected, they hiked to its bottom.

"When you enter, bow as low as you can. Address him as Master. Only speak if he asks you something. Relax, you'll be fine. Just don't do or say anything that might dishonor him."

They stopped in front of a small building. It was, in fact, the smallest building in the town. Jay thought it was likely some trick. He imagined entering and seeing a grand staircase that led to an underground palace.

"Go in, he's expecting you."

"You're not coming with me?"

"Oh no. I wouldn't dishonor him with my presence. Jay, this is a big moment for you. Even I have never spoken to Metrarch alone. You must tell me what it's like!"

Jay shuffled up to the door. He straightened his shirt, parted his hair, breathed in, and entered.

Inside, he found a room. There were no tapestries, royal rugs, or statues. It was simply a one-room home, smaller than Jay and Perl's. Two feathered sofas crowded a fireplace on Jay's right. To his left was a circular oak table. Behind that was a large, ornate hammock and beside that was a kitchen.

Standing by the stove was an enormous man with his back to Jay. He wasn't muscular, nor fat, just large. He was wearing heavy brown robes with a golden rope sash. He loomed over a pot of porridge, gently stirring and swirling it. The man spooned some into a bowl, which looked more like a teacup in his huge hands.

Jay thought that Bobo had brought him to the wrong house. The man carried his porridge to the table. He sat in his creaking chair and blew a soft breeze over his still steaming meal.

The man's face was old, with loving wrinkles around his eyes and lips. Full grey hair flowed royally down to his shoulders. His joyful eyes were an earthy brown-green. He was radiant, otherworldly. He knew this man must be Metrarch.

As he lifted a spoonful of porridge to his mouth, Metrarch caught sight of Jay. "Wahoo! Have you been standing there a long time?" His voice was deep and jolly.

Jay shook his head no.

"Well come here and let me fix you some grub. I heard you had a long journey, isn't that so?"

"Yes, sir—yes, master." Jay was so awed by Metrarch that he nearly forgot every commandment Bobo gave.

Metrarch pulled out a chair for Jay and retrieved a bowl of porridge and cup of water from the kitchen.

"I know some folks say, 'You can't have porridge for dinner!' but they've never had *my* porridge." He placed the meal and cup before his guest. "Now, don't tell me: your name is… Jay?"

Jay smiled, feeling honored.

"Well wahoo! I impressed myself just then. Here's a little secret: I call most people 'buddy' until I can remember their name."

Jay laughed.

"Yes indeed," continued Metrarch, "Jay, I may not be as young or handsome as I once was. I may not have the best memory either but… I forgot where I was going with that."

Jay laughed even harder this time.

"Jay, I love a good joke. But yes, Bobo left me a note, explaining things to me. That's how I knew your name. Though, I can't imagine why he wouldn't come in to speak with me."

Jay shrugged his shoulders.

"Well, anyway, I'm so honored to have you here."

"Really?"

"Yes! Jay, this is a momentous day. But don't let me keep you from eating, go ahead!"

Jay slurped on some porridge while Metrarch eagerly watched for a reaction.

"This is delicious!" And it was. Only Metrarch could make such a plain meal taste as savory as hickelberry pie.

"Wahoo! I seasoned it myself. The trick is to lightly sauté some moncetta before adding—well, I won't bore you with all the details. You didn't come this far to learn cooking from me."

"Well, Master, I was wondering about that. Why *did* you call me here?"

"You certainly deserve an answer. Let's finish eating, then retire to those sofas." As the two enjoyed their meal, Metrarch asked Jay lots of questions about his life on Onaga. "You haven't mentioned your parents, Jay. Do you mind me asking about them?"

"I don't remember them. Even when I try really hard, nothing comes to mind. Perl thinks they gave me up for adoption the day I was born."

"What a tragedy," Metrarch frowned. He put a gentle hand on Jay's shoulder. "Jay, I'm proud of you. You've lived a hard life, and yet, you're a fair-minded young man."

Jay was going to say 'thank-you,' but he found it difficult to speak. It was as if a froad was stuck in his throat.

"Was it hard," said Metrarch, "to leave Perl behind?"

"Where? At the barracks?"

"You mean she's here? In my Hearth?"

"Yes, Bobo let her come along, and my other friend, Sakona. Is that not okay?"

"Not okay? The only thing that's not okay is that they're not joining us for dinner!"

"Well, Bobo didn't want to overwhelm you."

"Oh, Bobo. Thoughtful Bobo. He loves and respects me, but he doesn't yet *know* me. If only he would come for porridge. I've invited him plenty of times! Come." Metrarch rose. "We must find your friends and show them the hospitality they deserve."

Jay and Metrarch searched the barracks but couldn't find them. So, they scoured all over the hill. As they passed other people, Jay noticed that only the younger, newer-looking members bowed before Metrarch. Everyone else either shook his hand or hugged him. In either case, wherever he went, Metrarch put a smile on people's faces.

Metrarch called many people by their names. But some he would call 'buddy' and shoot Jay a wink. He also never rushed anyone. Though he mentioned to Jay a few times that their porridge was getting cold, he patiently spoke with everyone who approached him.

It was then that a new feeling came to Jay, but not a good one. It was like anger, but more in the chest than the heart. Jay saw how important Metrarch was and how everyone loved him. Jay wanted to be like Metrarch. Jay wanted to be Metrarch. But he kept these thoughts deep inside himself.

Finally, they found Perl and Sakona walking along the beach with Loosha. The froad chased after waves and crustaceans—it was the best day of her entire life. Perl and Sakona were both surprised and nervous to learn that Metrarch had sought for them.

"I pray you two will pardon me for not realizing sooner," said Metrarch. "You two should have joined us from the start. Please come back to my home for some dinner."

Of course, the girls happily accepted his offer and soon sat at Metrarch's round table, stuffing their faces with porridge, fresh bread, and water. And while this may sound like a simple meal to you, it was nothing of the sort for them. They had only ever known stale bread kneaded with greyberry juice. Metrarch's warm, floury, homemade loaf was heavenly. Once everyone's stomachs were a good deal larger, they retired to the sofas.

Metrarch went to the kitchen and returned with a tray of vibrant fruits. There were jollos, myberries, clums, swallots, yimons, lerries, and hickelberries. He even had a few slices of my favorite meat: moncetta. It was partially smoked, thinly sliced, and unsalted (and though I prefer wholly-smoked and sautéed with diced swallots, it tastes plenty flavorful as is).

"Wahoo! What a platter. As you can see, eating is a very serious business in my Hearth."

Jay, Perl, and Sakona stared at the mouth-watering platter of sweet, candy-like fruits and savory moncetta. They gleefully and artfully tried every type.

"Some of these you'll find in the upper world, but most are found only here. If I were the money-making sort, I would start a business and sell these fruits. But if we win the war, draw back the sandstorm sea, these fruits will start to grow everywhere for everyone."

After a few more inquiries from Perl, Metrarch leaned back.

"I believe it's time I answer your question, Jay."

Chapter XI

JAY'S GIFT

"Before you ladies came, Jay asked me why I called him here. Brace yourselves for a long story from an old man."

"Maybe," interrupted Perl, "you can start from the end and then go back to the beginning and catch up to the end. That's how all the best stories go."

"I think that would confuse us," said Sakona.

"No, it works! Trust me."

"Indeed!" said Metrarch, "Perl is right, and she has clearly read the best stories. We shall start at the end, which goes something like this: and that's how we ended up on my sofa, eating fruit."

Perl smiled, thoroughly satisfied.

"Now, back to the start: A long time ago, very near the beginning, an enemy attacked Arland."

"The Kan'zi," said Jay with a somber look.

"Yes. So, Bobo has told you a bit. For generations, the Kan'zi waged war against your people. They would have succeeded if Lor Emai didn't intervene."

"Who's that?" Perl leaned in, intensely interested.

Metrarch smiled. His eyes danced with light, as a teacher's do when speaking on a favorite subject.

"Lor Emai is our creator. He made Arland and the Arlish. He's the most magnificent being in the Universe. Believe me—I've seen many. Lor Emai loved his creation and couldn't let the Kan'zi destroy it. So, he appointed an Arlish Hero and gave her a great power. With it, she defended Arland from the Kan'zi."

"And that's the power Jay has!" said Perl.

Jay lifted his chin, excited.

"Well, no. Not this power. When the Hero died, she gave her power to another. That person took up her title and defended Arland from the Kan'zi. The power was handed down in this way for thousands of years, and in all that time, the Kan'zi were kept at bay.

But three hundred years ago, the Hero died, and the power disappeared. Without the Hero to defend Arland, the Kan'zi invaded. But their strategy was different than in generations past. Instead of waging an all-out-war, they plunged the world into a sandstorm sea."

"Why would they do that?" said Sakona.

"It wasn't clear at first, but the past three hundred years have revealed their plot and purpose: their sandstorm sea swallowed cities, entire civilizations, history itself! I believe they want you to forget your history. They want you to forget the Kan'zi, Lor Emai, and the Hero of Arland. That way, it will be as if Arland has fallen asleep—no one will be awake to stop the Kan'zi. Think, can you fight an enemy you don't know exists? Or worse, can you ask for help from someone you don't know is there?"

Jay felt a twinge in his chest—it was a pure feeling of worry, the sort that is so strong, it moves you to doubt. He said, "This all doesn't make sense. Why would they want to conquer us? What good would it possibly do them?"

Metrarch paused for a moment in thought, then replied, "Frankly, Jay, we don't know yet. It's possible they want to do evil for evil's sake. In other words, they enjoy it. But I suspect there's more to it than that."

Perl wondered aloud if the Kan'zi used magic to conjure the sandstorm sea.

"No. The Kan'zi built temples in hidden places across Arland. I say temples, but they're more like factories. They consumed life—trees, earth, creatures, water—and expelled the remains as sand. This whole world was once as beautiful as my Hearth. Every grain of sand was once part of a forest, creature, or valley. This is why I was sent to Arland."

"Wait," said Perl, "Where are you from?"

"I lived in a world called Dovia—where Lor Emai lives."

"You don't look like you come from another world," said Sakona. "You look like the rest of us."

"It's not that I look like you or you like me. We both look like Lor Emai, our creator. He sent me to start a revolution, to lead the Arlish to war and destroy those temples. Then the sand will fade, and life will return."

"How can we do that when they're all hidden?" said Sakona.

"Well, now we are arriving at the end. This is the part that most concerns Jay. We discovered a map, an atlas, that belonged to the Kan'zi. We believe it was used when they first planned to build their temples. It likely contains their locations. But no one in my League can read the atlas, it's encrypted in the Kan'zi's power. But I believe you, Jay, have the power to read it."

Metrarch paused and gazed into each of his guest's eyes.

"And that's how we ended up on my sofa, eating fruit."

Perl applauded his story.

"So you're saying I have the power to read a map?" asked Jay. He tried to hide his disappointment (though he did not try very hard).

"Jay, your power is important! Without it, we have no hope

of winning the war."

"But how did I get this power?"

"I think you're truly asking, 'Where does power come from?' Like everything else in this world, it comes from Lor Emai, and who are we to question the gifts he gives us?'"

Jay leaned back and tried not to sulk. Can you blame him? This all was rather sobering business, first the adventure and now this. His 'special gift' was no more than the power to read a map! But Jay did not want to appear ungrateful or impolite, so he tried to brush aside his feelings.

"Alright then, let's take a look at that map—shall we?"

"Well, before I give it to you, you must become a member of my League."

"What? Why is that?" said Sakona, who was starting to grow a bit skeptical.

"This map is the key to our victory in the war. The elders of the League—including myself—want to know that you're committed to our effort. The Kan'zi have turned many of our allies to their side. The elders think they may specially target you because of your power.

"All three of you may join, if you wish, but only Jay is required. To join us, you must train to wield Vitex, you must learn our code, you must study our history. Finally, you must complete our Rite of Passage.

"But be warned: this war is dangerous business. I cannot, in good conscience, ask you to join us without making this perfectly clear: your lives will be at risk if you enter the war—no matter the side."

And that's all Jay needed to hear. His appetite for danger had grown since he left Onaga. Besides, he would learn to use Vitex, and that seemed like a swell thing. So, he snapped out of his self-pity at once.

"Sounds great. How do we sign up?"

"I think it best," said Metrarch, "if you speak with your friends about this first. It's always wise to hear from your loved ones before making a big decision. There's no rush."

Jay, Perl, Sakona, and, of course, Loosha stayed with Metrarch a little while longer. They bid him good evening and walked down the road to the lake. They took off their boots and dug their toes in the sand. This sand was clean, pure, and cool on their feet, unlike the sand from the upper world.

"What do you two think?" said Jay.

Sakona and Perl spoke at once.

"Well, I think—"

"You should probably—"

"Sorry," said Sakona, "You go first, Perl."

"Well," said Perl smirking, "We've come far. And it seems like we'd be in danger whether we join or not. Remember, Elska tried to kidnap you."

"Yes," said Sakona, "But is this the right team?"

"It certainly seems like it," said Jay.

"Yeah, look around you! Isn't this place beautiful?" said Perl.

"But so was Elska," said Jay, scratching his chin.

"What?" said Sakona, trying to hide the jealousy from her face. "Beauty can't tell you right from wrong."

"Maybe it can," said Jay, thinking out loud. "Sure, Elska looked… well, you know. Her power was beautiful too, but she was cruel. Metrarch, he's beautiful too, in a different way." Perl couldn't help but laugh at Jay for calling a man beautiful. But Sakona took him seriously.

"What do you mean?"

Jay ran his hands through his hair, thinking of how to explain himself. "While we were looking for you two, I saw the way he spoke with others. He was so kind and patient. It somehow made him more… beautiful? Ah, forget it."

Sakona made a special note of this.

"Right or wrong, pretty or ugly," said Perl, "these people are certainly the good people. That's obvious. And that's what matters to me."

"Me, too," said Jay.

"I don't want to discourage you, Jay," said Sakona, standing up, "but it's important to think this through: What if we go through this training, you become a member, and then you try to read the map and it doesn't work? What if they're wrong about you?"

"You mean what if I don't have the awesome power of map-reading? I'd cry," said Jay sarcastically. "But hey, even if I don't have that power, if I'm not special, these are still the good people. Maybe we could help them find the right person."

Perl and Sakona smiled. All three of them felt good about this decision.

"What should we do about Mackie and his pirates?" said Perl.

"Let's tell Metrarch. Who knows? Maybe they'd like to join the League." said Jay.

"Give them a sip of water," added Sakona, "they'll never leave."

The three laughed. They decided to find Metrarch and tell him all that they discussed. Before they even left the beach, they saw Metrarch and Bobo walking out of the town toward the lake.

"Bobo, why have you never come for porridge?"

"I didn't want to intrude, Master!"

"But I invited you, didn't I?"

"Well, well, yes, yes. But I thought you were being polite."

"I don't know why or how this all started, but too many of

you squires overthink me. When I say, 'I'd like you to come for porridge,' I mean just that!"

"Yes, Master. Yes, Master," said Bobo, bowing his lanky body low to the floor.

"And no need for bowing, Bobo. If you spent more time with me, you would know I don't care for it." Metrarch noticed Jay, Perl, Sakona, and Loosha. "Looks like we had the same idea! An evening stroll by the lake helps the food settle in my belly, too."

"Metrarch, we've decided to join you!" said Perl.

Metrarch smiled so very wide and let out his biggest 'wahoo' yet. But Jay frowned, thinking again of bad things. Metrarch was so loveable that it filled Jay with envy.

"This is grand," said Metrarch. "And you all agreed to this?"

"Yes," said Sakona.

"Sure," added Jay.

Metrarch's eyes stayed on Jay. He thought for a moment, then said, "Things are different than you expected. You think you don't have everything you want. But you do; it just looks a bit different is all. You have a special gift, Jay. It's something only you can do—the fate of the war rests in your hands. And you're not alone. You've got loving friends by your side."

Jay felt a bit lighter. This was a hard fact to face, but Metrarch was right.

"Now I don't know about you," said Metrarch, "but I'm ready for a swim. Won't you all join me?"

Metrarch entered the lake, followed by Jay, Perl, Sakona, and Bobo. They splashed and swam and played games for hours. When Jay rolled up his sleeves, the black mark was gone.

Chapter XII

A MADDENING MASTER

A clanging gong ended Jay's sleep. The sound so startled him that he thought he had died. When he realized he was, in fact, alive, he stumbled out of his room, rubbing his eyes. Adults packed the hallway. They were dressed, cleaned, and standing at attention.

Jay was certainly out of the loop. But, since it was his first day, Jay thought he would be shown grace. Perl, Sakona, and Loosha came out a moment later. They too looked sleepy, sloppy, and confused (though Loosha always looked that way).

Heavy bootsteps thudded down the hall. The men and women tightened their stance as a tall woman passed them by. She was flanked by two armored guards wearing wooden armor, like the sort Bobo wore on Onaga.

The woman stopped in front of Jay, towering over him and his friends.

"I thought you three wanted to join the League."

Her voice was harsh. She had a thick, rough accent, probably from a northern, mountainous country. Her limbs were sturdy as steel. Her face was aged and stoic as a marble bust. She was royalty, she was savagery. *She could kill you without you minding in the least,* Jay mused.

"Umm, yeah," said Jay. "We do."

"We do, what?"

"We do want to join."

A few people in the hallway chuckled, but one look from the woman silenced them all. "You mean to say, 'We want to join, *Master.*'"

Jay wasn't annoyed by this at all. He felt rather optimistic. "Umm, sure. We want to join, Master."

"I am Master Wald. Elder Wald. Master or Elder. Call me nothing else."

"Got it, Master," said Jay.

"Yes, Elder," said Perl.

Wald looked to Sakona, who rolled her eyes and said, "Yes, Master."

"Good. Now, you tell me you wish to join, but you did not wake early, you did not clean yourselves, you did not stand at attention."

"I'm sorry, Elder," said Perl. She was the most excited to learn Vitex. She would do or say anything to earn Wald's favor.

"How could we have known those things? No one told us!" said Sakona, but Perl punched her in the arm to shut her up.

"You chose to join us," said the Master. "It is your duty to learn our customs, not mine to teach them. Metrarch may want you here, but I made no such request. Tomorrow, you will be clean, present, and attentive before the gong. Now, to the fields."

Wald took her troop out of the town and into a field. For the next few hours, Wald ordered something rather strange: instead of teaching her troop histories or combat stances, Wald forced them to plow the field, plant seeds, and water the ground. It was hard work, but what made it most difficult was that it seemed pointless. Jay had a leg up on the others, having worked on farms before, but the girls quickly caught up to him.

Throughout the morning, Wald gave strict commands: "Don't confuse the hickelberries for myberries!" and "Yimons need partial sunlight. Partial!" and "Don't overwater the clums!"

"This is stupid," said Sakona. "She's using us to make her a garden."

"I don't mind," said Perl. "Didn't you try those fruits? They were unbelievable!"

"Still, what does this have to do with Vitex, or Arland's history?" asked Jay.

To receive an answer, they visited Bobo during their lunch break.

"Vitex is the energy of life," said Bobo, passing around bowls of freshly picked jollos. "It comes from other beings, like plants or creatures. By using a life form's Vitex, you kill it. You're taking away its life. But life forms won't give up their Vitex to just anyone. Think, think, if someone you didn't know asked you to die for them, would you?"

"No," said Sakona.

"Only if they were a really good friend," said Perl.

"Even then, I'm not sure," said Jay.

"Exactly. So, think of it this way: nature wants to know you like a good friend. She wants to know that you're on the same side. Farming—tending to a plant's needs—is one way we do that. It's an exercise."

"Why didn't Wald tell us that?" said Sakona.

"She can be a bit short and cold, but she knows her stuff. Give her time. Metrarch himself trained her. He trained all the elders."

"Why can't he train us? Instead of Wald?" said Jay.

"He doesn't train anyone anymore. Not sure why."

After lunch, they returned to the field. Wald ordered them to plow, plant, and water crops for another three hours. At the day's end, Wald asked Jay and his friends to stay while she dismissed her troop.

"You three are behind," said Wald. "You'll need extra training at the end of each day."

"Of course, we're behind! We just got here," said Sakona.

Wald squinted her eyes at the girl. "I will teach you a combat form tonight, and tomorrow I will test you."

"We get to use Vitex?!" Jay nearly collapsed in excitement.

"No. That would be dangerous. And I'd be surprised if you could, after only one day of farming. Now, here is what the form looks like."

Wald broke into a combat stance. Pointing her middle and index fingers together, then to the ground, she drew them to her chest. She moved forward, striking and swiping with every step. It looked like a dance—but with more punching.

Jay stood up, ready to give it a try, but Wald said, "Sakona, you are first. I hope you watched closely." Sakona stepped forward and put her pointer fingers together. "Wrong. You did not watch closely."

Sakona grumbled and Jay smirked. She stepped back and he stepped forward, but again Wald cut him off, "Perl, your turn."

Perl stood, wiping her hands on her trousers. She pointed her middle and index fingers together, then to the ground. But when she drew them up to her chest, out of the grass flowed flakes of Vitex! As the golden energy fluttered through the air, illuminating the field, the grass withered and faded. Perl froze.

"I'm sorry! I didn't mean to—"

"Don't be," commanded Wald. "Continue the form!"

Perl drew her fingers to her chest. The Vitex swirled and floated in front of her, twinkling and sparkling. She mimicked Wald's strikes and swipes. The Vitex followed her command.

Jay and Sakona watched the terrifying and beautiful energy

slash and soar through the air. It was amazing, breathtaking, and most of all, confusing.

"How did you do that!?" said Jay.

"You bent Vitex on your first try," said Wald, with a hint of shock. "Perl, you must be a prodigy."

"Not bad, kiddo!" said Jay.

Perl smiled and stepped back in line. Sakona folded her arms.

"I must consult the elders about you," said Wald. "Someone with your gift needs special attention." Wald nearly walked off that instant, but Jay spoke up.

"Hey, wait a second—I can do that too, Master."

Wald stopped, "Oh, yes. Go ahead."

Jay stepped up, feeling optimistic. If Perl could do it, he could, too. He pointed his fingers to the ground, then drew them to his chest. No Vitex appeared. He started over, drawing his fingers up from the ground to his chest, but again, nothing happened.

He shrugged it off and pushed through the rest of the set: he punched and struck as Wald and Perl did. When he finished, Sakona applauded him, but Wald shook her head.

"You did not step forward with your attacks. Did you expect to gain the upper hand on your enemy by standing still?"

"Whoops. But besides that, I did pretty good—right?"

"Good? You abuse that word. Good is our goal. It's the opposite of evil. Good is perfect. So, no. You did not do *pretty good*."

Jay's cocky smile faded. Until then, he had chosen to respect Wald, but now he furrowed his brows in contempt.

"Tomorrow, I will test you and Sakona. Perl, tutor them." And with that, Wald left.

"Did you see me? I used Vitex! I'm a prodigy!"

"That's great, Perl," said Jay, trying his best to put aside his own feelings. "Let's get this over with."

Jay and Sakona practiced the form for the rest of the evening. Perl corrected their mistakes and, though she was a bit proud of her skills, she was a natural teacher. Dusk came and with it that part of the day when all things become funny. They worked hard, but they had plenty of laughs, too, making silly jokes and teasing one another.

They left the funny part of the night behind and entered a new part. A deep part. The part in which the best conversations are had—when weariness feeds bravery.

"Sakona," started Jay, "Did you ever meet your mother?"

She peered into Jay's eyes, debating whether or not to reward his courage with an answer. "No. My father only spoke of her once. He drank a little too much Dalkan Ale that night."

"Yuck!" spat Perl. "That stuff is the worst!"

"How would you know?" said Jay.

Perl replied, "I've read about it. 'Nothing great comes from Dalk.'"

Sakona continued, "He said she was the meanest and strongest pirate in the world."

"Then why did he court her?" said Jay.

"I asked him, but he laughed and blushed."

"Strange," said Jay.

"Adults always hide stuff," whined Perl. "Why can't they spit out what they know?"

"Like Wald," said Sakona. "She showed us the form, but she didn't explain anything!"

"That's true," said Jay.

"I for one," said Perl, "want to know more about Elska. Why did her Vitex look different?"

"I suppose we should ask Wald," said Jay.

They had a large dinner at Bobo's house (stewed wooly gare, dehaired thankfully) and, as you can imagine, they slept well that night. Even so, they were careful to wake, wash, and dress before the gong.

After another long day of farming, they rehearsed the form for Wald, and they did so perfectly. But all she said was "Good."

Jay folded his arms, "That's it?"

"If you want an applause, join the circus," shot Wald. "And I think you mean, 'That's it, *Master.*' But come, I will teach you the next form—"

"Master," interrupted Jay. "Could you first teach us more about Vitex itself?"

"Yeah," said Perl, "and why Elska's Vitex was white. Are there other types?"

When Perl said Elska's name, Wald glanced about and, seeing no one, told them to sit.

"Vitex is life. It is our core existence. There are two forms of Vitex: Oftgaran and Dovian, Gold and White. Oftgaran is the Vitex of this world, the world in which Arland and Kan'zi exist. Dovian is the Vitex of the other world, where Metrarch comes from. It is the Vitex of our creators."

"But I thought Elska was Arlish—that's what Bobo told us," said Jay. "How did she get the White Vitex?"

"Yes, Elska is Arlish. She stole the White Vitex from this place a long time ago. White Vitex is an eternal power, it lasts forever. But Gold Vitex is finite, it fades after its use. It can only be summoned at the expense of something or someone's life—a sacrifice. You must consider this: when wielding Vitex, you are holding life in your hands. It must be treated as a solemn honor."

"I don't understand why something would give up its life for something else," said Sakona.

"It is because you do not yet understand the greater good. Nature knows we are fighting to save it, to save Arland. So, it willing gives up its power to us."

"But that tree or grass or whatever you're using won't be around to see the greater good."

"That's why it is called a sacrifice. It is no different than what we expect from each other."

"You would die for someone else?" Sakona shook her head in disbelief.

"If it means saving a life more valuable than my own, yes. We are no different than nature. In a desperate battle, I may sacrifice myself and give up my Vitex for another to use."

"So, Jay's power is the key to winning the war," started Sakona. "He's the only one who can read the Kan'zi map. If it was between your life and his, would you die for him?"

"Yes."

Jay looked up, surprised.

"This is what the League is built on," said Wald. "Sacrifice. In fact, it is what all good is built on. We must give up our needs for others."

Later that evening, Jay, Perl, Sakona, and Loosha walked (and waddled) to a flourishing flower field. They climbed a hill, sat at its top, and watched over the town.

"I'm not going to train anymore," said Sakona. Jay and Perl, who were rather shocked, asked why. "I don't agree with Wald or the League."

"About the sacrifice thing?" said Jay.

"But that's what your father believed," said Perl. "He died to save us."

Sakona said nothing. Jay could tell she was angry, so he didn't press her. After a long pause, she spoke again.

"I don't agree with them and I'm not going to. Besides, I need to repair the Rogue and see the crew."

*　　*　　*

The next few weeks were filled with hard work. Every day,

Jay and Perl woke and washed before the gong. They spent the entire day either farming or training. Training days were just as exhausting as farming days; Wald would make them run through obstacles, climb tall hills, and fence with one another. Dueling with sabers—Wald said—would help should they run out of Vitex.

She also taught them Vitex theory, saying it was more than a weapon; a wielder could bend Vitex into all sorts of rough shapes, like shields and blades. Beginners struggle to shape the power, but masters could bend Vitex to quickly serve their needs in battle. Therefore, they called it bending, for wielders bend and shape the power to their will. In these lessons, Wald always reminded Jay and Perl that "Vitex is still a mystery. We have yet to discover all of its powers."

In those weeks, Wald treated Perl kindly, but Jay harshly. She often made Jay repeat exercises twice and run extra laps.

One day, Perl and Jay came to Wald with a list of questions about Vitex. They were mostly Perl's questions, but when she voiced them to Jay, he too wanted answers.

"Master, can you tell us more about Dovian Vitex—White Vitex?"

"What more do wish to know? It is the life force of Dovia, the eternal world."

"Yes, but how did it get here if it's from that world? And do we have any more of it?"

Wald would have smiled if she was the smiling type. She valued curiosity. "Legends say that long ago, when the Kan'zi first invaded Arland, Lor Emai gifted one 'helping' of White Vitex to the first Hero of Arland. That gift was bestowed from one Hero to the next. To my knowledge, it is the only 'helping' in the world."

And this led to Perl's next question, "But if Metrarch is from

Dovia, doesn't he have White Vitex, too?"

"I suspect so," said Wald, nodding. She had clearly thought of this before. "But I don't know. I've only seen him use Gold."

"So you can use more than one," said Jay.

"When it comes to Vitex, it is hard to know things for certain. It is a mystery, after all."

"Okay. My next question is if Elska stole the Vitex, can we steal it back?"

"Not exactly. As you know, it's not a solid object. White Vitex behaves more like a liquid. Imagine that when Elska stole it, she didn't take it in her hands, but rather drank it into herself. To take it back, she would have to give it up willingly, which of course, she never would."

"She might have died when we fought her sloop. Did the power die with her?"

"White Vitex is immortal. It would survive and wait for someone else to 'drink it in.' Sometimes, that's what happened to the Hero of Arland: he or she would die in battle, then an apprentice would find the Vitex and become the next Hero."

"So the power is somewhere out there, in the sandstorm sea," said Jay.

"Perhaps. Perhaps not. Elska is stronger than you think. I don't believe you've seen the last of her."

"Got it. Last question," started Perl. "Which is better, Gold or White?"

"That remains to be seen. Gold relies on fuel and White does not, so in that sense, White is better. But in terms of raw power, I am unsure."

Perl smiled, happy to have her questions answered. Their training continued and after two weeks, Jay used Vitex for the first time. Though it was only a few blades of grass—a mere handful—he felt very proud. As was his habit in those days, he visited Sakona that evening. He climbed aboard the Rogue and searched its lower deck until he found her in the engine room.

"How's the ship coming along?"

"Fine," said Sakona, barely lifting her eyes from her work. She used a rusty wrench to tighten a bolt. "Finished the mast and hull today. You okay?"

Jay leaned casually against a piston. But it was piping hot and burning his arm, so as calm as he could, he shifted to another piston. His arm probably needed medicine, but he couldn't risk looking anything but cool in front of Sakona.

"I'm good. Had a decent day—I bent Vitex, so that's alright I guess."

Sakona dropped her wrench in excitement and asked, "Really? What was it like?"

"Like I sprouted another arm. I felt the Vitex, even though I didn't actually reach out and touch it. My chest felt hot, too. Like if I kept holding it, I'd start to burn. Kinda like these pistons."

"What?"

"Nothing. Nevermind."

Sakona thought of something that made her frown. She picked up her wrench again and continued her work.

"That's it? No 'congratulations?'"

"What do you want, a medal?"

"That or something else," Jay shot Sakona a half smirk. "I think I've earned it."

Sakona chuckled and rolled her eyes. She changed the subject, asking, "What did Wald say?"

"Just her usual 'good,'" he said, mocking her accent. "I never get anything more from her. She's always working me twice as hard as everyone else.

"She's a grumpy old lady. And you won't have to deal with her for much longer, right? Isn't your final test coming up?"

"Yep." Jay realized they were alone. "By the way, where's Mackie?"

"He's speaking with Metrarch—he and the crew want to join the League. I think it was the water."

"You sure you don't want to come back and train with us? It's tough and all, but—"

"Someone's got to take care of things while you and Perl play with magic."

"We're not playing, we're training."

"Right. Well go on and train with Perl. I'll be here, actually working hard."

"What are you, jealous? You could've kept training, you know!"

Sakona dropped her wrench and looked Jay squarely in the eye. "Get off my brig."

At once, Jay stormed off and walked back to the town, feeling heavier than before. As he came to the lake, he saw Metrarch sitting on the shore with a fishing rod. Metrarch waved Jay over to sit with him.

"Jay," whispered Metrach, "I'm glad you're here. I've been wanting to show you this." Metrarch handed Jay the fishing pole. "Have you ever fished before?"

"I almost died hunting a yavyu. Does that count?" whispered Jay.

"Not exactly. This is a much safer sport—but not many can do it. It takes patience. Keep a finger on the line until you feel a little tug."

Jay held the rod tight, but after a few minutes, he loosened his grip.

"I used Vitex today. First time ever!"

"Well wahoo!" Metrarch covered his mouth, "But—we best keep whispering, Jay. Don't want to scare away the fish. You're making great progress. I bet Wald was proud."

"She didn't seem very proud. She didn't seem very… anything."

They chuckled gently.

"I know exactly what you mean," whispered Metrarch. "You just take my word for it: she's proud."

Jay felt a tug on his line. He stood to his feet.

"Now reel it in—be stern. Reel and pull!"

Jay tugged and reeled until a green fish flopped out of the lake and onto the sand.

"Well done! You're a natural. That there's a Snooted Lye. They are pretty slimy to me. I wonder if you can catch us a Mullock for dinner. They're a bit crunchier," said Metrarch, licking his lips.

Jay cast his line back into the lake. "Our final test is in a few days. Any advice?"

"Oh yes. The Rite of Passage is very sacred, very tough, very important, very… well, everything! You've got to pass it to become a member of the League. But I'm sure Wald has prepared you well."

Jay spent another hour fishing. But even a new hobby couldn't settle his mind, for in one week, Jay would be tested in the Rite of Passage.

Chapter XIII

RITE OF PASSAGE

Six days later, Wald guided Jay and Perl across the training field, past the lake, to the edge of the Misty Wood. A thick fog floated over the dark forest. Far off, high above the trees, a glorious citadel peaked through the mist.

Wald paced back and forth while Jay and Perl stood at attention.

"Perl, name the ranks of the League."

"Ally, trainee, squire, knight, and elder."

"Describe them."

Perl grinned; she had studied for this.

"First, there are the allies—people who aren't officially members, but they're friends to the League. There are trainees, like us, who want to join but haven't completed their Rite of Passage. Next there are squires. They're members of the League—they've passed the test. There are knights. They've mastered higher forms of Vitex. To be a knight, an elder has to nominate you. Lastly, there are elders. They're Vitex masters and they govern the League."

"You've forgotten a rank."

"The League Master," said Jay.

Perl frowned.

"Jay, recite the Code of the League."

Jay stepped forward, took a breath, and spoke: "I trust in the maker of Arland, I will fight to defend his domain. To other's needs I will always tend… uh…"

"For good will my Vitex strain!" finished Perl.

But Wald held her gaze on Jay, "How is it you forgot the most important part of the pledge?"

Jay sighed and slouched, "I don't know, Master. It just happened."

"If I teach you Vitex apart from goodness, I've put a weapon in the hand of a madman. Never forget goodness. Good?"

"Good," said Jay, mimicking her accent. It was an accident, mostly, but Wald didn't notice.

"Remember, too, our pledge is not to the League, nor Metrarch himself, but to Lor Emai."

Jay and Perl nodded.

"Tomorrow is your Rite of Passage. Today you must review."

So, Wald drilled them for hours with no breaks. They sparred, studied, farmed, and used Vitex. Perl's powers had grown; she could wield Vitex as large as cannon ball and command it with total precision. But Jay still struggled to wield more than a pinch. And after wielding that pinch, he would often struggle to summon more for another hour.

You would think that this worried Jay, saying the Rite of Passage was only a day away, but that was not the case. Jay felt relaxed, likely because he had no idea what the test actually consisted of. It was all too vague for him to feel anything. Perl, on the other hand, had grown nervous for the same reason; with no idea what to expect, she expected the worst.

Soon, Perl couldn't contain her worry. "Master Wald, please tell us more about the Rite of Passage! How dangerous is it? Has anyone ever… died?"

"Died? No. But there have been close calls."

"What?!" said Jay. "How? Isn't it just a test?"

"Yes, though clearly not the sort of test you're thinking of," said Wald. "It involves much more than paper and quill. You must journey through the Misty Wood and complete a task there. I can say no more."

Jay and Perl stared at the Misty Wood and the astonishing structure which overlooked it. The wood somehow seemed darker than before. Jay even heard a few distant howls.

He tried to be brave and hopeful. "But there's nothing dangerous in there, right?"

"I know of at least three wooly gares, two packs of rolfs, and a few swarms of wookapods. It is rather dangerous."

Perl's jaw dropped while Jay fought to keep his shut.

When evening came and the Vitex dome dimmed to a gentle pulse of white light, Jay snuck out of the barracks and village. He came to a wide field and practiced his Vitex forms. But with each try he failed to summon more than a handful of energy. No matter how hard he worked, he couldn't use as much as Perl. You can imagine how frustrating it was, since Jay had farmed and practiced as much as she. What was he doing wrong? Finding no answer, he quit the field and fought his way to sleep.

When he and Perl woke the next day, they entered the barrack's hall. Seeing no one, they left the building and found Bobo waiting on the porch.

"Excellent, excellent, you're awake. And you have your swords, good. Come along, it's time for your Rite." Bobo turned to leave, "I almost forgot." He picked up a fishing rod and handed it to Jay. "It's from Metrarch."

It was a simple wooden rod with a comfy, fitted hilt and plenty of spool. Jay smiled, "Not bad! I'll leave it in my room."

"No, no, take it with you! You'll need it. The Rite of Passage will test you in many ways, including hunger."

"Did he get anything for me?" asked Perl.

"Ah silly me, silly me. How could I forget? He wanted me to tell you this: good luck."

Bobo brought the children out of the town, through the field, and past the lake. All the while, they never saw another person. The town, field, and lake were empty. But soon they came to the edge of the Misty Wood, where a mass had gathered— nearly two hundred in number.

"See lads? The entire League has shown up to cheer you on!"

Jay scanned the crowd, looking for Sakona. He hadn't seen her since they fought on the Noble Rogue. He saw Mackie Slook's sailors, many squires and knights, but no elders and no Metrarch. His heart leapt when he spotted Sakona coming toward him with Loosha by her side.

"You ended up coming, after all," said Jay.

"Of course!" said Sakona, playfully punching him in the arm. After a few awkward moments, she continued, "Look, I'm uh… I'm sorry."

But before Jay could reply, Bobo stepped before the mass and commanded a mighty speech, "Welcome all, welcome all, to another Rite of Passage! These brave young lads completed their basic training with Elder Wald and now shall prove themselves in the Misty Wood."

Bobo turned his attention to Jay and Perl. "Your challenge is this: enter the Misty Wood and search for a white tree. From it, you must draw Vitex and carry it to the inner sanctuary of the citadel. There you will be judged. Be warned: the white tree is sensitive. Drawing and sustaining its Vitex will be more difficult than any other life form. But be a friend to nature in the Misty Wood, and it will reward you. Be doubly warned: the wood is a dangerous maze filled with dangerous creatures."

"How long will this all take?" said Jay.

"The shortest run was two hours. The longest was three days."

"What!" Perl rubbed her stomach. "We haven't had breakfast yet!"

"That's part of the challenge. Perl, you're up first."

"You mean we can't go in together?" said Perl.

"Of course not. Your entrance to the League must be personal."

Jay and Perl felt uneasy, but Perl found her courage.

"I'm ready."

The mob cheered as she entered the Misty Wood. A long time had passed, and Jay's stomach growled. Sakona took him on a walk to distract his belly. But Jay kept looking back to the Misty Wood.

"Jay, you'll be fine."

"Who said I wouldn't be?"

"Your face."

"It's lying."

"I know. And think about it, they're making you take this test so they can use you. They need your gift, remember? If you fail, and they actually need you, it won't matter."

But that didn't make him feel any better. In fact, it annoyed him. Except for Wald, Jay was rather fond of the League and he wished Sakona would be, too.

Three hours later, Perl triumphantly marched out of the wood. She wore a white sash with an imprint of the League's emblem: a golden hand with sparks above the fingertips. She was damp from the mist—water dripped from her cap. The mass cheered.

"Well done, little missy. And in only three hours!" said Bobo.

"Thank you, thank you," she said, bowing.

"Ladies and gentlemen," bellowed Bobo, "I present to you Squire Perl!"

The mass cheered again. After a few minutes, all settled down.

"Jay," said Bobo, "it's your turn."

"Any tips, kiddo?" asked Jay.

Perl would have answered but Bobo cut her off. "Don't tell him nothing, nothing! He's got to go in blind, like you."

Jay felt that shy strain in his chest that comes from fear. He tried to think himself out of it: *If Perl made it, I can too.* But he knew that wasn't necessarily true. Perl's power was far stronger than his.

Jay heard a distant roar echo from the woods. Could it be a wooly gare? But he suddenly found himself smiling. It probably *was* a wooly gare. In fact, it could have been something worse, and what a thrilling thought that was! So Jay's daring side won. He boldly entered the Misty Wood.

Darkness and a ghostly mist shrouded the wood. Until then, Jay had never known humidity. There was no path, only wild shrubs and skinny trees sprouting in all directions. Most were blue, but some had hints of green and white. Like Jay, the trees dripped with sweat. Blue branches leaned lazily this way and that.

But the fog hid much from Jay's sight. He could only see about ten meters ahead. Beyond the fog, the wood sang wild songs—chirps and burps, howls and growls. What creatures lay just beyond the mist? It was a terrifying and exciting thought.

He bravely marched deeper into the wood with his sword in one hand and fishing pole in the other. But every step he took made him more confused. Without a path or map, he wondered how he would find the white tree in such a crowded place. What if he already passed it by?

For hours, Jay wandered around like this. Or did it only feel like hours? His legs began to ache, so he sat down and gave them a vigorous rub. But shortly after, a rustle sounded from a nearby shrub. Jay raced back to his feet. Next he heard a snivelling growl.

Out of the mist crawled three rolfs, daring and desperate creatures. Their yellow eyes deliciously locked on Jay. Their tall, furry ears stood alert. Their long snouts fanged with teeth. The center rolf—the pack leader—barked and the other two crawled toward their prey.

Jay dropped his fishing rod and pointed his sword with shaky hands. He stabbed this way and that to keep the creatures back, shouting with every wild wack. But then he remembered his Vitex and quickly summoned a handful out of the grass. It was a small supply, the size of his fist.

He took a deep breath and broke into a combat stance. He pointed at the front-most beast: The Vitex sped off and scorched the rolf's face, forcing the creature to flee. The other two rolfs dashed at Jay, growling for revenge. He tried to summon more Vitex, but none came, so he held up his sword again.

But another creature leapt out of the trees. Standing between the rolfs and Jay was Loosha. She shot her tongue at one, paralyzing it. The pack leader leapt at Loosha and bit her. Jay came to Loosha's aid and slashed at the rolf's back, who immediately released its bite and rushed away.

The brawl ended. Jay gasped for air and swiped the sweat from his face. Until then, he had fought with cannonballs and harpoons at a distance. Using a sword was personal and frightening. In fact, among all his adventures thus far, this changed Jay the most: it gave him a taste of true fear and with it, true courage.

Satisfied with her work, Loosha sat down and looked at Jay with her crossed eyes.

"Loosha! Did Sakona send you?"

"Croark!"

"Well, thanks for coming."

"Croark!"

"Keep this between us, but… I don't think I would have made it without you."

"Croark!"

"Are you hurt?"

A small imprint of the rolf's teeth remained, but no blood. Jay sighed in relief and sat next to Loosha, petting her head.

"You didn't see a white tree out there, did you?"

"Croark…"

"Of course, not."

Jay heard another growl, but this one came from his stomach. So, he and Loosha waddled on, now looking for a white tree and for food. Following the sound of rushing water, they came to a cool, slim river.

"Think there are fish in there, Loosha?"

But Loosha only ignored Jay, sniffing around the river. Jay cast his line into the pool and waited. An eternity seemed to go by, and Jay had nearly given up when he felt the slightest tug on his line. He yanked and reeled until a small blue fish flew out of the water and onto his lap.

"Croark!"

"Oh, now you care!"

Jay gathered some branches for firewood to cook the fish. He tried using Vitex to start a fire, but the air was too moist. So he gave the raw fish to Loosha who gladly swallowed it whole. Jay sat down with his back against a tree. He tried to think of a plan, but he soon felt drowsy. He fought to stay awake and alert, thinking a wooly gare might devour him in his sleep. In the end, sleep won as he drifted off into a unnerving rest.

Chapter XIV

THE WHITE TREE OF THE MISTY WOOD

When he woke, he was stiff, cold, and slimy from Loosha's oozings. Jay couldn't tell how long he had slept—the wood appeared as dim as before.

Jay stood and glanced around. Which way had he come from? And which way was he going? Thin, silver trees barred the landscape in every direction. Jay was lost. Slowly, aimlessly, he and Loosha wandered forward. Or were they wandering backward?

When another hour came and went, Jay and Loosha found a clearing. Jay thought they reached the forest's end, but as they moved further in, Jay found pale roots peeking out of the ground, like a yavyu breaching through the ocean. The gnarling roots stood to his chest and bulged fatter than Loosha. Jay tracked them to their source: a white tree.

Its sharp branches and finned bark coursed up the trunk and sprawled into deep, blue leaves. The trunk twisted round and round as it reached higher and higher. The white tree stood taller than any other tree in the wood. *Why did it take me so long to find?* Jay wondered. The tree's bark had many holes and gaps, like that of an old castle tower, with portholes and white stone.

"We did it, Loosha!"

"Croark!"

"Once I take the Vitex, we'll have to move fast to the cita-del."

"Croark?"

"Good question… where is the citadel?" Jay tried to peer through the foggy sky above the tree, but the mist was too thick. "Wait here, Loosha."

Jay started to climb the trunk for a better view, but the scaly bark nipped and pricked his hands. Halfway up, he had to stop. His hands were bleeding. He wiped them on his pants and kept climbing, baring the pain. When he reached the top, he saw a weathered tower of faded peach, with a dramatic, sloped roof. He smiled, then carefully climbed down.

"It's there!" he said, pointing. "We're close."

Wasting no time, he dropped out of the tree and spread his legs into a combat stance. He pointed his fingers and motioned at the tree to release some Vitex. Nothing happened.

He tried pulling Vitex from every part of the tree, but none came. Jay grew angry. He was hungry, cold, bloody, and now failing. He tried and tried for the better part of an hour, but nothing worked.

"I swear, I'm doing everything right."

"Croark."

"Well, I'm not going to sit here and starve. Let's just go to the citadel and see what happens."

"Croark!"

"If they ask, I'll say the tree's broken or something."

They quit for the castle. With every step he took, Jay felt more and more uneasy. He voiced his concerns to Loosha, but she was apathetic to his struggles.

Soon they came to the base of the structure. Before them stood its grand entrance. Vines and shrubs had overgrown much, but Jay could still make out its cobblestone walls. They were pale peach and orange. The gigantic doorway arched at the top and held a peculiar keystone: etched in its face were waves swirling round a crown.

The entrance stood tall—taller than a yavyu, though not as wide. Jay wondered what remarkable creature needed such a high passage. The white-wood door stood ajar. Looking within, Jay saw only darkness.

"You don't glow in the dark, do you?"

Loosha croarked with a frown.

"I didn't think so."

So Jay picked a few shrubs off the castle's side and pulled out a small pinch of Vitex and held the glowing flakes in his hand.

"This should last us for a bit."

They entered the citadel and found themselves in a long hallway. Jay's light was so dull and the hall was so long, he couldn't see to its end. He could only spot its walls and parts of the arched ceiling.

The structure was ornate. Every part of every surface was dressed in paintings, designs, and flourishes. The walls shimmered a deep, cold red—if you can imagine such a color—with splashes of white and gold. On the floors lay round tiles of obsidian.

The most dazzling feature of the structure was its scale. One could spend hours taking in all the features of a simple column section. How could any number of people build something so large and so lovely? From the broadest strokes to the finest prints, the castle was a work of art. Jay knew that he stood in the most beautiful building in the world.

He wished he could explore every corner of the room, but his Vitex flame strained his energy, so he and Loosha marched on. They moved by many corridors and antechambers, each glowing with spectacle. At last, the hall opened into an enormous chamber, so large that its boundaries were shrouded in shadows. But far, far off, Jay saw a light.

"Loosha, that must be the end!"

Together, they dashed toward the light. After a long run, they came to its source: a fire crackling in an immaculate, golden bowl. The bowl sat upon a long quartz shrine. Ten thrones flanked the shrine, curved in a semi-circle. Behind the shrine and flaming bowl stood a golden throne, raised higher than the others. Beside it, stood Metrarch.

"Do you bring us a flame from the white tree of the Misty Wood?" Long shadows dramatically danced across his face.

Jay thought of his question and realized that he could lie. The Vitex he held might pass for the Vitex of the white tree. He doubted Metrarch could tell the difference. And besides, hadn't he suffered enough? Blood still dripped from his palms.

The white tree didn't give up its Vitex, but was that Jay's fault? Suddenly, lying didn't seem like lying. It seemed like a good thing to try. He opened his mouth to speak. But the memory of Captain Zye probed in his mind.

"No, Master."

"What do you hold in your hand?" demanded Metrarch.

"Vitex… but from a different plant. I found the White Tree, but I couldn't bend it. I think it's… broken?"

Out of the shadows stepped Wald and the five other elders. They bowed to Metrarch and sat on their thrones. To Jay's surprise, not all the elders were elderly. There were Traylock and Gern, twin-brothers and young adults. Quil, the regal but mute woman, was middle-aged. There was Nul, a sour-looking old man of about Wald's age. Finally, there was Sageous—a shy, ancient woman.

For a long time, the council stayed silent. Grumpy Nul furrowed his black brows and began, "We cannot admit him."

"Well, how else can we read the atlas?" asked Gern.

"We'll find another way," shot Nul.

"What way?" said Traylock.

"I don't know. But he couldn't bend the Vitex of the White Tree!" said Nul.

"I did everything right," said Jay. "I didn't misuse my Vitex, I swear. I only used it in self-defense. I don't know why the White Tree wouldn't budge, but it wasn't my fault."

At this, the council fell silent again. A few scratched their chins, deep in thought. But Nul chuckled, "This all proves my point about him, it's as I told you before."

"Elders," said Metrarch, gently, "we should dismiss the boy—"

"No," demanded Nul. "He must stand our judgement. It's part of our Rite."

"Master Nul is right about the Rite," admitted Sageous. "Inability to use Vitex is not a mark of the League."

"No," said Nul, "it is the mark of the enemy!"

"We should never have sent for him," said Gern.

As if things couldn't get worse, Elder Nul asked for Wald's opinion. She sighed and spoke: "Of all the students I've taught, Jay is the most… gifted."

Her words stunned both the council and Jay.

"How can you say that?" said Nul.

"Master Nul, need I remind you that the greatest gift Lor Emai gave us is not Vitex, but Goodness itself? Jay is hard working, patient, thoughtful, but most of all, he is good."

Nul frowned and Jay blushed, shoving his hands in his pockets.

"But how can we even think of accepting one who can't

bend the White Tree?" said Nul. "The tree has long stood as our safeguard, keeping the evil-at-heart out of our League."

"Perhaps this challenge was unfair. It may not have been his fault, given his unique circumstance," said Traylock.

"Unique?" spat Nul. "Elders, you must see the risk we are taking if we accept him!"

"Enough," said Metrarch. "We will discuss this in private." Metrarch's tone lightened as he set his gentle eyes on Jay, "Take a torch and return to the hall. We'll summon you soon. And don't forget Loosha," he added, with a wink.

Jay took a torch from the golden bowl and returned with Loosha to the grand foyer. He waited a long time, his head filled with questions. What was Elder Nul talking about? What risk did Jay pose? But his mind drifted as he gazed at the hall's paintings.

The first he studied was of a woman kneeling in a grove. An orb of White Vitex descended from the sky toward her. An inscription below read *Glosha Storn, the first Arlo Kai.*

As Jay walked down the hall, he viewed more paintings. Each featured a hero, the Arlo Kai, doing something extraordinary. Some showed the Arlo Kai battling entire armies alone. Others showed the Arlo Kai subduing remarkable beasts—creatures Jay had never seen before. Jay did recognize one beast: a painting showed the Arlo Kai riding a yavyu. Jay had thought yavyu were rather stupid, simple creatures—he didn't know they were smart enough to tame and ride.

Moving on, Jay saw a painting of the Arlo Kai clashing with a dark monster. It was purple, scaly, and feathered; hideous—far uglier than Loosha. It was taller and slimmer than an Arlish. Somehow, Jay knew this to be a Kan'zi. He studied the creature with great interest.

After some time, Jay pulled himself away from that painting to a new one—where the Arlo Kai sat on a grand throne behind an altar surrounded by smaller thrones. Jay recognized the scene: it was a painting of the room he had just come from.

"If that was the Arlo Kai's throne, this must have been his castle!"

"Croark!"

Jay's eyes caught on the painting's inscription: *I trust in the maker of Arland, I will fight to defend his domain. To other's needs I will always tend, for good shall my Vitex strain.* But following the verse were two lines that Wald had not taught Jay and Perl: *I pledge this all to the King on High, I pledge myself to the Arlo Kai.*

Jay leaned back and scratched his chin, wondering why Wald didn't teach him the final phrase. Shortly after, mute Elder Quil found Jay and brought him back to the throne room.

"The council has decided," said Metrarch, "to admit you to the League. This decision was not made easily, so I trust you will accept it in humility."

Jay nodded. He felt relieved, yet sad, knowing he didn't quite earn it. At Metrarch's command, Jay knelt before the shrine. Metrarch drew an ancient broadsword and placed it on Jay's shoulders.

"Jay of Onaga, recite our pledge."

"I trust in the maker of Arland, I will fight to defend his domain. To other's needs I will always tend, for good shall my Vitex strain." And though, for a moment, he wanted to add the final phrase, he thought it best to keep quiet.

"I, Metrarch of Dovia, Master of the League of the Hearth, dub you Squire Jay."

Chapter XV

UNFURLING THE ATLAS

Perl, Sakona, and the rest of the League waited a full day for Jay. When night came, Sakona expected the League to return to their homes, but to her surprise, they pitched tents and slept at the forest's edge. The following day, they farmed and trained to keep busy, but no one left for the village. It impressed her.

At last, in the late morning, Jay emerged from the woods, sporting a golden sash. Loosha, Metrarch, and the elders followed close behind. Soon, he was surrounded by a cheering mass. Perl and Sakona squeezed through the mob and hug-tackled him.

"You did it!" cheered Perl.

"How do you feel?" asked Sakona.

"Hungry."

Metrarch waved for the crowd to settle.

"Today, we add two new squires to the League, and I'm sure a fine ally as well," he said, looking to Sakona. She nodded at Metrarch with a smile.

After more cheering, the League paraded back to the village. But on the road, Metrarch found Jay—who was stuffing his face with clums and swallots.

"Jay, be sure to thank Elder Wald. If she had not defended

125

you, I don't know what would have happened." Metrarch glanced around, cheekily, "You should have heard her when you stepped out of the room. She really let Elder Nul have it. Wahoo!"

"No way!"

"Oh yes. It was scary and hilarious."

Jay wiped his fruity face and found Wald in the herd.

"Hey Master, thank you for sticking up for me."

"I only spoke the truth. It's a shame that doing so is rare enough to warrant your thanks."

Jay noticed something unusual in Wald. Later that night, he would realize what it was: she seemed nervous and awkward. She had been vulnerable in defending Jay—something she was not used to doing—and it left her feeling shy.

Jay laid back in his bed and smiled. Deep down, Wald did have a heart. From that day on, Jay felt not only comfortable around her, but happy.

The next day, Metrarch called Jay, Perl, and Sakona to the war room atop the village hill. Once there, he seated them at a round table. Wald and Nul entered, holding an ashen-gray paper, tightly rolled.

Metrarch took the gray roll from Nul. "This is the atlas."

Jay smiled and tapped his feet. He stretched out his hands, excited to read the atlas and see if he really did have a special power.

But Metrarch pulled the atlas away for a moment and said, "Now Jay, when I open this, you must tell us everything you see, or hear, or feel. The Kan'zi are dark creatures—we're not sure what you'll find. Are you ready?"

Jay nodded, so Metrarch unrolled the atlas and carefully handed it to Jay. His eyes soared all over the grey paper, watching and waiting for something to happen. But his smile started to sulk. The map looked quite usual to him; sharp black ink marked the mountains, islands, and oceans of Arland.

Jay had nearly put the map down in defeat when he noticed a curious thing: its color began to shift. A feint, warm power glowed through the page. Suddenly, a deep red mark scratched into the paper. Jay yelped.

Wald leaned forward, "What is it?"

"It's alive!" said Jay. "Don't you see it?"

"No," said Metrarch. "Only you can see it."

"Tell us what you see!" demanded Nul.

The red mark moved along the map, leaving a gash-like trail. It was as if an invisible pen was writing across the page at that very moment.

"I see a red trail… like writing."

The mark carved to a stop on seven different spots and flourished into sharp symbols. Jay placed the map on the table and pointed to where the symbols appeared.

"Seven temples!" said Nul. "This is worse than we thought."

"They're spread out. It looks random to me," said Jay.

Metrarch scratched his chin, then said, "Only one temple lies in the Yellow Sea. Jay, show us the symbol in the south-east again."

Jay found the mark and pointed, which lay only a few leagues east of the Hearth.

"Destroying it would free the entire Yellow Sea!" said Nul.

"Send scouts to find the temple's exact location," command-ed Metrarch. "Wald, prepare a strike team and make sure they're ready to face the Kan'zi."

For the next few days, Wald trained Jay, Perl, and her squad especially hard. But no one complained—they knew what they were training for.

Nul's scouts returned, reporting the temple was near, only half a day's flight from the Hearth. Wald gathered her team; she selected twenty of her best men and women. Most were knights but a few were squires. To everyone's surprise, she also chose Jay, Perl, and Sakona.

The team armed themselves with bark and vine armor. On their way to the harbor, Metrarch and Nul stopped them.

"You must not bring the children, Elder Wald," said Metrarch. "Elder Nul thinks it's too dangerous."

"Is this your opinion as well, Metrarch?"

Metrarch scratched his chin, carefully choosing his words. "It will certainly be dangerous."

"Very well," nodded Wald. She coldly dismissed Jay and his friends. They watched as her two airships sailed up and out of the Hearth. Nul smirked at the children as he and Metrarch left for the village.

"They trained us for weeks only to leave us behind!" said Perl.

"They used Jay to read the map and now they don't need us," said Sakona.

Jay squinted his eyes in thought, "Sakona, how many people does it take to fly the Rogue?"

Sakona smiled—she knew exactly what Jay meant. "Not many at all. Follow me." She, Jay, and Perl crossed the village and flower field to the Noble Rogue.

"We're sneaking out?" asked Perl with a grin.

Sakona showed them on deck. The Rogue seemed mostly the same, but a few new pipes and gears spit out of the floor and zigged to the helm.

"These levers control the steam-release valve. As long as we keep the fire going, I can control the whole ship from here—except the sails. And by using water instead of greyberry juice, we should be able to sail faster!"

"Maybe we shouldn't do this," said Perl. "We might get in

trouble with Metrarch."

Jay said, "Didn't you notice? He said he agreed with Null that it will be dangerous, but not that we shouldn't go!"

"Yeah," said Sakona. "Plus, he didn't say we couldn't go—only that Wald couldn't take us."

Sakona took them to the engine room, where they found Loosha guarding a heap of coal. Together they fueled the furnace and warmed the engine to a slim steamy rumble.

"Jay, full canvas. Perl, stay by the bow," said Sakona, taking the helm.

"Aye, Captain!" they shouted.

Sakona worked her new levers and throttles until the propellers began to spin. The brig eased off the ground and sailed higher and higher toward the roof of the dome. As they neared the barrier of Vitex, Perl summoned a portion of her armor and created a shield around the deck.

"Hold on to something!" bellowed Sakona.

The Noble Rouge passed through the Vitex barrier and into the sandstorm sea. Sand splashed and swirled all about the ship. Perl stretched her arms out, trying to push back the waves. After a few more moments of pain, the Rogue emerged above the waves.

The three laughed with sneaky joy. They searched the horizon for Wald's strike team. Far off their port side, they saw her fleet sailing away. Jay angled the sails, Sakona turned the helm, and Perl stuffed more coal into the furnace. They sped after Wald. When they finished their tasks, they met back on deck.

"Well, we're definitely not going slower than them," said Sakona, peering through her spyglass. "As long as we keep the furnace going, we should be fine like this."

Perl glanced back toward the Hearth, "You think Wald will be mad that we followed her?"

"Not at all," said Jay. "She looked upset when Metrarch said we couldn't come. I'm sure she'll be happy to see us now."

"Besides, you two are members of the League now," said Sakona.

"Barely," said Jay.

"What do you mean?" asked Perl.

"I didn't bend the Vitex of the White Tree. I found it and tried, but it wouldn't budge. They accepted me anyway," explained Jay.

"So you didn't earn it!" shot Perl. "That's not fair."

"Maybe it wasn't your fault somehow," said Sakona.

"That's what they made it sound like, but I think the tree was broken or something," said Jay.

"So you're saying I could have gone straight to the citadel without any Vitex and still been accepted?" said Perl.

"No, no," said Jay. "I was a special case."

"That's ridiculous," said Perl, storming below deck.

"I told you it wouldn't matter," said Sakona. "They need you."

*   *   *

The morning faded. The distance between the Rogue and Wald's fleet neither grew nor shrunk. At times, Jay thought they weren't moving at all. Save for the war boats on the horizon, the sandstorm ocean looked the same in all directions. Its faded yellow waves ebbed and flowed in a never-ending dance.

The world seemed much sadder than it did before. The sky, though blue, felt more like grey. And the yellow sand was paler than he remembered. The Hearth was just so beautiful—the rest of the world now seemed dull.

Jay felt bad about Perl and wanted to cheer her up. He found her in the crew cabin, swinging from a high-up hammock.

He wasn't sure how to start the conversation. At first, he

thought to apologize, but he felt it dishonest to say sorry for something he didn't feel sorry about. He thought to skip the issue entirely and give Perl something new to think about.

"So, did you see those paintings in the citadel?"

"Yeah," she shrugged. "They were okay, I guess."

"But did you read the inscriptions?" This piqued her interest.

"No, what did you read?"

"Oh, nothing much. Just the pledge of the League. But there was stuff added to it, I'm sure you're not interested."

Perl flopped out of her hammock and climbed down onto the deck.

"Jay, you must tell me! Please!"

"It was one more line, at the end of the pledge. It read, 'I pledge this all to the King on High, I pledge myself to the Arlo Kai.'"

Perl's eyes widened as she paced around the room like a detective.

"The King on High," she started, "might mean Lor Emai, right? But, Arlo Kai… is that just another name for Him?"

"I think the Arlo Kai was the Hero of Arland. I saw that name inscribed below most of those paintings—paintings of an Arlish bending White Vitex."

"Ah ha! But why don't we still say that part of the pledge? Maybe they're hiding something from us!"

"Or maybe it's outdated since there's no more Arlo Kai?"

This was enough to put Perl in a good mood. Together, they returned to the top deck. And just in time—on the horizon, they saw black lightning frozen in time. Boney, jagged lines stretched high in the sky. As they drew closer, Perl realized what it was.

"It's a tree. A dead tree."

It was the largest tree the three of them had ever seen. It

was, apparently, so tall that it stretched above the sandstorm sea. But it's roots must have settled far beneath the waves. Wald's boats had already docked in the bed of two colossal branches. Sakona carefully landed with the League's ships.

The branches were as wide as the village in the Hearth. Old, decaying vines dripped down into the ocean. Chipped bark showed hollow parts in the tree. To Jay, it looked more like a cavern or hive than a lifeform. They left the brig and found Wald prepping her team. When Wald saw Jay and his friends approaching, she nodded at them in respect.

Once everyone was armed and ready, Wald gathered them around. "Nul's scouts reported the temple to be here, at the base of the last great tree. We will repel together, find the temple, enter, and destroy it. Remember, the Kan'zi are masters of deception. Stick together and stay sharp."

A squire with a young face asked why Metrarch sent so few soldiers.

"Our foe's power hasn't been tested in three hundred years," said Wald. "We didn't want to risk losing the entire League in one battle. It is possible that none of us will return."

While the adults readied for the long repel, Jay, Perl, Sakona, and Loosha stood silent and still. Wald's words wacked them with terror, but none wished to admit it. Sakona let it slip first.

"Loosha, why don't you stay with the ship... just in case."

For the only time in his life, Jay wished he was Loosha. She frowned and waddled sadly to the Noble Rogue. The three joined the rest who fastened repelling lines to their boats. Finally, Wald ordered them to equip their sand-goggles and thin, cloth masks to keep the sand out of their eyes, nose, and mouth. Together the team began to climb down the tree.

The climb was harsh; with each step the world turned darker and the vines seemed thinner. Even so, Jay thought the climb back up would be much harder. But then, a horrible thought dawned on him: he may never know for sure.

As they submerged beneath the sandstorm sea, the air grew thick and hot, and grains of sand whipped at their faces and hands. So, they hid themselves in the rotting bark of the tree. They climbed on and on. Every so often, Jay peeked out from the bark, but saw only a sheet of grey and yellow. Jay could only imagine what dying forest lay beyond the ocean, what forest the gigantic tree once belonged to.

To keep the team's spirits up, Wald called out to her troop, "This is the last great tree in Arland. Once, every tree was as large as this. Be honored—we are climbing through history!"

After an hour, they entered the thick roots and stood in the tree's base (a bend in one root left a shallow cave to shelter the team from the storm). Wald drew a pinch of Vitex from her armor to light their way. The team followed as she waded into the root, deeper into the tree.

At last, they came to a black stone wall with a narrow gate. Jay wondered if this subtle structure could be the temple. As he moved toward the front of the group, he saw letters etched at the top of the gate. Wald struggled to read them.

"It says 'Power,'" said Jay.

"How do you know that?" whispered Wald.

"Isn't it obvious?" But looking closer, Jay realized that the letters he read were in a language he'd never seen before.

Wald studied Jay. Turning back to the door, she said, "If it is power that blocks this door, it is power that will break it open." And with that, she drew more Vitex from her armor, composed a large ram, and smashed the gate open. "Prepare for battle."

But nothing happened. Not the faintest whisper sounded from the temple. Jay could only hear his own breathing.

They entered the temple. Inside, they found one long hall

with a dim light at its end. The jagged walls and floors were sharp and stern. As they marched on, the hall widened and heightened, as if it gained more strength with every step.

"Jay," whispered Wald, "do you see anything? Writings, creatures, anything?"

"No, Master."

Wald moved on with a bit more confidence. Soon they entered a large room—an atrium of sorts. Mighty pillars held a high ceiling. Red blazing torches lit the bare room. A slimy, stony staircase lay to the left, stretching toward a long balcony that surrounded and overlooked the chamber.

In the center lay a black throne, shrouded in a dark dense haze. Squinting his eyes, Jay saw through the fog. On the throne sat a Kan'zi. Its deep purple scales and feathers shimmered in the red light. Its long snout smiled, flashing sharp yellow teeth.

Wald did not see the creature. In fact, no one saw it but Jay. He ran in front of the team, drew a handful of Vitex from his armor, and cast it at the Kan'zi.

It splashed away the creature's shroud, but the beast itself seemed unharmed. Now seeing their foe, Wald and her team readied their weapons.

But the Kan'zi laughed. Its deep sinister voice echoed through the temple. It stood to its crooked feet and stretched out its claws. From its hand sped a bolt of red energy. It wildly splintered across the room and struck a knight in the chest, killing her instantly.

Everyone ran for cover as the Kan'zi zapped its red power all over the room. Wald and her troops returned fire, but the beast dodged their attacks. It clawed its way up walls and pillars, leaping this way and that, spitting its lightning upon the League. With every bolt he fired, the room flashed from black to blazing red.

Jay, Perl, and Sakona stayed behind Wald as she tried to keep her troops in line, "Stay in formation! Shields up, shields up!"

But her squires and knights were in shambles. Some cowered in cover, blindly shooting their Vitex around the room. Others chased after the beast in vain, shouting and stabbing their spears and swords, but the Kan'zi made quick work of them.

One brave knight, a young woman, formed her Vitex into a shield and bounded toward the creature, but before she could bash him, he vaulted over her and snatched her by the neck. His claws tightened.

Wald's stoic face suddenly filled with wrath. She drew a wealth of Vitex from her armor, formed a bulge around her fist, charged at the monster, and struck him in the jaw. He flew across the room and smashed through a stone wall.

The room fell silent. Jay, Perl, and Sakona followed Wald to the hole in the wall, but they saw nothing. Jay thought (and hoped) that Wald's punch had vaporized the beast. But they heard a clicking sound on the ceiling.

"What's that?" wondered Perl, aloud.

"It's him," said Wald.

His claws tapped tauntingly from somewhere beyond the room. The echo made it impossible to tell where he was. The team met in the room's center. Of Wald's twenty troops, only ten remained. Each stared into the darkness, searching for any sign of the beast, but they saw nothing. They could only hear the clicking of his claws.

In a flash, the creature burst out of the shadows, firing his red energy at Wald, but she summoned a shield of Vitex just in time. The colliding energy exploded, knocking the team in all directions. Jay found Perl and Sakona in the chaos and brought them up the stairwell to the balcony. They watched the fight from above.

"Metrarch sent you to die," roared the beast, "for I am Rone, the Powerful. I hold the great tree's life in my claws."

Rone summoned more energy and cast it at two fleeing squires. But Perl noticed something: as Rone's power sped farther away, it split into smaller bolts like the roots of a plant. Some bolts struck Rone's target, but others spread out and hit the structure.

"Look," she called, "his power is wild—it's destroying everything in its path!"

And it wasn't just his power; Rone himself was wild, carelessly shooting his lightning, cackling and jeering.

Jay thought of a plan. Perl liked it, Sakona didn't, but with no better option, they acted. Jay ran around the balcony to the right side of the room. Perl ran to the back side and Sakona stayed left. Jay and Perl fired Vitex down at Rone while Sakona hurled stones she loosened out of the wall.

Perl's first shot scorched the Kan'zi's face. He sought revenge, sending wave after wave of energy up at their balcony. They took cover as his red bolts shattered the temple around them. Rone's lightning struck the balcony, the walls, and the ceiling. Suddenly, the roof cracked, and a large chunk of stone crashed down onto Rone.

All fell silent. Jay, Perl, and Sakona peeked out from their crumbling cover. A mound of stone littered the floor. Rone emerged from the debris, disarrayed.

Wald approached the horrid beast. Rone lifted his claw to cast a bolt, but she moved faster: she formed a blade of Vitex and sliced off the creature's head.

Chapter XVI

LAST DAYS OF THE HEARTH

Rone was dead, but his temple remained. The strike team had to find a way to destroy it. Wald led Jay, Perl, Sakona, and the eight survivors deeper inside the abysmal structure.

In its lowest levels, they found a smoke-filled factory. Stoney gears and metal saws turned and churned, swirled and swiped. Pipes and vents swabbed along the floor and ceiling.

"This is the heart of the temple," said Wald. "The factory creates the sandstorm sea. It kills the tree and sends the dust and debris into the world, creating the ocean. But there's something else... what is this?"

In the center of the room rested a red block. It was a perfect cube, a meter wide, with no chips or scratches. Each face was an identical solid red. Strangest of all, it seemed that shadow and light had no effect on the block. Perhaps it was somehow its own source of light, yet it did not appear to glow.

Jay slowly drew near it, laying his hands on its surface. To you, this may seem a stupid thing to do because, for all Jay knew, it could trigger a terrible trap. But he felt drawn to it. As his hands explored the block's surface, he felt a deep, hidden warmth in his palms.

"It feels like... Vitex."

"It is as I feared," said Wald. "We must bring this to Metrarch at once."

Wald ordered two knights to carry the block out of the temple, but it was so heavy, another two knights aided them. Once the block was removed, Wald and her team drew the last of their Vitex and blasted the factory to bits, smashing machines, breaking pipes, and cobbling down pillars. When the room was beyond repair, all returned to the ships.

On the voyage back to the Hearth, Jay saw the ocean's waves calm. The sea sank lower and lower, like an enormous drain had come unplugged.

Back in the Hearth, they met Metrarch and Nul in the war room.

"You disobeyed Metrarch's orders!" said Nul. "You were not to bring the children."

"Well, to be fair," said Metrarch, "she didn't bring the children. They left on their own."

"And it is good they did," said Wald. "Without them, we would not have won. We faced one Kan'zi: Rone, the Powerful. He used a red energy, like Vitex. But it was wild and almost out of his control. Afterward, we found this block in the heart of the temple factory."

Wald's knights drew forward and dropped the cube on the war room table. It landed with a deep and metallic thump.

"It's full of Vitex, I think," said Jay.

Metrarch looked curiously at Jay but turned his focus back to the block. "It seems the enemy has found a way to harvest the power of life," he said.

"But why is it red, not gold?" asked Perl.

"The Kan'zi have never used Vitex until now," said Metrarch. "Nature would never give itself up to such evil creatures. This device must somehow force the Vitex out of a life form, the tree, in this case."

"By doing so," said Wald, "the Vitex becomes corrupt and unnatural. That is likely why it appears so different from our own."

"I will study this block further," said Metrarch. "For now, we have a difficult charge: to both mourn and celebrate."

After they buried and mourned the fallen, the League celebrated their victory. Rich music and dancing feet echoed in the streets. The savory smell of steamed fish and swallots lingered around every corner. And all were smiling, even Wald. This was their first real victory against the Kan'zi, and it was all thanks to Jay.

He felt proud. Everywhere he went, people thanked and praised him. Jay felt like a missing gear returned to its machine. He had purpose. Only he could see the atlas and only he could read the Kan'zi language.

He, Perl, and Sakona tried to enjoy the feast, but trainees and squires kept interrupting with questions: 'What did the Kan'zi look like?' and 'Can they use Vitex?' and 'How did you survive?' and 'Did you destroy the factory? Will the sand go away now?'

Perl enjoyed answering them all. Jay enjoyed the attention, but soon grew tired of the crowd. He walked down to the lake alone. He wished to clear his head of the day's events. But as he neared the water, he heard a screeching sound in the sky. Looking up, he saw three airships passing through the gold and white dome, entering the Hearth.

Jay wondered what ships these could be. Perhaps they were Nul's scouts or new members of the League. Jay squinted his eyes, studying the vessels. One sloop had a pale, birch hull and crimson sails—it was Elska's.

Jay's heart sank. His stomach churned in worry. Elska survived! And how did she find the Hearth? Jay hoped she had come to make peace, that Metrarch had invited her. But he knew this was not so.

Elska's fleet screamed through the air and circled the village. At once, Jay ran toward the town, shouting for help, trying to warn them, but he was too late. Her ships blasted their deadly cannons. Her volley struck the town, tearing apart home after home. And they fired more than just cannonballs—Red Vitex streaked down from above, setting fire to the land. Were Kan'zi on her ships, too?

Jay kept running and quickly came to the village. He soon found Bobo leading Perl, Sakona, and Loosha away from the battle.

"Jay!" called Bobo, "Come with us, we have to get out of here!"

"Can't we fight back?"

"You're too valuable. Let the others fight."

"How did they find us?!" said Perl.

"I don't know," said Bobo, "now come!"

Bobo took them out of the town toward the Rogue, but halfway there, Jay stopped.

"Get her ready for take-off. I'll be back."

"Where are you going?!" yelled Bobo.

"To find the atlas!"

Jay swept through the burning village streets. Squires, knights, and elders all fired volleys of Vitex at the enemy fleet. They crippled one, forcing the others to land.

A deadly battle ensued. Elska led her force against the League. Steel, arrows, and Vitex clashed and slashed through the streets. Past the flaming, smoky battle, Jay saw three Kan'zi shrouded in their black mist, raining Red Vitex upon the League. They were smaller than Rone, but no less deadly.

He would have helped, but he knew the atlas was the key to

the entire war. He ran up the hill to the war room. But near the top he dashed right into Elska.

She wore white, steel armor with a blood-red trim. Her twin blades dangled from a scarlet, leather belt. "There you are, you worthless scrap!"

She sneered at Jay with vicious hate, her nostrils flaring like a rolf. She pressed her fingers to her chest and conjured a heap of White Vitex—the immortal power hung hauntingly in the air. She fired it at Jay.

But her power never reached him. A shield of Gold Vitex appeared just in time to absorb the blow. Into the street stepped Wald.

She appeared like lightning. Even with no armor or weapons, Wald looked deadly as a wooly gare. She dug her black boots into the earth. She raised her iron-like fists into the air. Terror jolted down Jay's spine. His master stood so fierce, so mighty, he actually pitied Elska. A hint of fear glistened in his enemy's eyes.

"Run," ordered Wald.

Jay obeyed and ran for an alley up the hill. Once a safe distance away, he turned back and watched.

Wald drew waves of Vitex from bushes and savagely swiped them at Elska. The Elder pumped more and more power at her foe, as if to drown her in Vitex. She was ferocious. She was tenacious. In that moment, Wald was more than Arlish. She was a heightened form of man, or perhaps what man was destined to be.

Elska's eternal power shielded most of Wald's attacks, but some broke through and burned her armor. It knocked her off balance. As Elska turned to face her foe again, she saw Wald's fist—wrapped in Vitex—filling her view. Wald smashed and sent Elska flying off her feet, tumbling to the ground.

But Elska struck back—almost too fast for Jay to see. Faking hurt, she formed a sharp ray and beamed it at Wald, striking her neck. Wald collapsed.

Elska laughed. Rising to her feet, she fled the street. Jay ran back to Wald, tears filling his eyes. He knelt beside her. She was still breathing, but a black scorch marked her collar.

"Jay," she said, gasping for air, "take my Vitex."

"No! I can't," he said, his tears dripping onto Wald.

She took his hand, "Don't pity me. This is a good death; I've saved a life. Isn't that right?"

"Yes, Master."

"Jay, no matter what happens, no matter what others say, don't ever forget: you are good. Very good."

Wald lifted her shaking hands to her chest and pointed up. Out of her body fluttered flakes of Vitex, beautiful and potent. Wald breathed her last.

Jay sobbed, but he knew he couldn't stop. As the village burned around him, he took Wald's Vitex in his hands and marched up the hill. It was more Vitex than he had ever held, blazing with light.

Soon he came to the war room. Taking the atlas in one hand, Jay held Wald's Vitex in the other, like a torch. But he couldn't leave, for three Kan'zi appeared in the doorway, trapping him.

They cackled and snarled and shrieked. Raising their hooked talons, the Kan'zi readied their Red Vitex.

Jay pulled his arm back and hurled Wald's Vitex with all his might. The gold energy soared across the room like a dragon. The Vitex blasted through the building and beamed off the hilltop, vaporizing everything in its path. It was such a grand display, that Perl, Sakona, and Bobo saw it from the deck of the Noble Rogue.

When the Vitex cleared, the Kan'zi were gone, erased from existence. Jay gripped the atlas even tighter and sprinted down the hill. He dodged fire, arrows, and ruin, but at last, he came to the Noble Rogue. Once on board, Sakona raised the brig off the ground. She sailed to the League's fleet, which was still prepping to leave.

The League was in full retreat. Every squire, knight, and elder ran from the village to their boats, but Elska's force followed close behind.

"We have to cover their escape!" said Bobo.

He, Jay, and Perl manned the Rogue's cannons and fired at the enemy. Soon the League was on board their ships and lifting off the ground. But Elska stepped in front of her force and readied her White Vitex. As she stretched out her hands to fire, Metrarch emerged on the bow of his flagship.

"Elska!" he roared.

Seeing him, Elska stopped her attack and stared at Metrarch. Her face was sad and angry, full of pain. Metrarch's face showed pain as well. Something about him stopped Elska's attack, but Jay didn't know what.

"Shoot her!" demanded Sakona.

"No," said Jay, "she's stopped her attack."

"She killed my Father! Shoot her!"

The League's airships rose higher.

"Follow them," said Bobo. "We have to leave."

Sakona shot him a scornful look, then threw the helm starboard. The Rogue followed the League's fleet up and out of the Hearth, leaving behind their flaming, dying home. As they passed through the Vitex dome, Metrarch drew its energy into himself. The dome faded and the sandstorm sea swallowed the Hearth.

*　　*　　*

The fleet sailed silently south. Just over a hundred men and women escaped. Mackie and most of his crew survived. But many squires and knights perished in the battle. Wald was the only elder to die. When Jay shared the news of her death, the League deeply grieved. It moved Perl to total silence. For hours, she sat quietly by the bow of the brig, looking out at the ocean.

When they were far from the Hearth and night fell, Metrarch brought Jay, Perl, and Sakona onboard his flagship. It was a mighty, royal galleon. Its white sails boasted a sparking golden hand (the League's symbol). They entered the captain's cabin and found the elders and Metrarch waiting for them.

"Bobo told us you recovered the atlas," said Metrarch.

"Yes," said Jay, presenting the map to the elders. The council was relieved.

"Wahoo! Jay, your heroic deed may have saved us the war," said Metrarch.

"Surely," said Elder Nul, "here is one thing we can celebrate on this dark day."

"Jay, Perl, and Sakona, the council has decided," said Metrarch, "to send you three on your own quest. We want you to take the atlas and find the hidden Kan'zi temples on your own.

"The League has drawn the attention of the enemy. We will take advantage of that. The elders and I will start a new Hearth. This one will be a fortress. We will gather more members and prepare for total war. Meanwhile, you and your friends will spy out those temples."

"It will be challenging for the enemy to find and follow so few of you," said Nul. "When Rone declared himself 'the Powerful' to you and Wald's team, it revealed something to us: the Kan'zi have returned to their old ways."

"In ancient times," explained Metrarch, "the Kan'zi were governed by a council of 'Superiors'. Each Superior was known for a particular trait, a vice. One of these vices was 'Power', so we think that the Kan'zi have declared Superiors again. Each temple is likely ruled by a Superior—and the temple will reflect their trait."

"This is why Rone was alone," said Nul. "For a life of power-seeking leaves one with few friends."

"But don't be afraid," said Metrarch, "your special gift will help you find and understand the enemy."

"What if we run into a Kan'zi?" asked Jay.

"We'll kill 'em!" said Perl.

"You should avoid a direct confrontation at all costs," said Nul. "Just find the temples. Once you do, come back to us and we'll plan an attack together."

"And," said Metrarch, "if your ship is truly the one the legends speak of, you should have no problem outrunning the enemy."

"It is," said Sakona, proudly.

"And you've modified it, yes? Can it be flown with just you three?" said Nul.

"Yes, sir," said Sakona.

"Wahoo," said Metrarch. "Take the atlas and depart as soon as you're ready."

"That's great and all," said Jay, "but Metrarch, how did Elska and the Kan'zi find us?"

At once, the council fell silent. Their eyes dodged around the room as Metrarch stood still. After a few moments, Nul spoke. "We should not speak of her…"

But Metrarch waved at Nul to be silent. He flashed his sad eyes at Jay, saying "Elska was my student. My first student."

The council leaned in and stared at Metrarch. Seeing their faces, Jay realized that even *they* had never heard this before.

"I trained her to use Vitex—she was a prodigy. But the Kan'zi tempted and turned her to their side. She betrayed me and the others I came with from Dovia."

"There were others?" asked Jay.

"Yes. But she killed them all."

"And stole the White Vitex?"

Metrarch thought long and hard before answering.

"Yes. She killed them all but spared me."

"Why?"

Metrarch ignored the question. "She vowed to never return to the Hearth, but our attack on the temple must have provoked her. I should have foreseen that."

"So Elska's not the Kan'zi leader?" asked Perl.

"No, she's only their pawn. The Superiors rule the Kan'zi. But don't underestimate her. If you see her on your quest, you must run. Do not face her alone."

The three thanked Metrarch and returned to the Rogue. Once on board, they rejoiced.

"Our own adventure, can you believe it?!" said Perl.

"It will be nice to be on our own," said Sakona.

But Jay stayed quiet, so Perl asked, "Aren't you excited?"

"I am," he said, with a half-smile. He was still thinking about Wald.

A while later, Metrarch boarded the Rogue. He gathered them around.

"This adventure will be challenging. It is sure to test and stretch you three. When things get hard, remember that you're fortunate to have one another. So, trust each other. You're a family now."

Chapter XVII

THE ADVENTURE BEGINS

As they sailed away from the League's fleet, Jay felt a giddiness swirl in his spirit. At last, he could have his very own adventure. With a loaded craft, the world was in his reach. Soon, Jay would know what undiscovered lands lay just beyond the horizon, the unseen wonders that awaited his gaze. He found it all good, but in the way Wald found things good.

With each passing day, he felt better about Wald. He never felt perfect, of course, only better. Gratitude slowly replaced his sorrow. He was thankful for everything Wald taught and did for him. But Perl stayed sad. She would still go silent when Jay mentioned her name.

They had a long journey ahead of them, so Jay thought it best to try and rally his newly christened crew. He gathered Perl, Sakona, and Loosha on deck and began, "Isn't this great? We're on our own adventure and before you know it, we'll be back in the action. We just need to keep doing our jobs for now—Perl, you'll watch over the engine room, Sakona, you'll work the helm and sails. Okay, sailors?"

"Well, well, who made you boss?" said Sakona, playfully.

"Yeah!" said Perl, who wasn't being playful at all.

"Well, I'm the only one who can read the map, so…"

"That should make you the map guy, not the boss," giggled Sakona.

Perl raised the vessel's log, "I should be boss since I'm doing all the planning."

"And what *are* you planning?" said Jay. He and Sakona gathered around Perl.

"Jay, you said there was a temple in the south west, right?"

"Aye," said Jay, unfurling the atlas and pointing to the spot. "Somewhere in Fallengard by the looks of it."

"Well that's the only other temple in the south. If we find that one next and destroy it, half the entire world will be freed."

"Well," said Sakona, "she's got my vote."

They changed their heading and sailed for Fallengard. Soon their excitement faded. Real adventures can be, at times, rather dull. Much time is spent travelling and planning—this adventure was no different. To pass the time, they ate, three to four meals a day. Metrarch supplied them with food and water, plus Jay had his fishing rod.

The fish of the sandstorm sea tasted chewy as rubber and dry as ash. There's only one way to cook them well and Jay knew how; he wisely baked them in the boat's furnace to retain their moisture, then doused them in a clum and hickelberry juice reduction.

Though Jay found the adventure itself a bit dull, life on the Rogue never was. Living so close to Sakona excited him and kept him on his toes. He always had to look and sound his best.

One morning, Jay sat by the stern and cast his fishing line into the ocean. Sakona found him there, "So you're the boss *and* you can fish?"

"Oh, you know; I'm a man of many talents," shrugged Jay.

"Let's hope you're better at catching fish than yavyu." They both laughed as Sakona took a seat next to him. "I wanted to check up on you… about Wald. How are you feeling?"

Jay's smile vanished. "Better, I think. She died to save me. I should be thankful, not sad."

"It's okay to be sad. Look, maybe she didn't do it for you, maybe she just really hated Elska."

"Oh, is that what you think?" asked Jay, offended by the thought.

"I'm trying to help."

"I get it—you didn't believe Wald would die for anyone, you practically said so when we were training. But she did. You were wrong."

"Fine. But just because Wald died for you doesn't mean you should do the same for anyone else."

"Why not? That's what the League is all about!"

"Please, Jay. I don't need to lose anyone else." And with that, Sakona stood and walked away, leaving Jay with much to think about.

Later that day, they found a cluster of stone pillars stretching out of the ocean, layered like steps. Curious, they sailed nearer to the rocky highlands and saw nests and eggs lining the cliffsides. But where were the creatures who laid them?

"We need to land so I can oil the propellers," said Sakona.

"That won't fit into our schedule," said Perl, looking over her log. She had chosen that they should arrive in Fallengard in two weeks. How she decided on this number is a mystery to this day.

"I don't know if this is the best spot," wondered Jay. "What if—"

"I know you two think your quest is too important to stop, but we can't risk it. The next island is hundreds of leagues away."

"What do you mean, *your* quest? This is *our* quest, we're a team!"

"No. You two work for the League, so it's your quest. I'm along for the ride."

"But it's a big deal!" pled Perl. "The League, Metrarch, even Lor Emai!"

"I don't even know if I believe that stuff. That's why I didn't join, remember?"

"Sure," said Jay with a frown.

When Sakona landed the Rogue on top of a pillar, Jay took Perl to explore the cliffs. Carefully, they climbed down to a rocky landing and looked out at the sea. But a childish sound whimpered nearby. In the shadows of the cliff, wedged between two large stones sat a crimson egg.

It was immense, reaching up to Jay's waist. They stared at it in wonder. It whimpered again.

"Oh, the poor creature!" said Perl, rushing toward it.

"Careful! Don't break it!"

Perl placed her hands gently on the cold, gooey egg. "Look, Jay!" He stepped closer. Through the thin shell, Jay could see the small creature's shadowy form. It nervously swam around and around. "It must have fallen from its nest. We have to help it!"

They carefully lifted it out of the stony wedge. Jay scurried up the cliff to the top of the pillar. He leaned over the edge and took the egg from Perl, who held it high above her head. But when he placed the egg down, he heard a huge moan and splash from below.

Looking back over the edge he saw a yavyu breaching through the waves. It was followed by another, then another. Soon a pod of more than thirty yavyu surfaced and surrounded the pillar. Jay grabbed Perl's hand and hoisted her up the cliff. She grabbed the egg and the two dashed back to the boat.

Sakona already stood by the helm, starting the propellers. "What's that sound? And why do you have that egg?!"

"It fell from its nest. We're going to put it back," said Jay.

Suddenly, a yavyu swooped over the brig. Its small eye darted across the deck. Spotting the egg, it roared.

"No time for that," said Sakona, "let's go!" She shoved a throttle, pulled a lever, and the Rogue took off. "Throw the egg overboard, the mother will follow it!"

"No! It might crack and die!" shouted Perl.

"Then get to the engine room, we need a lot of steam."

Jay set the sails and the Rogue sped off. But the mother yavyu let out a behemoth groan. The other yavyu flocked to her. The whole pod chased after the Rogue.

Sakona spun the helm back and forth dodging tail fins and jaws. Under attack from all sides in all ways, Sakona sailed higher and higher. But the pod drew nearer and nearer.

"Jay, ready the cannons!"

A shadow fell over the Rogue. A colossal structure eclipsed the sky. A hatch opened in the object and out came a large metal claw, snatching the Noble Rogue and hoisting it into the shape. The hatch shut behind them.

Chapter XVIII

A COUNTRY IN THE CLOUDS

The claw dangled the Rogue toward the floor. Sakona quickly lowered her vessel's feet-like landing gears to keep the hull from damage. The claw released its grip. The Rogue touched down with a gentle thud.

They were in a long, wooden room that resembled an airship's cargo hold but much bigger. The outer wall—which sported many portholes—curved in, toward the floor.

"Are we… on another airship?" wondered Jay.

"We can't be. No ship could possibly be big enough to hold another one," said Sakona.

A cheery voice called out from nearby. "Hello, newcomers!"

Jay, Perl, and Sakona leaned over the Rogue's side and saw a smiling man. He wore slim white robes with green lining and a superior headpiece.

"Um, hi!" said Perl.

"Where are we?" demanded Sakona.

"You need not fear the yavyu now," chirped the man, "you're onboard the Exodus, the greatest vessel in the world!"

"That can't be," said Sakona.

"Oh, but it can! My name is Yohun. Come with me. Our captain, his Joyous One, will be thrilled to meet you."

"Just a minute," said Sakona. She pulled Jay and Perl away from the side, out of sight. "We should leave. Now." When Perl and Jay questioned her, she said, "This ship swallowed us whole—I don't trust it."

"He saved us from the pod," said Perl. "We should at least say thanks."

"Fine, but I don't want to stay any longer than we have to."

"And," said Jay, "let's leave someone to watch the Rogue."

In the captain's cabin, they found Loosha sitting on the egg. It was quite the sight—since the egg was twice her size.

"Loosha, get down from there!" called Perl.

But she croarked and growled.

"It's her mothering instincts," said Sakona. "She's protecting it!"

"Alright Loo." Jay had taken to calling her Loo since it sounded stupider. "Can you stay here and watch the egg and the Rogue?"

Loosha croarked and wagged her stump tail. The matter settled, Jay, Perl, and Sakona walked down the gangplank to meet Yohun. After another greeting, they followed him through the vessel.

Even below deck, they could tell the Exodus was a masterpiece, unlike any other. Most every plank of wood had a carved design, even the supply crates and barrels had artsy details. Some halls were etched with scales to look like the belly of a humongous beast. Others were carved with puffy billows to look like a passage in the sky.

More impressive than the design was its size. Passing through one of its six engine bays, they saw massive turbines that dwarfed those of a normal airship. Jay and his friends were amazed and terrified all at once. Who could have built such an ark? More importantly, who could be trusted to captain it?

They began a long climb up an immaculate, green stairwell. At the top, two tropical trees danced in the wind afront a blushing blue sky. Perhaps the ark had landed in a tall forest. But when Jay and his friends summited the stairwell, they learned the truth: the deck of the Exodus was, itself, a forest. It was thick, with lush, viridian trees, budding berry bushes, and mossy, fine grass. The climaxing community weaved its way through every corner of the top deck, arching over the port and starboard sides, grasping their roots through wide portholes and hatches five decks below.

"Our vessel is entirely self-sustaining," said Yohun. "We eat the forest's fruits, we use its wood for repairs, and we burn some for fuel."

As wonderful as this floating world was, Jay felt uneasy about it all. It was mostly Yohun. No matter what he did or said, he always smiled. Jay thought he might be wrong to find such a thing weird, but as he scrutinized, he found that Yohun's smile was different than a usual one. Yohun's mouth was wide and arched to be sure, but his eyes didn't squint.

As they walked on, they saw many more people. They all shared Yohun's smile. They seemed happy—but Jay sensed that in all of them, something was missing.

Soon they came to the door of the captain's cabin, but it looked more like a holy shrine. Silver obelisks towered over alabaster doors. The inside was just as fancy. When Jay, Perl, and Sakona entered, they saw long green and white banners hanging from the ceiling and shining armor stands. The armor was royal, metal, and spotless. It matched the style that the Colonel and his guard wore on Onaga, but without a hint of rust.

Drawing deeper in, they found a large smiling fellow sitting at a solid, granite desk—though it appeared more like an altar. He wore a green sailor's coat and a round feather hat, the kind a pirate would wear in the Blue Eye.

When he saw his guests, he leapt to his feet and wrapped them each in a big hug.

"Welcome, my new friends! I am the Joyous One." And he was. Unlike Yohun and the others, he seemed truly jolly, with squinted eyes and all.

Yohun bowed low, so the others did, too.

"Thank you for saving us, sir," said Jay.

"You're most welcome, friends! That is our goal: to save everyone we can from the world below."

"But we should get going—" started Sakona.

His Joyous One laughed, "But you just got here!'"

"There's a war, you see, and we have a part to play," said Perl.

"War… what an interesting word. It sounds familiar."

"You don't know what it means?!" asked Perl.

"It's a fight between two groups of people," said Sakona.

"Ah, now I remember. Yes, I read of it once in my ancestor's books. You see, friends, we have no reason to know that word because it doesn't exist up here."

Jay's mouth hung open, "That can't be."

"The Exodus is a paradise," said the captain, "a utopia. It is how all things should be. My ancestor Warek built it long ago, before the sandstorm came. He was the Galleran King; the King on High."

Jay eyed Perl, thinking of the secret part of the League's pledge. "Sir, what does that mean? The King on High?"

"It means King of the Galleran Kingdom: the greatest country in Arland—before the sand came, of course. Now this vessel is all that's left of Galleran."

"Perhaps," started Yohun, "his Joyous One's guests would enjoy a meal and rest before they depart?"

"Yes," said the Captain. "Stay for the night. Enjoy my world in the clouds, far from the troubles below. See how you feel in the morning."

Jay, Perl, and Sakona spent the night on the Exodus. Yohun spoiled them with luxurious rooms, new clothes, and ripe fruits: jollos and yimons. The next morning, they felt well rested.

"This place is amazing," said Perl.

"I haven't slept this well since… I can't remember," said Jay

"Yes, but we should go soon," said Sakona.

"I agree," said Perl, "but maybe another day would be okay."

"Yeah. Our quest is so important," said Jay, "we should be very well rested before we leave."

Sakona rolled her eyes, "Fine. If that's what you think is best."

But they spoke again in the morning and chose to stay another day. By the third morning, they stayed the night without ever speaking of it.

They remained a full week. They spent their days wandering in the wood, eating jollos, sleeping, and smiling. But no matter how much they rested, they still felt off. Their minds felt peace, but their souls felt anxious. It was that abysmal sense of knowing you've forgotten something, but not knowing what you've forgotten.

On the eighth day, they walked in the wood, and Sakona tried to address that feeling. She had felt it the worst, for she was an active person—always sailing or fishing. I don't think Sakona could have really rested even if she wanted to.

"This has been a nice break," said she, "but we should go."

"Go where?" asked Perl.

"Back to… where we came from," said Sakona, struggling to remember.

"Yes, and where was that again?" wondered Jay. "I can't seem to remember."

"Neither can I. But it was important. We were doing something," said Sakona.

"Yeah, it was a task…" said Jay.

"A quest!" said Perl.

"And people were counting on us," said Sakona.

"But if we can't remember, it must not have been too important," said Jay.

Sakona paced around, annoyed by the feeling. "It *was* important. It was a battle. We were fighting the K-, it started with a 'K' and we were helping the good guys. They were the…" She gazed at the clear blue sky, as if to ask it for help. At the moment, a name pierced through her misty mind like a gust of wind. "Lor Emai."

At once, they remembered.

Jay's head fell in his hands, "How long have we been here?"

"Days," said Perl. "How did this happen?"

"This place is so peaceful," said Sakona, "It's like it somehow enchanted us! We need to leave."

They went to the captain's cabin again and found his Joyous One resting by his desk.

"Sir, thank you for everything. But we're leaving," demanded Sakona.

"I don't understand. Does this place not make you happy?"

"It did," said Sakona, "but we have a job to do. We're on a quest and it's not our time to rest yet.

"But surely the world below cannot bring you joy. It's too dangerous and painful, isn't it?" asked the captain.

Perl and Sakona didn't know how to respond, but Jay did. He'd thought a lot about pain since he decided to follow Bobo to the Hearth. "Honestly sir, I think we'd be happier doing what we've been called to do—no matter how painful—than to ignore our duty and sit up here forever."

For the first time in his life, His Joyous One frowned. He cast his mighty gaze down, pitying himself. "No one who has come aboard my vessel has ever wanted to leave. I don't know what to say. It must be nice having a duty—having something to do. Who called you on your quest?"

"His name is Metrarch," said Sakona. He serves Lor Emai, our maker. And he would welcome your help in the war."

Jay eyed Sakona with surprise.

His Joyous One smiled again. "Then I shall look out for him. Best of luck on your quest."

They left his cabin and went below deck, but when they came to the cargo hold, the Rogue was gone. They ran up and down the halls of the Exodus, looking for her. In one hall, they found Yohun skipping and smiling, so Sakona shoved him against a wall.

"Where's my ship?!"

Remarkably, Yohun kept smiling, which only angered Sakona more. And I understand why: I, too, hate when people don't take my threats seriously.

"We sent it to the mill and furnace to use as fuel, since you won't be using it anymore."

"I *will* be using it. Where's the mill?"

"Oh! Sorry about that. Level three, starboard side."

They rushed to the mill and when they entered, they saw the Rogue still intact, sitting by the glow of a red furnace. They sighed in relief.

"We made it," said Jay.

Suddenly, from the shadowy roof of the firelit room dropped a mechanical arm. It held a huge circular saw, spinning fast, and lowering toward the Rogue.

"Loosha's still on board!" cried Sakona.

"I'll look for a way to turn it off," said Jay. "You two go find

Loosha!"

Perl and Sakona ran to the brig and climbed on deck. The air was thick with the furnace's heat. The cold metal claw moved closer and closer.

"We can stop it!" said Sakona, starting to sweat. "Grab a cannon ball." Sakona heaved a cannon away from the guard rail and angled it up toward the lowering blade, which now dangled ten meters above the helm, between the ship's main and aft masts. She aimed at the center of the blade, wanting to blast it clean off of the mechanical arm.

"But if we shoot the blade, it might splinter and hit us!"

"We have to try. Perl, load the cannon!"

Perl hesitated, but loaded the shot. The blade was upon the helm; it sliced the top-most handles, shooting woodchips around the boat. As Sakona lifted the lighter to the fuse, the blade abruptly stopped.

"I got it!" called Jay from afar. Perl and Sakona sighed in relief as the blade retracted to the roof. Jay joined them on deck with the mill operator, who apologized for almost shattering the ship though, of course, she smiled through her apology.

When she left, Jay, Perl, and Sakona entered the cabin and found Loosha still sitting on the egg.

"She's useless," said Jay, out of breath.

"Loosha!" Sakona dashed to her pet, "Have you eaten anything since we left? Have you even moved?"

"Croark…"

Sakona fed her stupid froad while Jay and Perl warmed the Rogue's engines. As quick as they could, they sailed out of the Exodus.

"Sakona, thank you so much," said Jay.

"For what?"

"If you didn't speak up, we might never have left."

"It would have been nice to stay," said Sakona. "But this quest is important to me, and I guess I didn't realize that until now."

"Jay," said Perl, "the captain said his ancestor was the King on High. Do you think one day, he might become the next King? If we ever clear the sandstorm sea?"

"He didn't seem fit to be a King. But maybe so. Or maybe that King had more than one child."

Chapter XIX

NORY SLOOK'S BALLOON

The Noble Rogue sailed away from the Exodus as fast as Sakona could fly her. Even with the wind, progress felt slow, but that was an illusion: the Exodus was so large, it loomed over the small sloop for an hour before the Rogue passed it by.

When the enormous ark finally drifted over the horizon, Jay, Perl, and Sakona sighed in relief. At once, they swore to never again stay in one place for too long.

When they left the Exodus, they found themselves in the Blue Sea. There, the sand appeared not yellow, but a pure, creamy blue. The sea and sky appeared as one and the same. At noon, the ocean's color was so saturated, it looked like the Rogue was gliding through a cold, heavenly void.

At dusk and dawn, the sea turned navy, reminding Jay and his friends of water. It was a sour sight, for they were fresh out of water and already felt parched.

And they were lost. After spending a week on the Exodus, they could be anywhere in the Blue Sea. Perhaps they had only just crossed over. Or perhaps they had passed Fallengard already. They chose to keep sailing west and if in three days they found no land, they would return and try a different way.

In the meantime, Jay and Sakona practiced their swordplay

by sparring. Jay was talented, but Sakona was better. She struck with speed and grace, knocking Jay on his butt many times which made Perl laugh.

"Sure, laugh it up," snarled Jay, rising to his feet. "But you won't be laughing when you see how hard this is. You're up next."

"I don't need to practice," said Perl, circling the deck and greyberry juicing her plants (she had gathered and potted many shrubs and flowers to use as Vitex fuel).

Sakona rolled her eyes, "There's a lot more to dueling than what Wald taught you."

"I know. What I'm saying is I don't need to use a sword. I've got Vitex."

"Perl, you can't always use that," said Jay. "What if you run out of fuel?"

"Or if you need to keep it a secret?" said Sakona.

"I'll be fine. You two are just jealous, anyway."

"Of what?" Jay shook his head.

"That I'm a better fighter," said Perl, very matter-of-factly.

Trying to keep from anger, Sakona forced herself to laugh and walk away. But Jay didn't want to give up. He was about to keep arguing when he spotted an orb in the distance.

"Guys… what's that?"

Sakona used her spyglass and shared what she saw: it was a big blue balloon, with a cabin hanging below. Someone, or something, flew it from the cabin—pulling cords and spinning a helm.

"Someone's flying it!" she said.

"Let's catch it so we can ask for directions," said Perl. But as they sped toward the balloon, it turned away and floated faster.

"Is it running from us?" asked Jay.

"It's got no reason to," said Perl.

They chased the balloon until it started to land.

"Look, it's heading for those ruins!" called Sakona.

She pointed to an old battlement, which stuck high out of the ocean. As the Rogue drew closer, Jay, Perl and Sakona saw shorter, slimmer towers, each stretching beneath the sandstorm sea.

Perl pieced the amazing sight together: "The towers must belong to a castle! And that means the main keep is beneath the waves. It's been swallowed by the sea!"

For a moment, Jay and his friends stopped their chase to gaze at the marvelous ruins. They were dark green with some hints of yellow. The stone slabs which formed the towers were not perfect squares. Instead, they had rounded edges. A rather artsy fellow must have chiseled them to appear as such. Torn tattered banners billowed from the stone towers. But time had faded their once proud colors.

It was such a pleasant sight to spoil one's eyes on, and Jay, Perl, and Sakona were doing just that when the bizarre balloon started to land on the castle's main tower. They remembered the urgency of their quest: they were lost and perhaps this balloon-sailor could give them direction.

So, the Rogue landed beside the balloon—since the tower was a wide space, able to fit four or five crafts. Looking over the Rogue's guard rail, Jay, Perl, and Sakona watched the balloon's pilot dash out of her cabin, away from the Rogue.

"We're not here to hurt you!" yelled Sakona.

"Yeah, we just need directions!" said Perl.

The pilot turned around. When she saw Jay and his friends, she relaxed.

"Aye?"

"Yes, of course!" said Jay.

The three marched down the gangplank to meet the pilot. She was a young woman—a few years older than Sakona—

kooky, with braided black hair. She wore a weathered tricorn hat, a silver sailor's coat, and flowy white trousers. From every piece of clothing dangled little trinkets. In place of her right leg was a pseudo pegleg, though it wasn't a true peg. It was actually a soontaplum wine bottle turned upside down. Clearly, this fantastic woman had travelled the world maybe more than once. She also smelled like rotten meat, but the three tried to ignore that.

Sakona piped up first, "Were you running away from us?"

"Oh no, no. Well… yes, yes. Sorry about that."

Jay scratched his head at the wacky woman, "Why did you run?"

"I like running! Well… no, that's not true. I saw yer brig! Last I knew, the Rogue was sailed by… unless… are ye three pirates?!"

"No, no, we're not," said Jay, "or not anymore. Her father was Captain Zye, but he stopped pirating, right?"

"Yeah," said Sakona, frowning at the memory of him.

"He's gone, and now we're on a special quest to…" but Jay remembered it was a secret. So, he changed the topic, "How'd you know the Rogue?"

"Well that's because I was a pirate myself! Well… no, that's not true. My family was, but I didn't want to join them! Well… no, that's not true either. I was, uh, cast out."

"Is *that* true?" said Perl.

"Aye. Since then, I've become an explorer! I've traveled the world and journaled all I've seen and heard. Nory Slook's my name!"

"Slook…" Perl paced in thought. "Wait, are you related to Mackie Slook?"

"Mackie! Why, he's my brother! How do you know 'em?"

Before they could answer, they heard and felt loud thumps beating on the stone tower. Gazing off its edge, they saw the red shadow of a creature beneath the waves. Its growl echoed up the tower—a scratchy growl with rythmic clicking and chomping.

"Kruski! Crawling up the tower!" said Nory. "Follow me."

"What's a kruski?" said Perl.

But Nory was too excited to answer. Jay, Perl, and Sakona followed as she raced down the battlement to an old dusty room—an armory. Inside they found swords, lances, cannonballs, black powder, and armor.

Jay licked his lips at the sight of such weapons, but Sakona faced Nory, "Shouldn't we run?"

"And risk letting kruski destroy the entire castle? Why, ye have no idea where ye are, do ye? Grab some gear and ready for a fight, if you're brave enough!"

They already had swords, so Jay took three sharp lances and Sakona took two cannonballs. Nory swiped a set of armor with a royal green cape. But Perl didn't take anything.

"Perl," started Jay, pulling her aside, "take a weapon… or at least a shield."

"Stop bossing me around, I'll be fine."

Jay rolled his eyes. "Okay, but you can't use Vitex anyway—not in front of Nory—we don't know if we can trust her yet."

"But she's Mackie's sister!"

"That doesn't mean she's good. Just take a shield!"

"Look, I've got my cutlass, same as you."

"Let's go," cried Nory. "I hear them coming!"

"Wait… them?" asked Jay.

"Aye. You see, kruski is the plural form of krusk and—" but another loud thump cut her off. "I'll explain later. Let's go!" They left the armory and found a cannon pointing out a window.

"Wait," said Sakona, "they might come by here!"

Sakona loaded the cannon and aimed it out the port. They could hear the kruski drawing nearer. With every thump came the sound of shattering stone, loud as lightning. Then came the clicking and chomping sounds.

They were near. The room shook with every thump. Dust fell out of the ceiling and fogged the room in an ugly brown haze. But as quickly as the sound came, it started to fade—the creature, or creatures had left.

Nory peeked her head out the window. "Here, kruski!" she called, clicking and whistling at the beasts. "Right here!"

She leapt back as a massive claw snapped through the window, breaking the stone to bits. The coral-red claw wiggled around the room, searching for prey. Many bumps and barbs on the creature's crook scraped and hooked on the wooden floor, bending and cracking the boards with ease. Jay and Perl dashed back, but Sakona stayed by the cannon. She lit the cannon's fuse and fired—the cannonball exploded against the claw, shattering the shell. The creature roared and crawled back into the sandy sea.

"That's one!" called Nory. "Let's go."

They ran up the tower to the roof, and save for the balloon and the Rogue, they found it empty. But the tower began to shake. The boom of creature's claws digging into the tower echoed for leagues. Then clicking and chomping and hissing joined the booms. Finally, two kruski crawled over the tower's ledge, onto the roof. They were round with rosey red shells, two sharp claws, and ten small feet. Their jagged jaws wrapped around half their bodies. Their mammoth mouths sagged when they spotted their prey.

While the others stood frozen, Jay leapt forward and hurled a lance at one, striking its shell. But the krusk clawed out the spear and snapped it in half with a deafening cry. It dashed at Perl, snapping its pincers. She ducked under it and swiped her sword with pride. But the sword bounced off its thick, red shell, without leaving a mark.

The krusk snatched Perl in its colossal claw—it moved her to its mouth and opened its prickly jaws. Thinking fast, she wedged her sword in its claw like a lever and tried to budge it open. But the sword was too slim and made too small an opening. She cried for help.

Jay hurled another spear at the creature. It sped through the air and struck near its eye. Enraged, the monster dropped Perl and bounded at Jay. Sakona leapt to his aid, slashing at the krusk with her cutlass, but it easily knocked her away.

So Perl drew Vitex from weeds growing in the stone and formed a long whip of energy. With a wild cry, she slashed the creature off the roof.

Nory gazed in wonder at Perl's power. But with one krusk left, she snapped to attention, "Let me handle this one."

She smiled and pulled a piece of rotten meat out of her coat. The stench almost made Perl puke (Sakona was used to the smell from her old pirate crew and Jay was, well, a boy).

"This is a chance I'll never get again. Don't attack the krusk!" she ordered. Nory sliced off a small piece of meat and held it high above her head. She whistled and clicked. "Here, krusk. Here boy… or girl." The krusk smelled the meat and lingered forward. "Put your weapons down!"

They obeyed. Nory chucked the piece in the air. The creature snatched it and shoved it in its mouth. It lowered its claws and seemed to relax. Nory sliced off another piece and threw it to the creature, who gobbled it whole.

"Now for the real challenge," said Nory. She drew near the creature with another slice in hand, taking small steps.

"She's crazy!" said Sakona.

Suddenly the creature snatched her in its claw and drew her to its mouth. Jay, Perl, and Sakona readied their swords, but they saw the krusk wasn't eating Nory; it was licking her—the way Loosha did to Jay's boot.

Nory laughed, "Why, thank you, friend!" She tossed the krusk more meat as it placed her down. "I saw a tribe of Crowlans tame kruski. It's easier than it looked; imagine that!"

"It doesn't mind that we just killed its pack," wondered Jay aloud. "Strange."

"Quite," said Nory. "My rotten meat must have lured them up here."

"So, you were hunting them from the start!" said Perl.

"No, that meat was going to be my dinner! Not sure what to do now."

"Let's get a fire going," said Jay. "I'll try to catch us some fish."

Nory lured her new pet krusk away from Jay and his friends to search the roof for wood. When the three had recovered from the tiring and terrifying battle, Jay found enough energy to get mad at Perl.

"Perl, you almost got yourself killed! You should have taken another weapon or armor like I said!"

"And you used Vitex," said Sakona. "I think Nory saw. What if she's with the Kan'zi?"

"I didn't need another weapon and I proved that," said Perl. "I didn't die."

"Thanks to me," snapped Jay.

"And you didn't die thanks to me!" snapped back Perl. "What's the problem here?"

"It's you!" said Jay.

Perl tightened her face and marched away. Jay's words hurt her, since she admired him so much. If Sakona said something like that, Perl wouldn't mind, since she didn't think highly of her. But she thought the world of Jay.

She found the tower ledge and sat with her legs dangling down, kicking the stone with her heels. She wanted to throw something into the sea, but she couldn't find any loose rocks.

You may find her reaction a bit immature, and maybe it was, but it also worked in her favor—time and space helped her calm down. After a while, she heard someone approaching. She hoped it was Jay, but it turned out to be Sakona.

"What's on your mind?" she said, seating herself with Perl.

"I don't know." Perl looked away for a bit, but when she turned back, she found Sakona waiting quietly for an answer. "I should have taken the weapon—deep down, I knew that—but why didn't I?"

Sakona shrugged. She was, clearly, the best listener of the group.

"I think I just want something," continued Perl.

"What do you mean?"

"Well, you're the captain—you pilot the brig. And Jay, he's the one who can read the map and see the Kan'zi. I guess I just want something to do, I'm wondering why I'm on this crew. Being the best fighter sounded nice, but maybe I'm not."

"Perl, you're a great fighter. But you bring something else to our team: knowledge. You're smart. You've read a lot about the world and I'm sure that will come in handy."

"You think so?"

"Of course."

These words were more of a bandage to old wounds than a true cure. Sakona was still learning how to encourage and value someone properly. But for now, Perl felt much better. They returned to the campfire together.

Perl sat across from Jay in silence. After a few awkward minutes, Jay spoke up.

"I'm sorry for what I said."

"I'm sorry for what I did."

The sky dimmed. Jay caught a few fish—they were barbed and scaly, much sharper than the fish in the Hearth. Perl and Sakona stewed the fish over Nory's fire while Nory played with her new pet who she lovingly named 'Rako'. She even fashioned him a saddle out of the armory's leather armor and chainmail. The savory smell of sandfish lured everyone to the fire.

"So yer with the League—eh?" Nory plopped down, seating herself near the fire. "I saw ye use that Vitex."

"How do you know about them?" Perl wanted to know if Nory was a friend or foe.

"Aye, I found their Hearth on my own. Well… no, that's not true. They found me and brought me there."

"Are you a member? A squire, or knight?" asked Jay.

"Oh no, they wanted me to be, but I turned them down. Well… no, that's not true. I could never bend Vitex. Metrarch said it's because I lie too much. But I'm trying to do better!"

"You're doing great," said Jay. At once, the three felt relieved. It seemed Nory was a decent enough lady.

"So how'd ye meet my brother, Mackie?"

"He helped us escape the Blue Eye," said Jay. "We came to the Hearth where he and his pirates joined the League."

"Imagine that," wondered Nory, "my brother has joined the League. Say, is that what your quest is all about? Is it for the League?"

Jay looked to Perl and Sakona. They both nodded.

"Yes," said Jay.

"Glad to see the Rogue's been redeemed. I always thought that such a legendary vessel was meant for more than pirating."

"Nory," said Sakona, "what stories do you know of the Rogue?"

"You'd be surprised how often I find her in old history

books and letters! Let's see… it once belonged to a boss of the Obsidian Chain—a cartel in the Boonbar Isles. I've heard it also fought in the War of the North, I believe as a flagship! And, of course, that it belonged to a Mendacian Princess."

Their old craft with royal-blue sails now seemed even more beautiful than before. Her grand banister ebbed like ocean waves, the cabin portholes arched like palace windows, and the dark hull shined with scratches and scars that showed its place in history.

By then, the fish were cooked. They ate in silence (for as you know, fighting giant monsters leaves you with quite an appetite). With full bellies, they each yawned and laid down to sleep.

Jay lay with his back to the fire. The castle towers loomed large against the expansive, black sky. Some towers had sharp points, others had flat tops. But from each, dangled old, torn banners. As faded as they were, they seemed familiar.

"Nory, maybe tomorrow you can tell us the story of this castle," said Jay. But Nory only snored. So, Jay curled up and fell asleep.

Chapter XX

DUNGEON DESCENT

While the others dreamed sweetly, Jay woke to a strange sound: a windy whisper calling his name. It was so quiet that Jay thought he had imagined it. But the whisper called again. Now uncertain, he left his friends and followed the sound.

It steered him down the dark tower. At its base, Jay found himself in the center of the castle, the throne room itself. Though smaller than the Arlo Kai's, it was still a marvel to behold. Its perfect symmetry delighted the eye. Great green statues of knights stood in place of pillars, holding up the arched roof. The floors, walls, and windows sported gold and green stripes, angled and slanted forward. The room itself pointed to the throne.

The royal chair was carved of an ancient tree and held an organic design. Branches sprawled out its crown. Mighty trunks splayed out of its feet. A shinning, jade cushion adorned the stump-like seat. Jay wondered, *Who had deserved such an immaculate throne?*

Most people in Jay's position would happily sit upon that throne and play King. But Jay made no such move. Though the sight was spectacular, it was sad as well. Cobwebs had overgrown the throne like weeds. Dust slept on every surface of the hall.

And while the room was filled with all manner of trinkets, tassels, and tables, it was empty of people, and therefore felt lonely. This place had seen better days, and Jay dared not dishonor it by sitting where he shouldn't.

But his emotions soon changed. Suddenly, he felt a breath of air. It brought with it such fragrant smells, more potent than the flower field in the Hearth. Jay felt a warmth, as if some invisible fire formed to heat the chilly hall. Finally, Jay saw a slim, white form like a man, standing by the throne. It looked like White Vitex, but far more luminous. For a moment, Jay panicked, thinking Elska had found him. The form was so resplendent, Jay had to cover his eyes.

The light faded and Jay peeked through his hands—the form was gone, but the smell and heat remained. So he sensed his way around the castle, following the trail of smell and heat.

It charmed him out of the throne room, down a stone spiral staircase, and into the castle's dark dungeon. Once there, the smell and heat vanished. Cold musty air filled the room.

But far down the dungeon hall, Jay saw a light. As he drew near it, he heard someone screaming. He ran toward the sound and came to a large cell. Inside he saw a vortex of Gold Vitex, swirling and glaring. In its center stood Perl and Sakona, crying and wailing.

"Jay, help us!"

The Vitex had not yet touched them, but it swelled with each passing moment.

"I'm coming!" Jay searched the room for anything that might help him. But it was bare. He stretched out his hands and tried to bend the Vitex away, but it would not obey him.

"Jay, please!"

He heard the whisper again, only this time it wasn't calling his name. Instead, it said a word that Jay had never heard before.

It was long and musical, but unspeakable; Jay couldn't repeat it even if he tried. It came from a creature with more tongues. It was so complex that I cannot write it down for it uses letters and harmonics we have yet to discover.

Though he couldn't repeat it, he knew its meaning at once, for when he heard the word, he was, in a sense, filled with it. Courage.

Jay courageously stepped into the Vitex ring. He wanted to pass through and carry Perl and Sakona to safety. But the moment he entered, he felt the Vitex burn and sting him. The pain was so terrible, he leapt back, out of the ring. He shivered.

"Perl, can you bend the Vitex away?"

But the Vitex swirled faster and louder, drowning his voice. He tried again to brave the ring, ready to bare the pain. He ran into the Vitex storm. It burned and stunned, it shocked and nipped until Jay leapt away again. The Vitex splashed closer to his friends.

"Help!" screamed Jay, "Nory!" But no help came.

"Jay, save us!" called Perl.

"Help us!" howled Sakona.

"I can't, it's too painful!"

At once, Perl, Sakona, and the Vitex vanished. The room faded, too. It was all some sort of dream or vision. Jay fell to his knees and breathed in relief.

When he calmed down, he lifted his head. Wiping the sweat from his eyes, he found himself, no longer in the dungeon, but a large crystal cavern. Gems, minerals, and precious stones painted the scene in phosphorescent light. There were large green gems, small purple ones, sharp red crystals, and round yellow ones.

If he wasn't so shaken, Jay would have enjoyed the other-worldly sight. He stood and listened for the whisper, but he heard nothing. He felt and smelled around the cavern, but he felt and smelled nothing. So he made his way through the cavern, into the castle and up the tower. But when he came to the tower's roof, he found it was already morning.

When his friends awoke, Jay brought Perl, Sakona, and Nory to the cave and told them what happened. "Then I saw… some people trapped in a ring of Vitex. I tried to save them, but it was too painful, I just couldn't do it. Then it all disappeared, like a dream."

Perl paced in thought, "What could that mean?"

"That sounds intense," said Sakona, "are you okay?"

"Maybe you're going crazy!" said Perl.

"What about the language?" asked Sakona. "Were they Kan'zi words, like the ones in the atlas?"

"No, those are harsh and short. Monotonous, too. This was different. What do you think, Nory?"

Nory paced about the cavern with hands on her hips. "I think ye met Lor Emai himself!"

"How can that be?"

"Because we are in a special place. This castle is High Alacon, the capital of the Galleran Kingdom. From here, the Galleran King (known sometimes as the King on High) ruled and, with the Arlo Kai, he planned his wars with the Kan'zi. At least that's what me books say. I'm not sure how much ye know about these things—"

"A lot," said Perl.

"But tell us more," said Jay.

"Well, according to legends, the Galleran Kingdom loved and served Lor Emai. Even though He wasn't actually the king, they were still His people. The Galleran King and Arlo Kai came to this very cavern to seek his advice."

"So Lor Emai lives here?" said Sakona.

"No, no. He lives in another world, Dovia. This place must

somehow be powerful enough to summon him for a time."

"Look at these gems," said Perl, "I can feel Vitex inside of them. Maybe he uses the crystals' power to appear."

"If that was Lor Emai," said Jay, "why did he send that vision?"

"Maybe to test you," said Perl.

"Oh. Then he's probably not too thrilled with the results," he said.

"You must've learned something," said Sakona.

"Well, sure. Saving people hurts, it comes at a cost."

"That's just like Vitex," said Perl. "It hurts the life form you draw it from." She and Nory started to wander and gaze about the cavern.

"Just like Wald," said Jay.

"I don't think you failed," whispered Sakona. "I think you made the right choice."

"There's so much Vitex here," called Perl. "I bet the League would love to know about this place."

"Maybe this could be their new base—it *is* a castle, after all," said Sakona.

"New base?" asked Nory. "What happened to the Hearth?"

"Elska and the Kan'zi destroyed the Hearth," said Jay. "Metrarch and the others are looking for a new home in the Pipyan Mountains."

"What a tragedy."

"But going there would slow down our quest," said Perl.

"Well," said Nory, "I can go to them and show them this place. It'd be wonderful to see my brother again, anyway!"

Later, they returned to the castle tower, ready to continue their quest.

"Nory," said Sakona, holding up the atlas, "can you point us toward Fallengard?"

Nory's face went pale, "Fallengard… that's a strange place. Dangerous, too."

"Why is that?" said Jay.

"A war's brewing there—a civil war. If yer quest must take ye there, then ye must go. But I'd avoid it at all costs."

Perl and Sakona looked to Jay. He took the atlas and studied the red mark on Fallengard. It etched in the center of the country.

"Thanks, Nory, but I don't see any other way."

"Let me leave ye with something." Nory went to her balloon and returned with gifts. "Sakona, here is a gladiator's shield from Lemuk—it is said to have survived a Crowl's headbutt. If you learn that a block can be as strong as an attack, you'll be a great warrior."

Sakona took the shield with a smile and, "Thanks!"

"Perl, this bow and quiver of arrows comes from Dalk. It is said that nothing great comes from Dalk, and I agree. Unfortunately, it's the only bow and arrows I have. So, may it keep your enemies far from you."

Though a little confused, Perl took the weapon.

"Jay, this is a lance-fishing rod. The blade retracts into the rod, should you need to hide your weapon."

"Thank you, Nory."

"May these weapons aid you on your quest."

Nory boarded her balloon, Rako squeezed on top of the cabin, and Jay, Perl, and Sakona boarded the Rogue. Nory floated away in search of the League and the Rogue sailed south west for Fallengard.

*　*　*

They sailed for three nights. When day broke on the third morning, the sky brightened, all except for one spot. On the horizon, leagues away, a cloud-like mark sat in the dark. As they drew nearer to the mark, they realized it was Fallengard.

A pitch-black wall surrounded the entire island. The wall stretched high in the sky and curved in at its top. In fact, it appeared more like a dome or shell.

When most people saw Fallengard, they were struck by a sudden uneasiness, like when one wanders too far into the woods at night. But Jay smiled as he stared at the awesome black wall. His mind raced with all sorts of thoughts. He wondered if the Gardish built it to keep something out or in. He wondered what secrets and dangers lay in the hidden city.

Sakona sailed the Rogue to the dome's top (which took the greater part of an hour). There, at the top, they found a small, circular opening. But before they could enter, five ships surrounded the Rogue and a voice called from the nearest:

"This is the Gardish Militia. Fallengard is closed to outsiders. Leave now or be destroyed."

Jay walked to the Rogue's edge. "We're here to help. There's this evil monster called a Kan'zi—"

"We need no help. Leave. Now." The Gardish ships aimed their cannons at the Rogue.

"We're leaving! Don't worry!" said Sakona, turning the helm away.

Sailing down the dome, away from Fallengard, Jay paced back and forth. "Well, that was… unexpected."

"Maybe we can sneak in," said Perl.

Before they could form a new plan, Sakona spotted something nearing Fallengard that changed everything. "Wait a second… Look!" At the base of the wall, sitting quietly in the sandy, blue ocean, they saw a craft with red sails and a pale hull. "It's Elska."

"Maybe she hasn't seen us yet," said Perl.

"We have to hide," urged Jay, "remember what Metrarch

told us."

"Or we can kill her," said Sakona.

At this, Jay and Perl felt uneasy. Perl spoke first, "That's wrong. We don't go picking fights."

Jay said, "She's pretty strong, too."

"If we kill her," said Sakona, "we don't have to worry about her anymore," said Sakona, folding her arms.

"Now's not the time," decided Jay. "Not when we're alone, against her entire crew."

"What if we go to that little island," said Perl, pointing off the port-side bow. A small, dusty plateau lay nearby. "We can hide out there for a bit. Looks like there's a village, too."

Though unhappy about it, Sakona went along with the new plan. She flew the Rogue down to the island, Lemuk, and docked in a cave outside the village. Jay, Perl, Sakona, and Loosha left the Rogue—after a debate over the egg's wellbeing.

Now you may have forgotten about the mysterious egg, but Jay and his friends had not. Before they left the Rogue they chose to leave it locked in the captain's cabin. I know what you're thinking: *but don't eggs need to be sat on?* Jay and his friends thought about this, too. First, they recalled the pillar where they found it. No yavyu was sitting on it then. So, they concluded this egg was not the sort that needed constant sitting. Second, the sandstorm sea carries with it a scorching heat. The Arlish have grown used to it, but by your standards it is as blistering as a desert. Surely the natural heat would incubate the egg. Of course, motherly Loosha didn't want to leave the egg, but Sakona dragged her away.

As they walked toward the village, hot, dusty sand swirled around their legs. Lemuk was a flat plateau that lay just beneath the sandstorm sea. So, blue sandwaves rolled over the island and splashed nearly as high as one's waist. The waves completely covered Loosha, but she didn't seem to mind.

They came to the village at last. Steep limestone walls guarded the city from the sand. Still, the village was a sad and arid place. Worn, gray buildings littered the streets. They were old and falling apart. The people, on the other hand, looked lively. The town was full of a weird energy. Some wore pirate garb, some wore explorer trinkets, and others wore elaborate dresses and masks. Most gathered toward a sizable building in the town's center.

In case Elska came, Jay, Perl, and Sakona wanted to blend in. They followed the crowds to the center building. It was a wooden coliseum, adorned with yellow banners. They entered and took their seats in the highest stands.

Soon, a Game Master stood in the arena and spoke in a bellowing voice. "Welcome pirates, smugglers, crooks, and gangsters to Lemuk's Dueling Ring! We have a special treat in store for you…"

Sakona looked around and under her seat.

"What's wrong?" asked Jay.

"Where's Loosha?!"

"Our first contestant," said the Game Master, "will face a rare and wild beast, far from its home in the Pipyan Mountains…"

Jay, Perl, and Sakona stared at the coliseum's raising gate: into the arena waddled Loosha.

Chapter XXI

TO SAVE A FROAD

Jay, Perl, and Sakona rushed out of the coliseum and found the entrance gate. It led down a long tunnel which ended in the arena itself. But an armored woman guarded it.

"That's my froad," said Sakona. "Give her back!"

"She was kidnapped fair and square, she was. Welcome to Lemuk."

"Give her back, or I'll *make* you give her back," threatened Sakona, letting her fingers drift over her blade.

"I'd like to see you try."

Sakona nearly drew her blade when the Game Master appeared at the gate.

"What's taking so long?! I've been shouting the same name for five minutes. You're making me look like a fool!"

"Hey tough guy," said Jay, "there's been a mistake. That's our froad in there."

"Save it, kid. That froad is staying and dying there," snapped the Game Master. But he studied the three further. "Unless, one of you'd like to join her. Been a long time since we've had a kid compete."

"Jay," said Sakona, grabbing his hand, "you've got to fight for us." She frowned and looked up to Jay with her big brown eyes.

"I, uh…" Holding Sakona's hand made his heart race. He would have done anything for her. But then he remembered the last time she asked him to do something. In the Blue Eye, she used him to steal her brig back. Was she just holding his hand and batting her eyelashes to control him? He couldn't give in so easily again, he had to keep control. "I know Loo's important and all, but this is kinda dangerous, right?"

Sakona frowned even more than before, breaking his heart. "Jay, she listens to you. You've got the best shot at getting her out of there."

Back in power, Jay was starting to feel playful. He gave a flirty grin and took a step toward her, "Is she more important to you than me? What does she have that I don't?"

"My goodness," said Sakona, rolling her eyes and shaking her head. "You want to talk about this now?"

"Well," shrugged Jay, "if I die in there, I'd at least like to die with some answers."

Sakona tried in vain to shake away her smile

"What are you two talking about!?" said Perl, clueless to their flirting though not clueless to common sense. "We're not sending Jay to his death for an animal."

But the Game Master cut in, "Alright, alright. I'm sorry—you can have your froad back." He raised the iron gate. "Go on."

"Like you said, she listens to me," said Jay with a wink. "I'll get her."

But as soon as he crossed through the gate into the tunnel, the Game Master slammed it shut. He trapped Jay in the arena.

"You want your froad, go get her," roared the Game Master in laughter. "Win to earn your freedom. Good luck, kid. You'll need it!" He walked down the tunnel, into the arena.

Jay ran back to the gate and tried to tug it open while Perl and Sakona tugged from the other side. But it was no use, and a score of guards came to take Perl and Sakona away.

"We'll get you out of there!"

"Maybe we can win!" said Jay. "Loosha can paralyze people, after all!"

As the guards tried to peel Perl and Sakona away, Perl muscled her way back to the gate. "Remember the same thing you told me with the kruski: you can't use Vitex in there. It'll give us away—especially if Elska shows up."

"Got it."

The Game Master returned to Jay. He offered him a sword and bronze armor set. "Take it. You can't go in there with a fishing pole."

"Actually…" Jay stuck out his fishing rod and pulled the trigger to extend the lance blade. Jay watched the Game Master to see if he was impressed, but the armored man only laughed.

"Let's get this over with," sighed the Game Master.

"You know, on second thought, maybe the armor wouldn't hurt."

Jay tried to wear the armor, but it was far too heavy. In the end, he wore only the helmet and leather under-armor. The Game Master took Jay down the dark tunnel to another gate. There, things suddenly became real to him. He lifted his helmet's visor and peered at the bare arena through rusty iron bars. There was nowhere to run and nowhere to hide. His stomach felt uneasy, like he had swallowed a cannonball.

He thought of his vision, *Maybe this is what it was all about? It is a ring… and I guess I'm making a sacrifice?*

Perl and Sakona took new seats near the front. They figured to jump in the arena and help Jay if things went poorly.

"Ladies and gentlemen," boasted the Game Master, "joining the froad is 'the Bronze Boy'!"

Perl and Sakona nervously cheered.

Jay stepped into the arena and found Loosha. She was totally unaware of the world around her. Her crossed eyes darted around the coliseum.

"Loosha, between you and me, I'm not doing this for you."

Realizing it was Jay, Loosha croaked and sat on his boot.

"Up first, we have Big Blen from Dalk," called the Game Master. "It's said that 'nothing great comes from Dalk,' so prove us wrong, Big Blen!"

Jay's helmet was a bit too large. He shifted it around until through the narrow slits, he saw Big Blen. He was a substantial man, sporting rusty armor, a sharp helmet, and a black mace.

"Umm, Big Blen," said Jay, "we're not actually here to fight. We just—"

But Big Blen bounded at Jay with his mace held high. Jay gasped and dodged his strike. Big Blen swiped and swung after the boy, but Jay dodged and leapt faster and moved quicker.

Blen chased Jay to the arena wall, and nearly clobbered him.

"Loosha, do something!"

Loosha turned to Blen, shot her tongue, and paralyzed him. Blen fell to the ground with a loud thump.

"Next time, let's start with that move."

"Great job, Loosha!" called Sakona, from the stands.

Across the coliseum, Perl spotted a young woman taking her seat. She had fair skin and blonde hair. Perl covered Sakona's mouth.

"Shh! Elska's here!"

"Where?!"

"Don't look now, she's across the arena from us."

"She might not recognize us—and Jay's wearing that helmet."

"Right."

"Is she with anyone?"

"No, why?"

"In case we have to fight."

Back on the arena floor, Jay and Loosha readied for their next tussle.

"Now," called the Game Master, "the Bronze Boy and the Froad will face a swarm of deadly selovates."

The mob cheered. Out of the gate poured five green selovates. They were horrid bugs—each about Loosha's size—with sharp pincers and small black eyes. They crawled toward Jay and Loosha, snapping their pincers.

"Loosha, stick 'em!" called Jay.

Loosha shot her tongue at the selovates, but nothing happened.

"Oh no," said Sakona.

"Their shells must protect them from her saliva!" said Perl.

Loosha shot her tongue again and again, but the selovates kept crawling closer.

"It's not working, Loosha," said Jay.

He drew his lance and dashed at the swarm. But the bugs bit and snipped; they cut through his leather armor and slashed his skin. This enraged Loosha. She galloped into the fray, mounted a selovate, and with one bite, chomped off its head. Jay whipped his lance around and crushed two more.

The last two selovates leapt at Loosha. Jay hurled his lance. It cut through the air and sliced through both bugs. The crowd cheered louder.

"Well, that was close!" called the Game Master. "Lucky for you, they weren't fully grown selovates."

"Is Elska still there?" asked Sakona.

"Yeah," said Perl. "She's leaned forward, watching close."

"For our last lash," said the Game Master, "we've captured

for your viewing and hating pleasure, a Rash Tallon!"

The mob booed as a figure stepped into the arena. It, or he, wore brown, hooded robes and a carved wooden mask. He stood stable and still, with no weapons at all.

The crowd jeered and mocked, shouting "Get outta 'ere, ye beast!" and "Kill 'em, Bronze Boy! Kill 'em!"

But Jay only shrugged. How could he kill something or someone that stood no threat? Jay didn't know this at the time, but the Rash Tallons were not some creature or monster—they were Arlish like everyone else and they were the true natives of Lemuk. But people still treated them like animals. Jay walked cautiously toward the figure.

"Hey. Are you a gladiator?"

But the figure didn't reply. It stood silent and still. Jay looked closer at the Rash Tallon and saw that his hands were bound in chains.

"If I free you, will you hurt me?"

The figure shook its head.

"In case you're lying, my froad can paralyze you. It's about all she's good for, but it works." Jay lifted his lance and slashed down on the chain, breaking it open.

The mob booed louder. They spat at Jay, cursing 'the Bronze Boy.' Bottles and rubbish flew at Jay, Loosha, and the Rash Tallon. They fled to the arena gate. Soon, the Game Master raised it and took Jay, Loosha and the Rash Tallon through the tunnel to safety. As soon as they left the coliseum, the Rash Tallon ran away.

"What'd you do that for?!" The Game Master marched up to Jay in a rage. "I gave you a perfectly good Rash Tallon to kill and you freed him! I ought to—"

But thundering bootsteps stopped the Game Master. He turned and saw a gang of twenty. Each gangster looked tougher and uglier than the last. They stood beside an old man in a wheelchair.

"I wish to speak with the boy," said the man.

"Yes, of course. Anything for Kal Korro." The Game Master excused himself.

Kal was a rugged man. His crippled legs and cheap clothes made him look quite normal. If it weren't for his guards, Jay would not have found the man special. As Jay studied him through his helmet, he saw old, worn muscles with plenty of scars. Jay imagined that this man was like a balloon, who was once bold and strong, but now had lost some air.

"That was an interesting brawl, Bronze Boy." His crackly, old voice hissed out of his jaws. "Though your froad did most of the work. But I think you've got what it takes to make it big time. I'll cut to the chase, kid: I'm looking for a new gladiator to sponsor in the Fallengard Dueling Circuit. You interested?"

"Why me?" Jay posed this question to stall. He would need Perl and Sakona's help to make the choice.

"You've got the most important thing: spectacle. A boy and a froad. Now that's weird stuff. The crowds will love you, and when the crowds love you, the game masters make sure you stay alive. That's why ours here sent you a free Rash Tallon to kill. I, myself, didn't have spectacle till Arrow Anslo shot my legs. People came from all over the south to see me duel from this wheelchair."

"Hey, speaking of that, why did everyone boo the Rash Tallon?"

"Why didn't *you*? They're disgusting creatures, always clicking and whistling at each other, never speaking a lick of sense!"

"But what did they do that's so bad?"

"Don't you have ears, kid? I just told you!"

That's when Jay realized the Rash Tallons were victims of a

common form of hate: the baseless kind, the kind people use to try and feel better about themselves.

"If I go with you, what's in it for me?"

"The good stuff: fame and fortune. In Fallengard, you'll have whatever you want."

"You can get passed the Gardish Militia?"

Kal Korro laughed, "You kidding me? They wouldn't dare to stop my gang. So, are you in?"

As Jay thought it over, a woman carved her way through Korro's guards. Jay peered through his helmet's visor and saw Elska's piercing eyes. He gulped.

"Hey, who are you?" said Korro. "Back off my gladiator."

"I'm just here to congratulate the Bronze Boy and his froad." Elska studied Jay. She smiled. She knew who he was.

"Good, now scram. You can see him again in the Fallengard Circuit."

"I will."

Korro's gang eyed Elska. Their hands stayed on their weapons. Korro rested his right hand on an old, black dagger. Elska backed off. Even she seemed to respect the legend. She left the coliseum.

"I'm in," said Jay. "But I have two friends with me."

Perl and Sakona raced to the gate and wrapped Jay in a hug so big that it knocked his helmet off.

"You fought pretty well," said Perl.

"Jay, thank you so much. You saved her life!" She placed a gentle kiss on his cheek.

Jay's face turned redder than a krusk. For a long time after, he felt warm sparks on that cheek. Dazed, he spoke the smartest thing he could think to say, "Yeah, I did."

Sakona stooped down and hugged her froad, "Loosha! I'm so glad you're okay."

"Croark!"

"Jay, we saw Elska in the coliseum," said Perl.

"I saw her. She knows it was me."

"What should we do?" asked Sakona.

"We're going to leave. Kal Korro is taking us to Fallengard."

Chapter XXII

THE BLACK-DOMED CITY

Jay and his friends walked (and waddled) through Lemuk's dusty road. They followed Kal and his gang, but even so, they felt on edge. They knew that Elska might be watching them. As they neared the city docks, they meandered by a few Rash Tallons, who gave Jay a slight nod. It seemed that Jay made a few new friends.

Finally, they boarded Kal's yacht. It was a craft fit for a king, with four mighty propellers and three golden masts. Billowing bronze tapestries shaded the deck's royal sofas and round tables. Servants floated from guest to guest with drinks and food. Kal had many friends. Some seemed as harsh and rugged as him, but others wore noble tunics of saturated dyes.

At first, Jay, Perl, and Sakona felt too awkward to sit—thinking they didn't belong. But Kal convinced them to rest on a lovely purple couch.

The propellers quietly spun until the yacht eased off the ground and into the air. As they sailed away, Perl snuck toward the stern and spied the horizon, searching for Elska's craft. But after a few minutes, and seeing nothing, Perl returned to her friends.

"I didn't see Elska's ship following us. We might be safe in

Fallengard."

"I hope so," said Jay.

The yacht came to the dome's top, and, as Kal predicted, the Gardish Militia let them pass. The yacht sank through the dome's hole and entered Fallengard.

Jay gazed at the dark city in wonder. It was a cluttered place. The homes, though tiny, overlapped each other. It was clear this place had outgrown itself long ago. Most of the city lay in the wall's shadow. A single shaft of light stretched from the dome's hole to the city's center. In that zone, the buildings stood tall and grand, carved from pure white stones, glimmering like gems. The tallest building was a round castle of pale cobblestone. Its battlements were pointy like flames.

"That monastery belonged to the Mystics," said Kal, wheeling over in his chair. He held a cerulean drink in his hand. "They're led by Alfex. But they left when the war began."

Jay scratched his head, "What's a Mystic?"

"It's a religious person," said Perl. "Right?"

"Yes. They're a religious, spiritual group. Some people think they have magic powers, too."

A loud boom echoed from below. Jay searched the city but saw nothing. "What was that?"

"Explosions—below the city," said Kal. "The war is fought underground, mostly."

Sakona leaned over the guard rail, "In caves?"

"Mines. That's what Fallengard's known for. That, and the Mystics." Kal took a sip of his juice. "The coliseum's down there, in the mines. We'll head there soon, but first I've got some business to do on the surface. We'll land now and leave again tonight."

The yacht sailed away from the bright zone and into the shadows, landing in a cramped harbor—squeezed between two other airships. Soon after, Jay, Perl, and Sakona set out to explore the city, leaving Loosha to lounge about the yacht. They wanted to search for clues to try and find the Kan'zi temple.

As they started down the city streets, Jay noticed that the homes and shops had no windows. They each had small metal doors with long black bars. The Gardish people kept their heads down and gazed away from Jay and his friends.

"Maybe that Mystic Monastery in the city's center is actually a Kan'zi Temple!" said Sakona.

"But isn't that a little too obvious? Besides, it doesn't look much like the other temple," said Jay.

"Yeah," added Perl, "they work from the shadows, remember? That was the brightest spot in the city!"

"But isn't this whole country a little busy for them?" asked Sakona.

"Maybe it wasn't this busy when they first came," said Jay.

Suddenly, a gang of men and women slid in front of Jay and his friends. They sported brown, dirty clothes, matching crimson caps. and blood-red blades.

"That's a nice rod, ye got there," said one, pointing to Jay's lance. "Why doncha give it 'ere and you and your friends can run along?"

Perl and Sakona drew their swords, but the bandit laughed.

"Doncha know we're Ashen Blades? We take what we want. Now hand it over."

Jay pulled the rod's trigger, drawing its blade. He pointed it at the bandits and said, "Don't *you* know we're... Icy Spears? We take what *we* want. Now hand over your swords."

"Icy Spears?!" the bandit was caught off guard. He hadn't expected his day to go quite like this. "Say... how come I've never heard of you?!" Jay's trick would have worked on the Colonel in Onaga, but this bandit was smarter—though only a little.

"Fine, take my rod," said Jay faking a frown. "It's from Dalk anyway."

The gangsters all murmured in disgust.

"But boss," whispered one, "nothing great comes from Dalk! We ain't gonna turn no profit on that."

"Shut it, fool. He's just tryin' to trick us!"

"It was worth a shot," said Jay, raising his blade.

But the lead bandit let out a sharp whistle. Other men and women emerged from alleys and doors—each wearing red caps and drawing their Ashen Blades.

Jay, Perl, and Sakona ran, but the Ashen Blades ran faster. The mob neared their prey, when Jay spotted a long bush.

"Perl, look!"

When she saw the bush, she and Jay drew its Vitex and splashed it at the gang, then kept running.

"Doesn't this city have guards?!" shouted Perl.

They came to a long street blocked by a hill of trash—a high pile of chairs, tables, barrels, crates, and other junk, perhaps three stories high. At first, Jay wasn't sure they could climb it. But the sound of the mob grew louder and louder.

They leapt into the trash and climbed up and over the hill, tumbling down the other side. Once there, they found a group of armored guards.

"Are you all deaf?" said Jay. "We're being chased by a mob!"

"What's this?" said the guard leader. "Out passed curfew? You've broken the law!"

"Let me try this again," said Jay. "Are you all deaf?"

"And those weapons! You can't parade your weapons in public. You've broken another law!" More guards gathered around.

"How do you expect us to protect ourselves?" said Sakona.

"Saying you're all deaf," added Jay.

"And you're children! Without an adult! Why, you've broken

three laws!"

"Oh, shut up!" said Perl. The guards gasped. "Look, a bunch of thieves are chasing us. I'm sure stealing is against the law, too. Right?"

The guard leader looked up with hungry eyes, like a rolf who smelled fresh meat (or like myself when I smell smoked and salted moncetta). "Where are they?"

"On the other side of that trash hill," said Sakona.

"You mean the wall? You came from the other side?"

Looking now, Jay and his friends saw that the trash pile was not just a single hill, but a long barricade which stretched down the street, out of sight.

"Well," said the guard, "you three are safe here. The Ashen Blades will never control this half of Fallengard, no matter how hard they try. But where are your parents?"

"No clue," said Jay.

"They kicked me out," said Perl.

"Mine are dead," said Sakona.

"Ah, orphans. Come with me, we have strict rules for orphans."

They would have fought back, if not for the full platoon of guards which surrounded them. They dropped their weapons and followed.

Marching down the streets, Jay found that the people and homes matched the other side. The people were shy and the tiny, overlapping homes had no windows.

Soon they came to a four-story home with a sloped roof and charming chimney. The leader approached the door and pulled on a rope which fed through a slim hole into the house. The rope was a doorbell, for after the leader pulled it, they heard a feint ringing beyond the door. A few moments later, there sounded many bolts and locks opening before the door finally did. A lowly, older lady named Eera stood timid in the doorway.

"We've got three children for you, Miss Eera. They had these weapons. We'll leave them with you. If they're ever adopted, you can gift them to the parents."

Eera waved for the three to enter. Her home was wooden and warm. A comfy rug and chunky chairs sat around a roaring fireplace. Without a word, she brought them to the dining room.

A few round tables lay about the room, and around the round tables sat many children. But there was something odd about the sight. After a few moments, Jay realized what it was: the room was silent. Not one child spoke with another.

The old lady showed Jay, Perl, and Sakona to a table and left to fix them a meal.

"We have to break out," said Sakona, "but how?"

Perl turned to the children at their table. "Has anyone ever escaped this place? Hello?" But the children kept quiet and ate their food.

Jay whispered to the boy who sat beside him. "Are you not allowed to talk?"

"We can talk." The boy's voice was soft, like it hadn't been used before.

"Then why are y'all so quiet?"

"What's there to talk about?" said the boy.

"What do you mean?" said Jay, puzzled. But the boy didn't reply, so Jay thought for a moment and said, "There's always stuff to talk about! Like, this food and if we like it or not. Or we can swap tales and share about things we've done."

But the boy rolled his eyes, "If I did that, you'd use it against me."

"Why would you think that?"

"That's how it is," said the boy with a shrug.

By then, Eera returned with plates of green, leafy food, a

truly unacceptable meal by all modern standards. Jay and Sakona ate theirs, but when no one was watching, Perl swiped hers off the table and into her pocket.

Eera rang a bell and the other children lined up by the door.

"What should we do?" whispered Jay. "We can't stay here!"

"Don't worry. I've got an idea," said Perl.

They followed the other children and the lady. She showed them out of the dining hall to their rooms. She put Jay in a small bedroom with the boy from their table. She took Perl and Sakona to a bedroom down the hall. She locked the doors and went to bed.

Jay gazed about his meager quarters. Two small beds huddled a nightstand, which held a dim candle. The pale blue walls made the room feel cold and empty. The boy had already tucked himself in.

"I'm Jay, what's your name?"

"What's it to you?"

"You don't trust me?"

"Why would I?"

"C'mon, kid. What are you afraid of? Have some courage!"

"Courage?"

"You don't know what it means? Well, it's like bravery."

"Bravery?" The boy looked just as confused as before.

Jay tried with all his might to explain it, but the word was too complex. It irked him a bit, but he was more confused than anything. *How has this kid never heard such a common word before?*

Soon, Jay gave up and instead shared about himself and his life on Onaga, hoping the boy would do the same. When he spoke long enough, Jay asked "Did you know your parents?"

The boy shuffled in his sheets. After some time, he finally answered, "Yes. They wanted to cross the barricade. At night, we tried, but the militia found us. They took me away and I haven't seen them since."

"Sorry to hear that," said Jay. "Do you think they're still out there?"

"I don't know. It was years ago. But I promised myself that if I'm ever adopted and leave this place, I'll look for them."

"That's a good thing to promise." Jay laid down and closed his eyes. He almost fell asleep when the boy's voice stirred him awake.

"Pardon, what was that?" said Jay, wiping his eyes.

"Kipper. My name's Kipper."

"It's a pleasure to meet you, Kipper."

Suddenly, Jay felt a rumbling, like a wind had shaken the wooden home—but Fallengard had no wind! Kipper still laid in his bed, as if unaware of the rumble.

"Kipper, do you feel that? What's going on?!"

"It's an earthquake," he yawned. "There's been a lot since the war started—since it's fought underground and all."

"Oh," but that didn't make Jay feel much better. He laid down again and tried to sleep, but then another strange thing happened: he heard a small 'poof' in the hall. Jay sat up. The doorknob fell off and thumped on the ground. The door swung open as Perl and Sakona entered the room.

"C'mon, Jay!" said Sakona.

"How'd you get out? And in here?"

"Dinner!" said Perl. "There was Vitex in the leaves. Now c'mon!"

"Wait," said Jay. "Kipper, will you come with us? We're going to escape." Kipper seemed torn, so Jay added, "C'mon buddy, you can look for your parents!"

So Jay, Perl, Sakona, and Kipper tip-toed to the living room. They found their weapons stored in a chest by Eera's desk. But the front door was locked with several bolts and a chain.

Jay flopped his hands to his sides, "How can we get out now?"

"Why doesn't this city have windows?" groaned Perl.

"We can get more leaves from the kitchen and Perl can blast the door open," said Sakona.

But the kitchen door was locked, too. Jay had an idea—it was rather nasty, but they had no other choice. Jay and Kipper dug through the trash bins in the dining hall and found a few, half-eaten leaves.

"That's not much," said Perl, "but I'll try my best."

She took the leaves in her hand and pulled out a small ball of Vitex (to Kipper's great surprise). She hurled it at the door—it broke the chain and one lock, but the door stayed intact.

Sakona sulked, "Those were all the leaves we could find!"

"The chimney!" said Jay.

"We can't climb out a chimney," said Perl.

"Yes, we can," said Jay. "We need to press our hands and feet hard against its sides. I had to when we first built ours on Onaga."

"And only one of us needs to climb it bare," Perl pointed to a rope above the door; the rope which worked the doorbell. First, she pulled the outer end inside. She followed it to its source: a bronze bell deeper in the house. Quietly, carefully, yet quickly, she untied the cord from the bell and returned to the group.

"One of us can climb up with this line and lower it to the others."

"Leave it to me," said Sakona, who was anxious to be rid of the orphanage. "I'm used to climbing the mast on the Rogue." She took the rope from Perl, tied it around herself, and started her climb. She crawled up slowly.

"I thought you said you're a good climber," said Perl.

"Yes, but not with all this rope wrapped around me!" said

Sakona. "This thing weighs as much as I do!"

Before long, she came to the roof and rested. She tied the cord around the chimney's top and dropped in the loose end.

"Alright," said Jay. "Let's go one at a time. Perl, you first."

Perl took the rope in her hands and started to climb. But Jay and Kipper heard a door open from somewhere in the house. Eera was awake.

"We can't wait for Perl to finish. Kipper, you've got to go now!"

"But what if the line can't hold us all at the same time?"

"We'll need to have courage." But Jay realized that Kipper still didn't know what that meant. "Courage is when you're afraid, but you climb up anyway."

Kipper nodded, and nervously neared the rope. He grabbed ahold and started to climb. Jay followed right behind him. After much tugging and sweating, they flopped out of the chimney. Their clothes, hands, and faces were black, covered in soot. They looked quite silly but they were too tired to laugh.

"I think I see the barricade from here," said Jay. "We can run along these rooftops until we reach it. Will you come with us, Kipper?"

"No, I've got to find my parents. They're probably still on this side. You three should go to the city's rim. The farmers there are friendly, like you. Thanks for helping me escape. I'm glad I trusted you."

So Jay, Perl, and Sakona said goodbye to Kipper. They leapt from roof to roof until they reached the barricade. They climbed down the building and up the barricade again. They ran through the streets and didn't stop until they came once more to Kal Korro's yacht.

Chapter XXIII

TO SAVE A BOY

Jay, Perl, and Sakona dashed aboard Kal Korro's yacht, still covered in soot from the chimney.

"Next stop, the mines! But it looks like you've already been there," said Kal, laughing at his own joke. He took a swig of his gaudy drink. It was soontaplum wine, an acquired taste with a tangy kick. But I digress.

When the yacht lifted into the air again, Jay, Perl, and Sakona sighed in relief.

"Kal," said Perl, "This city sucks."

Kal let out a hearty laugh. "What makes you say that, lass? Not that I disagree."

"One side has too many rules, and the other doesn't have any."

"Yeah," said Jay. "How did that happen? How did the war start?"

"I don't care much, so I don't know much. But from what I gather, the Lords who ran the city wanted more control. They made more and more laws, but bad ones. They hurt people—made 'em poor. So the people turned to crime. The Ashen Blades formed and grew big enough to start the war."

"You said something about Mystics? Are they the Lords?"

asked Jay.

"No; Alfex and his Mystics used to live here—in that monastery. They helped the city by caring for the poor, the elderly, and other needy folk. They worked with the Lords. But the war was so dangerous, the Mystics decided to leave. Since then, the city's fallen apart."

"What will happen if the Ashen Blades win?" said Sakona.

"No more Lords," said Kal, with a grin. "This place will be as crazy as the Blue Eye. But don't worry yourself with that, we've got plenty on our plate. Tomorrow we enter the dueling circuit. Jay, if you win, you'll become rich and famous. Even Alfex himself will know your name."

Perl let out a fake yawn. "What's so special about Alfex?"

"Don't you know? He's leader of the Mystics. But legends say he's three hundred years old! He was here when Fallengard was founded. If you win the circuit, I'm sure you could meet him."

"But didn't you say he left Fallengard?" said Sakona.

"Yes, but he didn't go far—he left for the Mystic Mountains, just south of here."

Kal wheeled away to find another drink while the three and Loosha gathered close together.

"This dueling stuff is a huge waste of time," said Sakona. "We made it to Fallengard. We should ditch Kal and look for the temple!"

"But where do we start?" said Perl. "This place is huge—it could take us weeks to find it."

"Weren't you two listening?" said Jay. "Kal said that Alfex is three hundred years old. If that's true, he was here before the sandstorm sea. He's got to know about the Kan'zi!"

"If he himself isn't a Kan'zi!" added Perl. "How could an Arlish live for three hundred years?"

"We have to meet him to find out," said Jay. "And the only way to meet him is if Loosha and I win the circuit."

"No offense, Jay, but that sounds like a longshot to me," said Sakona. "That first arena was dangerous enough. Who knows what you'll face here?"

"Is that a lack of faith in Loosha or in me?" asked Jay with a smirk.

"Croark!"

But Sakona pressed her point, "This isn't a joke. If we need to talk to Alfex and we know where he is, let's go look for him!"

"Well, maybe. But," started Jay, but he didn't have a comeback. So, he started to mutter a lot of nonsense, "Someone as important as him must have defenses. He's not the sort of guy we can just walk up to."

"That's a huge assumption. You don't know that!"

"Look, there's a clear path in front of us. It's hard, but it's clear. And I'd prefer we do it that way."

"But why?"

Jay didn't reply, or rather he couldn't reply. The truth was, he didn't know the answer yet.

The fancy yacht floated over dark overlapping homes and narrow streets. They drifted through the city until they came to a large crevice—a shaft in the ground. It was a blanket of gray shadow. And yet, the airship sank lower and lower, into the crevice. Soon, the yacht entered the underworld.

Jay and his friends could hardly see a thing. Kal Korro's yacht sailed toward a far-off beam of light that pulsed on and off. The world beneath the city was a series of large mines, wide enough for two airships to pass each other. It looked like a cave, but the walls and roof were flat as a crate.

The yacht sailed nearer to the pulsing light which wasn't actually pulsing—it was spinning. It belonged to an underground lighthouse. Looking deeper down the cavern, Jay saw what must have been more lighthouses with chromatic spinning lights, each spaced a few kilometers apart.

Now underground, they heard the constant sound of battle raging. Boom after boom echoed from afar, like a large drum. Regardless, their voyage continued. They sailed over a deep, black wound in the ground—a gorge devoid of life and light. Kal said it was the Black Fissure, and that no miners who entered ever returned.

The mine grew wider and wider until, at last, they came to a village. Its sharp buildings made the mine look more like a true cave. The homes, shops, and plazas were made of rusty metal and circled a stupendous coliseum of alabaster stone. Even from afar, Jay could tell it was much larger than the one on Lemuk. Three lighthouses surrounded the city, dancing their beams across streets and alleys.

"How can people live here? It's always dark!" said Perl.

"Maybe they don't have a choice," said Jay.

"Some people like the dark," said Sakona. "The Blue Eye never got very bright."

Soon the Yacht landed and Kal guided Jay, Perl, Sakona, and Loosha to a small inn across from the arena. Inside, a large, happy woman met them. She wore a long purple smock and a golden yellow flower in her hair.

"Well, hello! My name's Padea and this is my brother Pud," she said, gesturing to a grouchy man, sitting in a rocking chair. "Welcome to our inn."

"Our inn?" said Pud. "What a joke."

"You're right—I should have said *my* inn, saying you don't lift a finger while I'm around!" she teased.

"I never asked for your help!" he moaned.

"If it were up to you, these kind people would never get

their room." She made a face to Jay and his friends that said, 'can-you-believe-this-man?'

"Sit down and relax!" said Pud. "You're on vacation!"

But Padea ignored him. "Sorry about him. My brother's a lazy oaf."

Kal wheeled over to the woman and shook her hand, then he pointed to Jay.

"You're looking at the next dueling champion," he said. "The Bronze Boy and the Froad! Take good care of them, they enter the ring tomorrow." He dropped a few coins in Padea's hand.

"You're the next champion?" said Padea with wonderous eyes.

"That's me," returned Jay with a smolder.

"You're so young," said Padea. "You must be quite the gladiator!"

That almost made Perl laugh, but she caught herself and said, "He's come a long way."

"Well Jay, I'll see you tomorrow," said Kal, spinning his chair to leave. "Sleep well."

"Wait, we've got to strategize! Teach me some moves or at least tell me what I'm up against."

"We'll save it for the morning. Meet me by the gladiator gate. Good night."

Padea showed her guests to their suite. And in that short time, Jay and his friends learned that Padea loved to chat.

"Sorry about my brother. He hates seeing me work, but I can't sit still! It's all too exciting down here. How could I sit around all day like him when there's a gladiator in our inn!"

"You're not like the other Gardish," said Perl. "Where are you from?"

"Oh, I'm from the overworld—but I live in the city's rim. I own a farm. I know what you mean, though. When I go into town, everyone looks away, as if I'm not there. It's so rude!" Padea took to the oven and cooked up some grub. "Isn't this exciting? Why, this might be your last meal!"

You might think that comment would have seized Jay with fear and chased away his appetite, but it didn't, and that is for two reasons: first, Padea was a cook to rival Dovians. She baked fresh bread kneaded with hickelberry juice instead of that dreadful greyberry spat. She also seared a ribeye nathlagoon steak. The only thing she lacked was, of course, water, and though the three missed that drink dearly, they found this all to be a fair substitute.

But the second reason was more important than food and drink. When Jay had heard the words 'dueling champion,' he was gripped. He had thought about little else since they arrived on Fallengard. He fancied himself wearing that epic title like a new coat. His desire for the title blocked out logic and reason.

But Perl and Sakona cut through his daydream. When Padea had left, Perl said "Jay, you shouldn't go tomorrow. I don't think it's right."

"What? Why not?"

"Well, killing monsters is one thing, like those selovates. That's like hunting. But you can't kill other people. That's wrong, and you know it."

"Well, duh. But I wasn't going to. Loosha can paralyze them, like Big Blen."

"You better be careful."

"I am careful!"

"Perl's right, Jay," said Sakona. "Fights are wild. You can't control the outcome."

With this on his mind, Jay hardly slept a pinch that night. He was too worried. Not so much for his own life, but more for the lives of his coming foes. He surely didn't want to kill anyone. Meeting Alfex wasn't worth someone's life. He wanted to find

Kal and quit. But he thought of Loosha, *She can paralyze people. I won't have to kill anyone.*

In the morning, Jay, Perl and Sakona found Kal at the coliseum. Jay equipped his leather armor, bronze shield, and helmet. Perl and Sakona gave him and Loosha a quick hug.

"Kal, what am I going to face? Monsters, other gladiators?"

"That's the thing… I don't know. I haven't fought in this circuit for ten years. A lot has changed."

"What?!"

"Be ready for anything, then nothing will surprise you!"

"That's it? That's all you've got for me?"

"What do you want? I'm your sponsor, not your trainer. Now get in there and make us some money."

Kal took Perl and Sakona to their seats—they sat at the front, almost on the ground level—leaving Jay and Loosha at the gladiator gate.

"Welcome ladies and gentlemen," called the Game Master. "This pair of duelists hail from Onaga. Don't let their age or size fool you—they're a deadly duo." The gate lifted. Jay and Loosha entered the arena. "Sponsored by Kal Korro himself, I give you the Bronze Boy and the Froad!"

Jay gazed around the coliseum, it was packed with people, all shouting and cheering for him! He felt a force of nervous energy deep within, looking for a way out. He raised his rod-lance and shield high in the air and cheered back at his fans. Eventually he pulled his eyes away from the crowd to the arena floor. Steaming geysers, yellow grass, and tall mounds filled the battlefield.

"The Bronze Boy and the Froad will face another duo. This pair hails from the north and sponsored themselves. Today is their first duel. Let's see what they're made of. I give you Flare and her Selovate!"

A woman emerged from a far off gate, clad in a ramshackle

suit of green, crusted armor. A selovate's exo-skull served as her helmet. By her side was a fully grown selovate—nearly as tall as the woman herself. The creature had six spikey feet and two crooked green pincers. Its drab shell looked identical to Flare's armor.

Jay gulped. "Loosha, your tongue won't work on either of them. Selovate shell is too tough. You have to try something else, okay?!"

"Croark!"

"Try not to be stupid for a few minutes, alright? Then we can be champions."

"Croark!"

The woman drew twin blades and dashed across the field, toward Jay. Her selovate crawled close behind. Jay drew his rod-lance and held his ground.

Flare lunged at Jay, spinning her blades like an airship's pro-pellers. Jay blocked and dodged; he swiped his lance to hold her back. Loosha, despite Jay's warning, shot her tongue at the sel-ovate. When nothing happened, she whimpered and ran away. The enormous bug chased after her, pinching and nipping.

"Wait, Loosha! Useless blob."

Flare pulled one sword to her side then lunged it forward to stab Jay, but he rose his shield just in time. Her blade pierced the shield and nipped his arm. But the sword stayed stuck, so Jay tossed the shield away. Now he only had his lance, but his foe only had one sword.

With the longer weapon, Jay had an advantage. He pushed forward, swiping and thrusting his lance. Flare ducked and leapt from his attacks. To try and turn the tide, she parried his strike, spun, and stabbed at his heart. But with the hilt of his rod, he bumped her sword away and jabbed his blade at her face.

At once, Jay felt awful about his strike—he thought it would kill the woman, so he pulled back as quick as he could. But the blade already caught her skull-helmet so when he pulled his lance, it knocked her helmet off. She was a young woman with fair skin, blonde hair, and captivating eyes. She was Elska.

In a flash, Perl and Sakona stood by Jay. Perl had suspected it was Elska, and when she was proven right, she and Sakona jumped out of their seats and into the arena. Sakona held her sword and shield up high. Perl drew her bow and readied an arrow.

"Stop!" called the Game Master. "This is unfair—"

But Elska held up her hand and said, "It's fine. I accept the challenge."

She slowly circled Jay and his friends. Her eyes never left Jay.

"What's the matter?" said Perl, "Run out of Vitex?"

"The Kan'zi and I prefer that these simple people don't know of greater powers," said Elska, gesturing to the crowd. "I won't use my Vitex unless you do. And you know I would win. You saw what I did to Wald."

Perl screamed in anger and fired an arrow. Elska leapt aside and dodged it, but Sakona lunged after her slashing and striking with hate. Elska dodged her too, ducking and strafing in cold apathy.

Perl aimed her bow but couldn't find a safe shot—Sakona was too close! And Perl didn't trust her aim, she was still new to archery and had only practiced a bit.

"Perl, go help Loosha!" said Jay. "I'll help Sakona."

They split up. With Jay's help, Sakona pushed Elska back. Jay saw shock in Elska's eyes as Sakona angrily hacked at her foe.

"You killed my father!" she shouted with a stab.

"I don't seem to remember him," taunted Elska. "I've killed lots of people. Can you be more specific?"

The arena's geysers rumbled and spat out a thick mist. Elska vanished into the fog.

The mob stood to its feet, cheering and shouting. Many yelled, "C'mon, I can't see nothing!" and "Clear that fog!" while others saw it as a surprising and welcome turn of events.

Jay and Sakona rushed up the nearest mound and stood back-to-back. Even from the higher point, they couldn't see more than a few feet ahead of them. Suddenly, they heard Perl, crying "Help!"

They followed her voice and found her standing alone, with her bow drawn.

"Are you okay?" asked Jay.

"Where's Loosha?" asked Sakona.

"She's out there, somewhere—she's in trouble!"

Through the mist they heard growls, hisses, and croarks. They gasped when they heard a crunch. But out of the fog waddled Loosha, smiling and chewing on something.

"Loosha! Did you… eat that selovate?"

"Croark!"

"But it was so big!"

"Croark!"

Elska leapt out of the mist with both her sabers. She sliced Sakona's leg and cut away Jay's lance. As she moved to strike him, Perl summoned a desperate wave of Vitex from the grass and blasted Elska.

The Vitex pummeled into her and sent her soaring through the air, across the arena. She tumbled to the ground. Perl's strike was so remarkable that it cleared most of the fog from the field.

The mob cheered louder as Elska stood to her feet. She dropped her blades and pointed her fingers, ready to fire her invincible White Vitex.

But at that moment, the coliseum quaked. Titanic booms sounded with cracks and blasts like lightning. The crowd gasped as the arena rumbled. Jay, Perl, and Sakona gaped around in terror—it felt like the ground was falling out from under them. Even Elska put down her hands.

The arena's metal gate split in two. Into the coliseum poured the Ashen Blade army, shouting, "Retreat! They've broken our line!" Over a hundred soldiers sprinted through the field. Many had cuts and bruises. "Run! Everyone, run!"

Then came the Gardish Militia. Clad in iron armor, they pursued the Ashen Blades with a numerous force. Their arrows sped through the air and pinned down more of their foes. "Surrender, thieves!"

They set fire to the arena; the air filled with smoke and screams as the crowd fled. When Jay looked back to where Elska had stood, he saw only the fire's black smoke.

"We have to get out of here!" said Perl.

"No! We need to kill Elska," said Sakona, limping from her wound. "We're so close!"

But the blazing fire crawled nearer and nearer. Sakona realized their danger, so she leaned on Jay and Perl for support. Together, they fled the coliseum. The city was filled with panic. Soldiers marched all around, spreading fire from home to home. Cannons bombarded the coliseum; their savage strikes shattered the stands, reducing the massive structure to rubble.

"We have to get to Kal's yacht!" said Jay.

They zipped through the streets, dodging trouble on all sides. But as they neared the harbor, they watched Kal's yacht lift off and sail away without them.

Jay felt sick to his stomach. There seemed to be no hope for escape. But they heard a familiar voice.

"Children!" called Padea, dragging Pud by the ear. "Come with me, we've got to leave this dreadful place." Relieved, the three followed Padea and Pud to her airship—a small sloop with a single sail.

"Let go of me, you hag!" squealed Pud. "I can't leave my inn—" A series of cannonballs tore through the inn, leveling the building. "Never mind. Drag away!"

They boarded Padea's sloop and she tried to get it afloat, but the battle made her nervous. Her hands fumbled all over the controls.

"Why don't you let us take over?" said Sakona. "We're used to stuff like this."

Padea sat down. Sakona took the helm, Perl took the engine, Jay took the sails. Together, they lifted off and sailed away from the burning underworld.

Chapter XXIV

WARRIORS OF THE DIM DISTRICT

Hundreds of other airships filled the tunnel, each fleeing for their lives. Despite her bloody leg, Sakona skillfully sailed the sloop through the crowded mineshaft.

Jay, Perl, and Padea peered over the ship's side to the ground below. The rocks seemed to wobble and bobble; a few boulders tumbled out of their pockets, forming fierce landslides.

"It's another earthquake," said Jay.

Padea banged her fists on the guard rail, "Blast this war! Don't they know we live on top these mines? If they keep this up, the whole city will collapse!" Jay and Perl wondered if that could truly happen. Somewhere in this city was a Kan'zi Superior. Maybe that was the Kan'zi's strategy. Maybe Padea was right.

Soon they sailed out of the mines and back to the overworld. The city was silent and still—seemingly unaware of the battle below. With clear skies and easy sailing ahead, Padea took the helm again. She sailed the sloop over the junk wall and onto the Gardish side. Jay, Perl, and Sakona met by the bow.

"Jay," said Perl, ever ready for a fight, "This was a horrible plan from the start."

"Gee, thanks," spat Jay.

"We should have gone with Sakona's plan. Now look at her!"

Perl pointed to Sakona's leg. Her wound was deep.

"I'm fine," said Sakona, waiving off Perl with one hand and clutching her wound with the other. Even so, she winced from the pain.

Jay's heart sank, he felt awful—the kind of awful that moves you to tell the truth, "I'm sorry. That was a dumb choice. I think I wanted to win, but I see what that did."

Perl nodded, happy with his reply.

"We're flying to the Mystic Mountains. Now." said Sakona. "We know Alfex is there. Let's go already!"

"Yes," said Jay, "let's get back to the Rogue and fly there ourselves."

But Padea bumbled into their chat: "Why don't you three come to my farm and get some rest. I can patch you up nicely," she said to Sakona. "Afterward, I'll take you anywhere you need to go."

"Thanks," said Sakona, "but I think we should get back to our ship."

"Oh, but we're almost there! And I can make you some fresh bread!"

"But—" started Jay.

"I insist!"

Jay felt wary of Padea. He wondered if her kindness was just a facade. He remembered her nathlagoon ribeye and figured that another meal with her was worth the risk.

When Padea took the helm again, Jay took Sakona below deck. He sat her on a small barrel. He knelt and tied a rag around her leg to patch the wound he helped to make.

"I'm sorry about this," said Jay with a little frown.

Sakona replied, "We're cool."

Jay tried to make light of it by saying, "At least you'll have a cool-looking scar!"

"Add it to the others."

Since humor wasn't helping, Jay thought of a different approach. He gazed into her eyes and said something rather bold, "You'll still look just as beautiful."

Sakona looked down and blushed. She awkwardly tugged at her hair, trying to undo some knots. "Anyway... don't feel bad about it, Jay. Elska did this."

Jay chuckled, "Glad you see it my way."

Sakona stared off in hate, "She's a monster."

Jay argued in his head whether or not to say anything. In the end, he let out the smallest peep of what he was thinking, though more was to follow: "You know... she's an Arlish, too."

"Are you defending her?"

"No! Well, sort of? I'm saying... every time we face Elska, it fills you with so much hate."

"Well, duh! She's hunting us. She's hunting you."

"Yes, but you were bleeding with a fire all around us, and your first thought was still to kill her."

Sakona stood and stepped away from Jay. She bit her bottom lip, taking a moment to think. "Why shouldn't I hate her? She killed my father, Jay. She killed Wald, too! Doesn't that make you angry?"

"It does," he said with a frown. "I get it, I do. But when we spoke after your father died, you told me you 'hate death and wanted nothing to do with it.' What happened to that?"

"I do hate death—but she's trying to cause it. If I have to kill her to stop her from killing us, I will. I can't believe you disagree with me on this. What other option is there?"

"I'm not sure. But maybe there's another way."

"I don't see another way," said Sakona.

*   *   *

They came to the city's rim. It was known as the Dim Dis-

214

trict, since it sat in a dark corner of the dome's curved wall. Berry bushes drooped from the wall, like leaves from a willow tree. Farmers pulled themselves up the wall with repelling lines to harvest their crops. If it wasn't for the lack of light, the Dim District would be a desirable place.

Padea landed her sloop beside her home. It was a cozy wood-frame ranch with a thatched roof. A cobblestone fence surrounded her land on three sides and the fourth met the dome's wall. Padea farmed greyberries from the wall and hickelberries from the field. It earned her a modest living.

Padea took her guests and brother into her home and sat them at a long wooden table. "I'm back! Rellen, I'm back! Bring me some rags and greyberry juice!"

Rellen, a slim older woman with white hair, dressed in peasant garb, came and tended to Sakona.

"This is Rellen," said Padea. "She doesn't speak—she's a mute. Been working here for a few weeks now. Sakona, deary, can I get you anything?"

"A glass of water—I mean… hickelberry juice, please!"

The adults eyed Sakona.

"Water?" laughed Pud. "Aren't you kids too old to believe in such a thing?"

"Yes, sir," said Jay, to cover for Sakona.

The delightful evening passed by all too quickly. A roaring fireplace warmed Jay and his friends while the smell of Padea's cooking fostered their hunger. The dining room was a picture of comfort, with a fluffy rug, cushioned seats, and plenty of candles—for light was sparse in the Dim District, even during the day.

Padea cooked and cooked while Pud put his feet up and relaxed. He did, however, tell wonderful, scary stories of the underworld. On the other hand, Rellen was a mysterious woman.

She had perfect posture and fast focus. She seemed smart and nearly noble. Though she couldn't speak, her presence loomed large over the small dining room. All evening, Jay couldn't help but wonder why she was a mute.

When their stomachs were stuffed, Padea tossed the scraps to Loosha and turned to Jay. "So, tell us about your quest!"

"Well, I'm not sure if we should," said Jay, eyeing his friends. He felt Padea and Pud were trustworthy, but he wasn't sure about Rellen.

"Oh, they're fine," said Perl. The taste of dinner still lingered in her mouth. "I think they're safe."

"Oh, I'm very safe," said Padea. "Besides, Pud doesn't have any friends, so he's got no one to gossip to!"

Pud rolled his eyes but didn't deny the fact.

"And Rellen doesn't speak anyway," said Padea. "So that just leaves me, and I can keep a secret!"

So Jay told Padea, Pud, and Rellen of their quest—but to be safe, he left some parts out. He told of the secret war, of Vitex, of the old world before the sand, and of the Kan'zi. He didn't tell of the atlas nor of the League's location.

And when Jay spoke of the Kan'zi, Rellen leaned in while Padea leaned away. Rellen seemed curious, but Padea seemed afraid.

As he spoke these things, he realized how crazy his tale sounded. He spoke of life-energy and monsters and secret wars—it all sounded like rubbish. But to his surprise, Padea, Pud, and Rellen seemed to believe him. They didn't scoff once. Later on, Jay learned that they believed the tale because of their history with Mystics.

"We have reason to believe there's a Kan'zi Temple somewhere in Fallengard," said Jay. "That's why we're here. We've heard that the Mystic Alfex is three hundred years old—that's about as old as the sandstorm sea—so we think he might know where the temple is."

"That's some story," said Pud. "I've heard better, of course. But that's pretty good."

"So, you're not real gladiators?" asked Padea.

"No—we did that to get into Fallengard," said Sakona.

"But you're good at fighting?"

"Yeah, we are!" said Perl. "Why do you ask?"

Padea brought her guests out of the ranch and into her hickelberry field. "Look at the stalks."

"They're pretty sparse," said Perl. "Where are all the berries?"

"And what happened here?" said Jay, pointing to a few trampled plants.

"It's the Gardish Militia. A patrol comes every day and takes my crops—my neighbor's, too. We can't afford to lose anymore."

"Isn't there anyone that can help you?" said Perl.

"You tell me. I haven't been honest with you three. I went to my brother's inn to find a gladiator who could help me stand up to the militia. Then I met you and… here we are."

"So, you want us to stop the patrol for you?" Jay smiled, itching for another brawl.

"How many soldiers are in the patrol?" asked Perl.

"That doesn't matter," said Sakona, pulling Jay and Perl aside. "We have our quest and we're already behind. Remember what happened on the Exodus? And if we save the world, we'll be helping Padea anyway."

Jay took a moment to think, then said, "Isn't the world just a bunch of people with problems?"

"I guess," said Perl.

"What are you getting at?" said Sakona.

"I'm saying we can't pretend to save the world while ignoring someone's problem—that person is part of the world we're trying to save. So Padea's part of our quest."

"I'm not sure that makes sense," said Perl. "But I think that's what Metrarch would want."

"We can't stay here forever," said Sakona. "If we fight off the patrol, what's to stop them from coming back?"

Jay paced about and thought. He looked at Padea, then her crops. "What if we teach them to defend themselves?"

"You mean Vitex!?" said Perl. "That's against the rules!

"Sure," said Jay. "Only elders can teach Vitex. But remember, part of the League's code is, 'To other's needs I will always tend, for good will my Vitex strain.' I'd say teaching them Vitex would make both those lines true."

"But that still doesn't solve our problem," said Sakona. "It took you two weeks to use Vitex, even with an Elder teaching you. What makes you think they'll learn any faster?"

Jay smiled, "Because they're farmers."

*　　*　　*

When Jay shared his plan with Padea, she gathered her neighbors at once. Soon, nearly thirty farmers of all ages came to Padea's field.

Jay stood before Padea's neighbors and clasped his hands. "Padea told us of your problem with the Gardish Militia. We can't defend you, but we can teach you how to defend yourselves."

Perl stepped up, holding a hickelberry vine. She pressed her middle and index fingers to the plant, then lifted her palms into the air. Out of the vine came golden flakes of Vitex. The energy dazzled the eyes of the farmers. It was, perhaps, the brightest thing they had ever seen, since most never left the city's dim district.

As you can imagine, there were many gasps and shouts and

questions. Only Rellen stayed calm; she watched with a stoic gaze from Padea's home.

Jay did his best to field everyone's questions, but one left him stumped:

"So, you want us to defend our crops by using our crops?" asked a grumpy old lady.

"Well, yes," said Jay, scratching his head.

"What's the sense in that?" shouted another farmer.

"All good things come at a cost," stated Perl. "If you use this power just once, I bet you'll never see those soldiers again."

"Bunch of complainers you are!" Pud frowned at her neighbors. "This power sure does sound good to me. I'll take it!"

"Yes," said a young girl, "I think we can spare some fruits if it means we'd never have to give 'em to those guards!"

The farmers murmured for a time. Once they settled down again, Jay spoke. "We want to teach you this power, but before we do, you'll have to join the League."

"The League?" said a farmer. "Is that like a club?"

"Kind of," said Perl. "The League taught us this power, but they also taught us to only use it for good. That's what we want to do with you."

So Jay, Perl, and even Sakona explained the League to the farmers. They told them about the elders, Metrarch, Lor Emai and the Kan'zi. As they explained these things, a few farmers left, thinking it all nonsense. But some stayed, wanting to hear and learn more.

"We can't make you squires," said Jay, "since we're only squires ourselves."

"But I think we can dub you trainees, as long as you recite our pledge," said Perl.

Jay and Perl were making this up as they went.

"But what about the Kan'zi?" A wise, old farmer stroked his

mighty beard. "If we join your League, won't they come for us, too? We would be trading one enemy for another."

"The Kan'zi are your enemy whether you're in the League or not," said Perl.

But Jay knew this wouldn't be enough. These farmers feared the Kan'zi. They needed more than logic.

"You're right," started Jay. "The Kan'zi might come for you. That's why you need courage. Do you know what that word means?"

The farmers shook their heads. For some odd reason, the farmers, like Kipper, had never heard that word before.

"Every day," continued Jay, "you pull yourselves up the wall on ropes to pick berries, right? When you were young, were you afraid of falling? Or that the rope might snap?"

Oldest to youngest, the farmers all nodded their heads.

"How did you get over that fear?" asked Jay.

The wise old farmer said, "We pulled ourselves up anyway."

"That's courage," said Jay. "It's having fear, but going up anyway."

One by one, the remaining farmers recited the pledge of the League. Jay and Perl began to train their new friends. Sakona worked on a battle plan. In a few short hours, most of the farmers were able to summon Vitex out of their crops.

Jay was right: because the farmers spent their lives serving nature, most could easily use Vitex. The oldest farmers could even use ample sums of it.

The next day, the patrol came—about twenty troops and their leader, a sergeant. He led his soldiers around Padea's ranch to the farm, but Padea stood in his way.

"Step aside," ordered the sergeant. "This field belongs to me and my troops."

"No. I won't let you steal my crops any longer."

The sergeant drew his broadsword, and spat, "Back down."

Then, out of the hickelberry stalks, there came a score of farmers armed with nothing but their bare hands and sacks of berries. There stood men, women, and even a few children.

The sergeant stumbled, afraid at first. But seeing they had no weapons, he lifted his blade.

"Soldiers, attack!"

The patrol raised their swords and charged but the farmers stood their ground. First, they spread their legs into a martial stance. They clenched their hands into fists. Next, they aimed their pointer and middle fingers toward their berry sacks. Finally, they lifted their palms toward the sky. Out of their bags flowed golden waves of fiery Vitex!

The great power floated high in the air. One by one, the farmers hurled their Vitex at the patrol. Their power exploded all around—golden flakes stunned and burned the soldiers. The farmers' power stupefied the troops. Most fled the field at once, frightened for their lives. The bravest ones stayed a moment but fled when their sergeant did. In terror, he had dropped his sword and sprinted away.

The farmers cheered. Soon after, Jay, Perl, Sakona, and Loosha rushed out of the ranch and hugged Padea.

"It worked!" shouted Jay.

"Did you see the looks on their faces? They're never coming back!" said Perl.

The other farmers gathered around Jay and his friends. They each said their thanks and gave many hugs and handshakes. When all quieted down, Padea smiled and said, "Tell Metrarch that when he needs our help in the war, he'll get it."

The farmers roared, "Indeed!" and "So be it!"

"I know we've delayed you from your quest," continued Padea. "Let's get a move on. Rellen and I will sail you back to your boat. Rellen! Oh, Rellen!"

Rellen had not trained with the farmers, so she wasn't in the battle. Even so, she had watched Jay and Perl teach with great focus. She stared with unblinking eyes, studying every move. But now, she was nowhere to be found.

Chapter XXV

MYSTIC MOUNTAINS

"Rellen!" called Padea, again. "Rellen, it's safe now. You can come out!"

At last, someone emerged from the ranch; someone who looked like Rellen, and yet not at all. A slender old woman with pure white hair stood in the doorway, wearing radiant red robes. Even in such a dim place, she shone like a blazing torch. At once, every farmer fell to their knees and bowed to the woman.

"This city is so weird," said Sakona.

"Rellen!" said Padea with wide eyes, "you're a Mystic!"

But she ignored Padea and her neighbors. She strode to Jay, Perl, and Sakona and said, "Friends of virtue. Greetings."

"You can speak?!" asked Perl.

Rellen laughed. "Yes. I am a Mystic of Alfex. I came to Fallengard in disguise because I needed help. Alfex is in grave danger. I want you three and your froad to come with me to his monastery in the Mystic Mountains."

Jay thought it was all too easy and too good to be true. But he studied her robes—they weren't the sort you could fashion at home. And the farmers kept bowing. Surely, they would know a Mystic when they saw one. But why would Alfex need the help of three children and a froad?

"How can we help him?" said Jay. "What's the danger?"

"I can't say right now," said Rellen, looking to the farmers. "But what you said of these 'Kan'zi' yesterday, and how good you proved to be by helping these poor folk—well, I believe you're exactly the right people to help him."

Jay looked to his friends. They nodded.

"We'll come with you."

They said goodbye to Padea and the farmers. Rellen marched them into the city.

Gardish citizens, who always kept to themselves, now stood and stared. All were shocked to see a Mystic. Some bowed like the farmers, and others rushed away to find and tell their friends. But Rellen marched on, without ever stopping. They came to the city's center, the Bright District. The buildings here were taller, cleaner, and fancier. Red tiled roofs contrasted soft olive and teal walls. Each structure had white columns and the most immaculate doors.

They barely stepped foot in the Bright District when a force of Gardish Militia emerged and blocked the street.

"In the name of Alfex, let me pass!" bellowed Rellen, standing taller than the guards. "I must see the Sanctum of Lords."

The militia trembled, recognizing the mystic. They parted at once, and a few soldiers even formed an escort. Soon they came to the Imperial Palace, one of the most glorious monuments in all of Arland. Massive columns of white stone held a glossy, pyramid roof. Marble sidings stretched over twenty stories high, and tall, stained-glass windows stood the building's full height.

Light poured down from above onto the white palace, blinding anyone who approached. Jay gazed up and saw, far in the sky, the dome-wall's top hole directly above the superstructure. The Imperial Palace stood in the city's center. Once their eyes adjusted, Jay, Perl, and Sakona took in the breathtaking view.

Sakona was particularly enamored with the building, while Jay and Perl ranked it as the number two building in the world, behind the Arlo Kai's temple in the Hearth.

Rellen triumphantly led them into the palace, down its grand hall, and into a dark, round room. Every part of the round room was covered in paintings of Fallengard's history. How Jay wished he could sit and study them all! The only light which entered the room came from doorway. This was meant to be a secretive place.

There they found some forty men and women dressed in fine blue robes, though not so fine as Rellen's. They were seated in short thrones and they were shouting at each other. They argued back and forth, speaking over each other. Jay found it all immature. But these, he rightly assumed, were the Lords of Fallengard.

Jay sighed, thinking that he and his friends would have to wait a long time for their turn to speak. But Rellen bounded into the room like a raging yavyu.

"Overlord Cren, I have an urgent request!"

When the Lords saw Rellen, they gasped and whispered to one another. A woman with curly red hair and dark blue robes lined with gold, Overlord Cren, stood and turned her hallowed eyes on Rellen.

"A Mystic has come back to Fallengard," she said. "It's been a long time."

"Overlord, Alfex is in danger. These young warriors may hold the secret to his safety. You must grant us a fleet and take us to the Mystic Mountains!"

"And why should we?" demanded Cren. "In our time of need, where were the Mystics? Where was Alfex?"

"The war was too dangerous," said Rellen. "The Ashen Blades stormed our city monastery. We had to leave!"

"You left us!" said Cren. "I've realized something, Mystic. Before you left, we counted on you for everything. We went to you with every choice we made. But since you left, we've learned to fend for ourselves. That showed me something else. Why did this war start, Mystic?"

"The Ashen Blades of Lemuk invaded the city in secret and gained followers—"

"No. You and your Alfex started it. You wanted more control. You made more laws—built up our walls. The people pushed back, and rightfully so."

The Lords cheered for Cren and howled at Rellen.

"This is going very poorly," said Perl. "Maybe we should leave."

"I see why Kal didn't care for this stuff," said Sakona.

"Lords," said Rellen in a powerful voice. "I admit that our exit was untimely. And I admit that our laws did not help matters. But these, too, I think, stem from Alfex's dire case. He needs our help! Lords, who was it that helped Fallengard rise to such power? Who gave you your titles and raised you to be the leaders you are today? Will you deny that man the help he so desperately needs?"

For a long time, Overlord Cren coldly stared at Rellen. Finally, she spoke. "I grant you one ship."

Gardish Militia escorted them to the imperial harbor. They glided by many grand warships before coming to a decrepit schooner, a tiny thing meant for eight. She was called Dalk, named for the island that nothing great comes from. Begrudgingly, they boarded the embarrassing craft and sailed out of Fallengard. As they left the city's domed wall, Sakona spied Lemuk in the distance.

"We'd fair better in my brig."

"There's no time," said Rellen."

"I'm worried about her. We've been away for too long."

"As soon as we land," said Rellen, "I can send someone to fetch it for you."

"I don't trust anyone else to sail her."

"We cannot delay," said Rellen. "Don't worry, I'll send our best sailors."

"You better."

"Rellen, tell us more about Alfex," said Jay. "Is he sick?"

"Alfex is dying. He's sick, and no one can find the cause. But I have a clue. Before the civil war, when we lived in Fallengard, I caught Alfex leaving our monastery in the dead of night. I followed him, worried for his safety. I silently tracked him through the city. But he hiked down to the underworld and I dared not follow him.

"He repeated this ritual many times over many nights, and each time he seemed to grow worse. He looked sour and restless, as though he were poisoned. Soon after, he ordered the Lords to make foolish laws—the laws you heard Overlord Cren speak of. The civil war began.

"When you spoke of a hidden monster who works from the shadows, the Kan'zi, it all made sense. I believe Alfex might have found a Kan'zi in those caves, and it poisoned him, somehow."

"If that's the case, we can help," said Jay.

"Rellen, why did you stay with Padea?" asked Sakona. "What made you think you'd find help there?"

"It wasn't my choice. Other mystics had already spread throughout the main parts of the city, looking for help. I never thought I would find anything of worth in the dim district, but fate, it seems, was kind to me."

"So what's Alfex like? Besides sick," said Jay.

"He's a mighty man, a legend, a prophet. He's the noblest man you'll ever meet. He started our order of mystics to pursue

Virtue."

"Virtue! That's something we're taught in the League," said Perl.

Rellen smiled. "Then we are like siblings in the war for good. Virtue, as you know, is the height of goodness. It is order, justice, mercy, peace, and love wrapped all in one. Before he became sick, Alfex was all those things."

Sakona steered the Dalk south, down Fallengard's dome. Not far off, they saw three mountains shrouded in a pale haze. They sailed closer, toward the tallest peak. On it lay a peculiar village; the homes, streets, even benches were carved out of the mountain's marble. It was a village of pure white rock.

They landed on a cliff near the town and left the ship. The cold air chilled their bones. Only Rellen seemed unfazed.

"Welcome to our first monastery. Alfex is in that sanctuary." She pointed to a large building up the mountain that overlooked the town. It was a perfect block, with no windows or style. The other buildings had much more finesse to them. The block was the oldest building in the monastery.

As they moved through the town, Jay noted how bare it was. It was pale and empty. He hadn't seen such an empty place since he left his own home on Onaga. But the many mystics who seemingly soared through the town looked anything but empty. Each was tall, thin, and fair, like Rellen, with impeccable red robes.

But despite their unusual look, the mystics were Arlish. Legends say their oldest ancestors came from a land beyond Arland in the west, a country called Reathen.

Rellen stopped a younger Mystic in the street and told him, "Take an airship, a crew, and find this young lady's brig on Lemuk."

Sakona carefully described the Rogue and where she left it.

"If it comes back with so much as a scratch, you'll be sorry."

The man jolted upright, saluted Sakona, and dashed away.

They came to a long staircase carved in the mountain's side and followed it to Alfex's sanctuary, the block house. For Sakona's sake, they climbed slow—her leg, though healing, still pained her on stairs and slopes. At the top of the stairs, they faced the block house, which sat in the center of a perfectly cut, square plane. The only item of note was a thinly-etched path that led to the block's side.

Once there, they found a humble archway that declared the center of the cube, which turned out to be a courtyard. A single tree with deep red leaves grew out of the earth. From the courtyard, Rellen showed Jay, Perl, Sakona, and Loosha down a short hall and into a bare, dark room.

In the room lay a single large bed and in it lay a small old man. He was frail. A few white hairs drooped from his bald head. Brown spots and sores spangled his scalp and face. His boney hands and long nails clutched his blanket. His large blue eyes were lowly and sad. Jay took one look at the man and felt absolute pity. Gazing over his pale wrinkled skin and ghostly face, Jay knew this man, Alfex, was truly three hundred years old.

"Alfex," said Rellen, "these children have something to share with you."

With her help, Alfex sat up in his bed and gazed at Jay, Perl, and Sakona. They told him of their quest: the secret war, the League, the sandstorm sea, and of the Kan'zi. They explained that a Kan'zi Temple lay somewhere in Fallengard, and they aimed to destroy it. Alfex did not at all seem surprised. He nodded gently as they spoke.

"So you see, Alfex," said Rellen, "perhaps this Kan'zi is the cause of your sickness! We've lived with a monster all these years and didn't know it! If we help these children defeat the beast, perhaps you'll heal. What do you think? Have you seen such a beast before?"

"I know of the Kan'zi." Alfex's voice was hollow, like wind passing through a log.

"You do?" said Jay, but that was to be polite. He was not surprised.

Alfex nodded. "I was born many years ago in the caves of Fallengard. My people fled there to escape the sandstorm sea. They told me all about the old world, before the sand. But I could never imagine it. All I knew was the cave.

"One day, a few of my kin explored the Black Fissure. They came back changed—they feared each other and us, like we were hiding something. They were paranoid. They turned on us and tried to kill us. And their fear seemed to infect the others, like a disease—no one was safe. I remember my own mother chasing after me, trying to…"

Tears dripped from his wrinkled eyes. But he paused, took a breath, and continued, "When the massacre ended, I led the survivors out of the cave and into the sandstorm sea. We found this mountain—a true miracle. We climbed and made ourselves a new home, far from the terrors below. But my people were filled with strife and worry. Memory of the cave haunted them.

"So, I preached of love and peace. They called me a prophet, a mystic. They felt at peace, but I never did. For I had forgotten something, we all had: a very important word. It's like force or power, but something else. Without it, I knew we could never be complete.

"Years later, I returned to Fallengard. They had heard of me by then and sought my council on all things. They even had me appoint their Lords. But no matter how much power I had, I still worried. I had them build walls and raise an army, but it wasn't enough."

"What exactly were you afraid of?" asked Sakona.

"The Black Fissure. I grew old and close to death. One night, I left my quarters and found that terrible place. It haunted me since my childhood. I wanted to face my past, but it only made things worse."

"I found the temple you seek. I met a Kan'zi. Her name was Erlek. She was so hideous and evil—her minions readied to kill me. But I think she saw my terror, for then she offered me something: eternal life, if only I did whatever she asked. I agreed.

"For the next two hundred years, she used me to rule Fallengard. I was her puppet. Before her, it was a friendly country. Now the people are paranoid, like my kin used to be. She forced me to build the walls higher and wage war on Lemuk and Elos. She's spread evil and terror throughout the Blue Sea. And this civil war is her master stroke."

"How?" said Perl. "What's her plan?"

"Fallengard is the only country strong enough to keep order in the Blue Sea. This civil war will destroy it and any hope of peace. And I mean that literally! Have you felt the earthquakes? The mines grow more fragile every day. Soon, they will collapse, and with them, the country."

"How could you let this happen!?" said Rellen. "You've betrayed our order—you've given yourself to evil!"

Alfex raised his hand, asking for pity. "I feared death. I didn't have the power to face it when it came. Instead, I made a selfish choice and doomed our world."

"Alfex," said Jay, stepping forward. "That word, the word you've forgotten, is courage."

Alfex gasped. Another tear dropped from his blue eyes and rolled down his cheek. "Yes. I remember it now. For all these years, we've lived without it. And how can we face evil without courage? Somehow, Erlek must have hidden that word from us."

"That explains why Fallengard is so… afraid," said Sakona.

"Alfex," said Perl, "how did she keep you alive for this long?"

"She used a great, red power on me. She shocked it into my bones. But see how it's left me: alive, yes, but falling apart. She lied to me. My death can't be stopped now."

"Red Vitex," said Jay.

Suddenly, Alfex threw aside his blanket and rose to his feet. His legs wobbled and he leaned on Rellen for help.

"It's time we set things right. Erlek has tortured me all my life. Now she must be stopped. Bring me to the village."

Slowly, they helped Alfex out of his sanctuary, down the long, stone stairs, and to the village square. His Mystics flocked around him, awed to see him out of bed.

"My friends, my loyal friends," he said. "I've done a terrible thing. I gave up my will to a dark creature, a beast in the heart of Fallengard. She is Erlek—a Kan'zi Superior. This is why I've lived so long. This is why I'm sick and dying now.

"Find your courage. Yes, remember courage! It is the force that fights fear. A power of will, the might to act in the face of terror. Friends, forgive me and help this heroic trio destroy that monster."

His strength left him. He fell into Rellen's arms.

"Rellen, you must succeed me. Lead the Mystics and save the Blue Sea." Alfex inhaled. He knew his end was near. His eyes trembled with fear. Suddenly, he smiled, whispering to himself, "Courage. Courage. Courage."

Alfex breathed his last. Rellen clutched him tight as the Mystics mourned their fallen seer.

"Now we know where the temple is," said Perl. "Kal pointed out the Black Fissure to us on our way to the coliseum. What's our next move?"

"Why don't we hold off on that," said Jay, looking at the

mourning mystics. "Just for a moment."

But they heard someone new approaching. Peering past the crowd of mystics, Jay saw Elska marching toward them.

Chapter XXVI

UNEXPECTED ALLIES

Jay, Perl, and Sakona drew their swords.

"Rellen, watch out!" said Jay. "That woman is with the Kan'zi!"

Rellen and her Mystics turned to face her, but Elska put her hands in the air, as if to surrender. She came to the front of the mass and faced Jay and his friends.

"I just want to speak with you," she said with easy eyes and a stoic stance.

"Yeah right," snapped Perl.

"What if *we* don't want to speak with *you?*" said Sakona, pointing her blade at Elska. Her hand twitched, ready to strike.

"When you hear what I have to say, you will," Elska stood calm and cool. She let her arms fall to her sides. "I know you're looking for the temple. I'll bring you to it."

"We don't believe you," said Perl. "You're trying to trap us."

Jay looked around to see if any Kan'zi were sneaking by, but he saw none.

Sakona stepped toward Elska, raising her blade ever higher. "You want to kill us." But Elska didn't flinch.

Jay felt different from his friends. He thought back to when Elska destroyed the Hearth: seeing Metrarch, she stopped her attack. Her face was full of sadness, anger, and pain. Jay knew she was more than a monster. "How can we know you're telling the truth?"

"She's not!" said Perl. "Jay, she killed Wald!"

"And my father," said Sakona, grinding her teeth. Her grip tightened around her sword.

"I understand your point," said Elska. "So, I'll give you a truth to prove my good will. The temple belongs to Erlek, the Kan'zi Superior of Fear."

"We already knew that," said Perl, crossing her arms.

"Well, not the 'fear' part," shrugged Jay.

Perl rolled her eyes, "Well that part was obvious."

"Well, then, where is the temple?" tested Sakona. Of course, they knew it was in the Black Fissure, but Elska didn't know that they knew. Sakona hoped to catch Elska in a lie.

"In the Black Fissure. But that place is a maze—you'll need my help finding it. Meet me there in three days."

Jay's eyes squinted on Elska, trying to figure her out, "What's in it for you?"

But Elska only smiled again and said, "Three days, meet me there." She strolled away.

Jay and his friends stared as she glided down the village streets. Soon after, they saw her bone-white airship with scarlet sails glide away, down the mountain.

"Who was she?" asked Rellen.

"A witch!" said Perl.

"She works with the Kan'zi," said Jay. "But she used to be good."

"But she wants to help us," said Rellen.

"No. She's probably lying," said Perl.

"But she didn't lie about Erlek or the Black Fissure," said Jay.

"What are we to do?" Rellen put her head in her hands. "We

can't trust her, but we must find the temple!"

"We know it's somewhere in the Black Fissure," said Jay. "Maybe we can explore it for ourselves. Maybe we don't need her help."

"No," said Rellen. "The Black Fissure is as she described it—a maze. One wrong turn and you may be lost forever."

"Remember our instructions," said Perl. "We were only supposed to find the location of the temple, then report it to the League. I'd say we've done that."

"Elska only gave us three days," said Jay. "I don't think we can find the League that soon."

"Yes, we can," said Sakona. "Remember the castle we found with Nory Slook? Nory said she would find the League and bring them there. And that's only a day's flight from here."

"Right," said Jay. "Let's go. Then he'll send us back with an army."

"It's settled," said Rellen. "I'll recruit what soldiers I can—though I doubt the Lords will spare me any, since they barely gave us the schooner. I'll see to it that you can reenter Fallengard with ease."

Quick as a wooly gare, Jay and his friends boarded the Rogue. Sakona checked all over the brig for damage while Jay and Perl checked on their egg. It was sitting still, unmoved, and uncracked. With all in order, they set sail for High Alacon—the ruins of the Galleran Kingdom.

Soon, the Mystic Mountains faded into a thin haze. Before them stood a vast stretch of blue swirling sand and heavy gusts of wind. After a full day's flight, they spotted the ruined castle ahead. Several airships were perched on each tower. Among them, Jay spotted Metrarch's flagship.

"Looks like the League made it!" called Jay.

Sakona squeezed the Rogue onto the biggest tower. They

heard a familiar, raspy voice calling for them. Bobo rushed up the Rogue's gangplank to greet them.

"You're alive! And you've returned! Excellent, excellent. That will surely cheer up Metrarch."

"Of course, we're alive," spat Perl.

"Cheer him up? What's wrong?" asked Jay.

"Well, well, we haven't fared too well. We're alive and safe, to be sure. But we haven't found any new members. No one wants to join us."

"Why is that?"

"The Hearth was a special place. All we had to do was bring someone there and at once, they understood the war. Don't get me wrong, this is a great place. Thanks for finding it!"

"What do you mean? This place is special, too," said Jay.

"Well, yes, yes—the crystal cavern is amazing. But it's nothing like our green grass, flower hills, and oh! Of course—the water! We ran out of water a week ago so we're back to drinking greyberry juice. I forgot how awful it tastes."

Bobo took Jay, Perl, Sakona, and Loosha down the tower's winding stairs. They descended slowly, for Sakona's leg still pained her immensely. They entered the throne room and descended again into the castle dungeons. From there, they came to the crystal cavern.

The League completely transformed the cavern. Bold banners which boasted the League's emblem hung from every corner. Pitched tents of varied sizes rested all along the walls; twinkling greens and blues from the cavern's crystals danced along the flowing white fabric. Bonfires were sprinkled throughout, warming the hideout.

Though full of squires and knights, it felt far from lively. A sort of sadness sat over the room. League members meandered throughout the camp, trying to find something to do to occupy their time.

Bobo brought them deeper into the cavern to a small tent, perhaps the smallest in the hideout. Inside, as Jay suspected, they found Metrarch sitting with the Elders, plotting and planning. When he saw Jay and his friends, Metrarch smiled wide, jumped to his feet, and wrapped them each in a big hug.

"Wahoo! You're back. And you're all unharmed!"

"It's good to see you all again," said Jay.

"Have you found another Kan'zi temple?" said Elder Nul.

"Oh, that can wait! I should speak with Jay a bit, first. Come with me, son."

Metrarch brought Jay out of the tent to the edge of the cavern, out of ear shot of the others. There, Metrarch sat upon a large rocky stump and sighed. "It's been difficult here, Jay. Losing the Hearth has made things harder than I thought. It was an oasis, a paradise. Now we're back in the real world—though I think the Hearth was 'realer' if you get my meaning. Arland is hotter and drier than I remembered. I'm trying to keep everyone's spirits up, but it's hard when even mine are sulking."

"Bobo said you've had trouble recruiting new members."

"Yes. Back then, all we had to do was give them a glass of water and they'd join on the spot! It's hard now for newcomers to understand."

"Bobo said you built the first Hearth, dome and all. Can't you do it again?"

"Not by myself. Last time I had help."

"Right, the others from Dovia. Well, all the world can be like the Hearth one day, right?" said Jay, trying his best to comfort Metrarch. "If we destroy the temples and push out the sandy sea?"

"Metrarch's face formed a small smile. "That's right. We need to remember what this world should be, what it could be. I guess it just takes a bit of imagination."

"And this place isn't that bad," shrugged Jay. "It's safe, it's got history…" What Jay was really looking for was a 'thank-you for finding it.' But to his surprise, Metrarch was so somber that he said nothing of the sort.

"This was a special place," said Metrarch, gazing around at the glowing crystals. "In the old days, the Arlo Kai and the Galleran King came here to seek wisdom from Lor Emai. I hoped that by coming here, I might hear his voice, too. But all I've heard is silence."

"He hasn't spoken to you?"

Metrarch sighed and looked down. "Not for a long time. I don't know why he won't speak to me. Especially now! We're so desperate for help."

Jay wanted so badly to report on his quest. He thought it would encourage Metrarch. So, he blurted out: "I don't think so! We found the next temple, so I'd say we're in pretty good shape."

But this hardly turned Metrarch's mood. "You did? Well, let's gather the League. Perhaps your report will rouse our spirits."

They returned to the greater cavern and once all were gathered round a roaring fire, Jay began to speak.

"We've found the next temple. It's in Fallengard's deepest mine, 'the Black Fissure.' It belongs to Erlek the Feared."

The squires and knights cheered. For the first time since the Hearth, they had hope again. For weeks they stayed hidden in a dark hole and many were anxious to see the world again. They wanted to gather their arms and rush out of the cavern right away. Nul spoke to their desire.

"We must prepare for battle," said Elder Nul.

"But we don't have troops to spare," said Elder Traylock.

"We can't afford to lose anyone," said Elder Gern.

With these words, Traylock and Gern chilled the energy of

the room. Jay watched as a hundred heads dropped.

"What?!" said Nul. "The enemy is found—we must strike while we have the chance!"

"Elder Nul," said Metrarch, "if we strike and fail, who will be left to rebuild the League? There are so few of us already."

But Jay had grown frustrated with the council. He and his friends hadn't risked their lives to find this temple only to sit and wait. So, he said, "What are you all so afraid of? We can't wait! Erlek caused a civil war in Fallengard. If we don't stop her now, she'll destroy the country and any hope for peace and order in the Blue Sea."

"I'm sure we have some time to spare," started Sageous, but Jay cut her off.

"No, we don't. The war is waged in Fallengard's mines— more explosions rattle the city every day. We've felt the earthquakes ourselves! Soon the entire city will literally collapse."

"Erlek wouldn't do that," said Traylock. "That would bury the temple!"

"I'm sure Erlek accounted for all of that," said Nul scratching his chin. "The Kan'zi know how to tunnel—they work from the shadows."

Jay was shocked that he and Nul agreed on something, but he welcomed his help, nonetheless.

"Jay," said Metrarch, "we appreciate all you and your friends have done. But right now, I think it's best if we wait and—"

But Jay knew this wasn't about numbers. For some reason, Metrarch and the elders were afraid. "Have courage! Last time I was here, I had a vision from Lor Emai. He told me to—"

"Lor Emai spoke to you?" said Metrarch with a mighty frown. "That can't be."

"If he hasn't spoken to the League Master," said Gern, "He certainly wouldn't speak to a squire."

"He *did* speak to me. He told me to have courage even when it's hard, even when it hurts."

"Perhaps it wasn't Lor Emai," wondered Traylock aloud. "Perhaps it was a Kan'zi!"

At this, Jay threw his hands in the air and said, "You know what? We don't need your help. Elska offered to help us. She wants to lead us to Erlek's temple. Maybe she'll prove to be a better ally than you all."

"It's a trap," snapped Metrarch. "She'll try to kill you."

"But we have friends in Fallengard," said Perl, "they can help us fight."

"I forbid you from going. I forbid all of you from going. We will gather more troops and strike in a few weeks." With sullen strides, Metrarch left the crowd and returned to his tiny tent.

Jay, Perl, Sakona and Loosha walked and waddled away from the League. They found a lone corner in the cave and sat with their heads in their hands.

"I guess we'll have to wait," said Perl.

"Without their help, I don't think we can win," added Sakona.

But Jay wasn't ready to give up. "This is ridiculous. It's exactly what Erlek wants. She's the Kan'zi of fear, right? She wants us to sit here and be scared stiff! Look—we've got Rellen and her Mystics. We know exactly where Erlek's temple is, and we have friends to help us. We've got to try something!"

"But what about Elska? And the trap?" asked Perl.

"Yeah, about her… I think I've got an idea," said Jay, eyeing Loosha. "But my point is, with some help, I think we can win this."

"Croark!"

"With Loosha's help, of course," laughed Perl.

Bobo bumbled into their gathering. He had tip-toed behind

them and heard everything. Jay and his friends gasped, thinking he would report them to Metrarch. To their surprise, Bobo grinned.

"So, you're going to fight? Excellent, excellent. Elder Wald would be proud." Jay smiled. "You're going to need all the help you can get. Go to the Rogue and make ready to sail!"

They snuck out of the cavern, through the dungeon, out the throne room, and up the castle tower. On the Rogue, Sakona took the helm, Jay angled the sails, and Perl shoveled coal into the engine. Over the guard-rail climbed squires and knights armed for battle—twelve in total. Next, came Mackie Slook and his democratic crew of ten. They boasted of their unanimous vote to help Jay and his friends. Bobo, too, plopped on the deck.

"Excellent, excellent. Let's go!"

But someone else climbed onboard: Elder Nul, with his famous frown and furrowed brows. He sucked the cheeky joy off the boat. The grumpy Elder peered at his squires and knights. His eyes landed on Jay and squinted tight.

"It seems you'll need a general. Count me in."

The team smiled and cheered.

Jay nodded to his new ally. "Welcome aboard."

Jay let loose the sails and Sakona helmed the brig toward Fallengard.

Chapter XXVII

BATTLE FOR FALLENGARD

The Rogue sailed on until evening. When night fell, Mackie cooked and served boiled krusk to the crew, only after a long and elaborate vote. The vessel was too packed for everyone to eat in the mess hall, so Jay elected to take Perl and Sakona on deck. They sat by the helm and ate their crunchy meat.

Though they tried to start a conversation, nothing stuck. They were too nervous. Jay kept thinking of how Alfex described Erlek, searching the story for a clue on how to defeat her, but he couldn't find any. It only made him more afraid.

Finally, Sakona broke the silence with a strange question. "How do you forgive someone?"

"I don't know," said Jay. "I just kind of do it. I remind myself that what they did wasn't a big deal, anyway."

"But what if it *was* a big deal?"

"For me," said Perl. "It takes time. My own mother kicked me out when I was little. Things were normal when my dad was alive—he and my mom were so kind. But when he died, my mom started to go crazy. She started throwing out old furniture, saying it reminded her of him. She fired our servants and hired new ones. Finally, it was my turn to leave."

"That's terrible," said Sakona.

"Yeah. But it helps to remember what good came from it. That's the day I met Jay."

"Really?"

"I was in my parent's field, crying. I had no idea what to do with myself."

"I was working there as an extra hand," said Jay. "I saw Perl and asked if she was okay. She told me what happened, so we ran away together and made our own home."

"So maybe try that," said Perl. "Think about the good that came from it."

"You're talking about Elska?" said Jay.

Sakona nodded. "It's easy to forgive her now, when she's far away. But every time I see her, I think of my father. And it fills me with so much hate. There was something good that came from it, though. If my father hadn't died, I guess I wouldn't have grown so close to you two."

For the rest of the night, Jay and Nul planned the attack. They needed Elska to find the temple, but they knew she would betray them. So, Jay designed a plan to dupe Elska, a plan in which he and his friends would be bait.

*   *   *

Fallengard's mines lay dark as night, yet the Black Fissure was somehow darker. Jay, Perl, Sakona and Loosha stood at the gorge alone and waited. They were each fully armed. Jay had his cutlass, his rod-lance, and a vine wrapped around his arm for Vitex fuel. Perl had a vine, too, with her bow and arrow. Sakona wore her sword and shield while Loosha wore nothing but her usual ugly face.

Suddenly, they heard the tap of bootsteps clicking nearby. They drew nearer and nearer until out of the shadows stepped Elska.

"You made it," she whispered in relief. Her twin swords

dangled from her belt and she held a rusty lantern. Jay had never seen her look so uncertain. Elska's usual confidence was replaced with a hesitance. "Come with me."

She began to hike down the gorge and the others followed. Loosha stayed close to Elska—her angry, crossed eyes tracked her every sway. Perl stayed toward the back. Every few steps she let out a pinch of creamy blue sand from her pocket, leaving a trail.

Scaling down the gorge was dangerous. Every few steps, they would drop to a new landing two or three meters lower than the last. There was no railing, and some landings were so narrow it would make your toes tingle.

After descending twenty or so landings, they came to the gorge's base. Elska led them through a series of caves, each splintering off from the last in a random direction. Some were large and tall; others were narrow and short. Jay tried his best to remember the turns, but there were too many to track.

For the entire hike, no one said a word. They worried that by speaking, they might somehow break their fatal truce. All Jay heard was the pitter-patter of their steps and breathing. With every step, Sakona breathed faster and harder. Jay hoped it was because of her wounded leg, not because she was growing angrier.

They came to a stretch of rock with a slim crack. It was as thin as Jay and maybe a bit taller. Elska ducked into the crack and told the others to follow.

But that made them all more nervous than before, for if Elska betrayed them, how could they defend themselves in such a small space? They hesitated. They wished for another way. But with no other choice, they entered the sliver.

To fit through the crack, they entered single file. Loosha went first, followed by Jay, then Sakona, then Perl. The jagged sides scraped Jay's shoulders. His breath quickened as the air turned hotter and the walls wedged closer. The room slimmed to the width of a single boot, so everyone turned sideways and shuffled on. Now the sharp sides scraped Jay's nose and chest and the back of his head. Their feet stepped on each other—there was much kicking and cries of "Stop that!" and "Careful!"

It's amazing how quickly pain and discomfort can turn our moods. Jay seethed in anger. *How long will this go on for? Why would the stupid Kan'zi build their temple in such a ridiculous place?*

Finally, the narrow cave widened into a larger space, too large for the torch to light its end. Elska stopped.

"The temple is there," she whispered, pointing down the widened cave, into the shadows.

Jay, Perl, and Sakona held up their weapons—they thought that Elska's reinforcements might jump out of the shadows and attack them.

"Don't worry, they don't know we're here," said Elska. "You can never tell them I helped you. You can't or they'll kill me. Promise me."

Jay looked at her, puzzled. Many thoughts raced through his mind. Maybe she was genuinely helping them and the Kan'zi only forced her to join them. Or maybe she only said those things so they'd let their guard down.

"We promise."

Elska turned to leave but stopped, "By the way, I know that you told your froad to paralyze me if I made a false move—and I know that you're not alone." She nodded at Jay, impressed. She turned again to leave.

But Sakona's hand tightened around her sword. She wanted so badly to strike Elska, but she pulled her blade back, trying to stop herself. Her boots twitched back and forth, as if her anger was escaping her body through her feet. She took a deep breath and calmed down.

Elska noticed this. She smiled with pride and said, "Good choice, kid."

And that was the last straw. Sakona swung with all her might, but Jay grabbed her hand and yanked her back, letting Elska slip into the darkness. Her bootsteps echoed away.

"Jay, let go of me!"

"Quiet," whispered Perl, "We don't want them to hear us."

"Sakona," said Jay, "you have to try—remember what we talked about."

Sakona took a deep breath and relaxed. "You're right, I'm sorry."

Perl drew a small flake of Vitex from her vine to light their way. They crept down the cave until they found a black, stone wall. It stood far higher than Rone's temple, and it boasted a wide, iron gate.

A slim whisper of wind slipped through the air and sounded a hollow tune. A wicked voice screeched from within the temple.

"How did you find my domain?"

The gate opened. A thick, black fog oozed out. Through the shroud, Jay saw a horrid monster—a Kan'zi. Her clawed feet dug into the ground below. Her purple scales and feathers were sharp as blades. Her crooked back arched toward the floor. Her yellow teeth fanged from her jaw. Her green eyes glowed through the fog. She was Erlek the Feared. By her side stood more Kan'zi. They were smaller than Erlek, and had no shroud, but still looked cunning and deadly.

Erlek cackled, "Kill them."

Her Kan'zi minions rushed at Jay and his friends. In moments, Jay, Perl, and Sakona would be swallowed whole by a legion of monsters. But as the Kan'zi surrounded them, a blazing light scorched the air. The Kan'zi flinched away, covering their green eyes with their claws. The cave filled with a wave of Gold

Vitex that crashed down on Erlek's minions, washing them back against the black stone walls of Erlek's temple. Many would never stand again.

Behind Jay stood an army. Nul, Bobo, and the others from the League—each wearing royal, wooden armor and white sashes—cast their golden power at the monsters. By their side stood Padea and her farmers with satchels full of hickelberries for Vitex fuel. Before them lay two scores of Mystics, led by Rellen. Trained in the martial arts, they held staffs and simple weapons that proved deadly in the hands of a master. Beside them was Mackie and his pirates, with cutlasses and bows and arrows.

Nul held up a silver broadsword that glimmered in the light of the army's gold vitex. He pointed the shimmering blade to the temple: "Attack!"

Jay's army roared and rushed forward. But Kan'zi minions poured out of the temple and met the army. Red and Gold Vitex zapped and flourished through the air. Swords and claws slashed and cut. The Battle for Fallengard began.

Jay, Perl, Sakona, and Loosha fled from the temple entrance and joined the army. Jay stood back-to-back with Sakona—slashing his lance at the evil beasts. Sakona bashed the Kan'zi with her shield. Perl perched herself away and fired her arrows. Loosha dashed about the battlefield, shooting her tongue this way and that, paralyzing the enemy.

But Erlek barked an order from her gate. A hundred more minions gushed into the battle. They sprinted around the army to try and flank it. But Nul saw their advance and ordered the army to charge right and cover their flank.

Enraged, Erlek fired a grand bolt of Red Vitex across the field, more lustrous and gigantic than Jay had ever seen. He despaired, thinking the battle would end in moments. But Nul cast out a shield of Gold Vitex, equal in size to Erlek's attack. The two forces collided. Sparks and fractals raced across the room. The shield was gone, but the army was saved.

The battle raged on. Though the Kan'zi outnumbered Jay's army two to one, the Arlish seemed to have the upper hand. The Kan'zi fought with only claws and Red Vitex. But the Arlish had swords, shields, lances, bows, arrows, staffs, and Gold Vitex.

Jay smiled, thinking they might win the day! But the temple gate was drawing shut. Erlek had retreated into the temple.

"Perl, Sakona, we've got to get in there! We can't let Erlek escape!"

Perl drew a heap of Vitex from her vine and formed a thick wedge like a battering ram. Jay and Sakona followed Perl as she dashed through the battle, smashing a slew of Kan'zi. They came to the gate just in time. As it pressed near the ground, Jay, Perl, and Sakona slid underneath. It slammed shut behind them.

Chapter XXVIII

THE TEMPLE OF FEAR

The noise of the battle outside still echoed, but it was quieter, muffled. They stood in the temple's grand foyer and found it dark, still, and empty. A harrowing chandelier hung from a black, domed roof. It swayed back and forth, drifting light and shadow across the creepy, cracked floor. Dozens of pillars held the ceiling high, but they were warped and unkept. In the dimly lit room, they looked like skeletons.

As Jay and his friends glanced about the foyer, they saw many passages split off into the unknown. They couldn't see far, for dust and white sand swirled around the room, creating a thick and bitter fog.

"Our best bet is to find the throne room," said Jay as he studied the paths, reading the scratchy symbols above each port.

"What do they say?" said Perl, since only Jay could read the Kan'zi language.

"They're riddles," said Jay, staring at one passage with a path that sloped down. "This one says, 'Out of light and out of sight, here we keep those who do right.'"

"We can't waste any time," said Sakona. "Let's just pick a way and go!"

"Wait! I can do this," said Perl. She paced back and forth,

scratching her head with one hand and gesturing with her left. "For Erlek, people who are good are bad, and people who are bad are good. So, people who do right are actually wrong. And people who do wrong… go to a dungeon!"

"Works for me," said Jay, scurrying to the next passage. "What about this one, Perl? 'Best of my stewards, rich and toothy foes he skewers.'"

"That's easy! Rich and toothy are flavors; it's talking about a chef. That way is to the kitchen."

"Okay, but that doesn't help us," said Sakona.

"Here's another one," said Jay, coming to the darkest passage with a straight and narrow hall. "It says, 'Seated by great red fires, here shall I order my desires.' Sounds like the dining hall to me."

"Maybe not," said Perl, pacing again. "Maybe it's the throne room! Maybe she's making commands, not ordering food."

Jay pursed his lips in thought. "Sakona, what do you think."

"Perl hasn't been wrong so far and we're running out of time. I say we go."

"Agreed," said Jay.

They started down the slim, black hall. To light their way, Perl conjured a pinch of Vitex from her vine. Even so, the way was too dark. They each stumbled over cracks and bumps in the stony floor.

Suddenly, a sharp scream sounded from above. They gasped and looked around. A feint blue light streaked across the ceiling from an unknown window, but there was no hint of movement. Soon, all was silent again.

"What was that?!" shrieked Perl.

"That was terrifying," said Sakona.

"Exactly," said Jay. "Remember, we're in the temple of fear. She's trying to scare us."

"It's working… a little," said Perl.

"We've got to fight our fears," said Jay, trying to encourage his friends. "And what fights fear?"

"Courage," said Sakona.

"Right," said Jay. "So, let's be brave and keep moving."

Soon they reached the end of the hall which spilled into a wider space. Smoke filled the room, thicker than greyberry steam. It was so thick, Jay and his friends couldn't see past their own hands, let alone the room itself.

"We can't go in there," said Perl.

"We have to," said Jay.

"But we can't see! Anything could be in there. Anything!"

A terror crept up Jay's spine. Perl was right. They had no idea what evils awaited them. He stepped away from the door and searched for another path but found nothing. The only way forward was through the unknown room.

He wanted to embolden himself and his friends, but he didn't know how. So, Sakona spoke up, saying "Well, what's the worst that could be in there?"

"A Kan'zi," said Perl. "A lot of them."

"Well," started Sakona, "isn't that the whole reason we came here? To find the Kan'zi?"

"Good point," said Jay. Suddenly, he felt much braver, for 'something' is much less scary than 'anything.' Together, they linked arms and entered the room.

They inched their way through the haze, listening and watching closely. But to their great surprise, they reached the end of the room unharmed and passed out of the smoke.

After a sigh of relief, they crossed under an archway into the next room. It was long and bare, with a dim red light glowing at its end. But as they stepped in, they noticed that their boot steps no longer echoed. Instead, they creaked. They found themselves standing on wooden boards, not stone.

Jay realized what this meant, but before he could speak, the floor beneath them broke. He tumbled and rumbled through the floor until he landed in a pile of splintered wood.

He was in a bare hallway with white stones. It was terribly long and narrow, so narrow that two people could not stand side by side. Jay tried to spot his friends, but they were nowhere to be seen. He was alone.

Again, terror crept up his spine. Fighting Kan'zi wasn't so bad with friends by his side, but alone, it seemed a much scarier thing. He called out for Perl and Sakona, but the only thing he heard was his own echo. Standing up, he searched the area for a way out. Rather than one clear path, he saw several. He was in a maze. Slim, twisted paths curved in all sorts of directions.

Jay felt hopeless. He thought he might be trapped forever. At his most lonely, he heard a feint whisper calling his name. He felt a warmth float by. He had heard and felt this all before—it was Lor Emai.

Jay was amazed. His mouth opened, his heart beat fast, and his knees shook, filled with fear. But this was a different sort of fear, a good kind of fear. Lor Emai was so great that it was somehow right to fear him. And yet, Jay wanted to draw closer to him. This filled Jay with both joy and wonder, "How are you here?"

But Lor Emai didn't answer. Instead, his whisper and warmth floated away. Jay followed the voice and warmth, chasing them down a path with many turns and bends. It led him up a staircase and out of the maze. He now stood at the far end of the room he started in, next to a leather door with a beaming red torch. At once, the voice and warmth vanished, but Jay was not alone, for Perl and Sakona stood waiting for him.

After they embraced, Jay learned that both Perl and Sakona had taken similar journeys—tumbling into a maze alone, but following a whisper and warmth to its end. With new joy and courage, they readied to move on, drawing near to the glossy door.

"This must be the throne room," said Jay. "Get ready."

But as he put his hand on the doorknob, he fell to the ground in pain. His hand burned. It felt like he grabbed a pure ember and couldn't let go. As he lay on the floor, wailing in pain, he saw a vision: flashes of Erlek casting Red Vitex at Perl and Sakona, swarming them in her power. But the vision ended as quickly as it came.

"Jay!" Sakona rushed to his aid. "What's wrong?!"

"Are you okay?" Perl took his hand and helped him sit up.

"I don't know." The pain faded, but his hand trembled all the same.

Jay remembered his vision in the crystal cavern—the vision Lor Emai sent. The memory gave him no new moral or lesson. But having faced the fear before, he felt ready to face it now. He rose to his feet and kicked open the door.

They entered Erlek's throne room. It was filled with boney altars, weathered chests, and pale urns. High, skeletal columns held the arched roof. Torches blazed around the room, flickering black shadows along floor. Unlike Rone's temple, Erlek's Vitex factory and throne room were one in the same. Enormous stone mills churned while steel saws swiped and slashed. Pipes and tubes pumped out thick, hot steam.

Beyond that, beyond all the chaos and terror, were ten Kan'zi minions. Looming over them was Erlek. She sat on her tall, iron throne shrouded by the dark fog.

Jay whispered, "Erlek's on the throne. Do you see that fog?"

The girls nodded. Jay held his rod-lance tight. Sakona rose her shield. Perl drew her bow.

"You should leave while you still can," bellowed Erlek. "I have a thousand more minions ready to slash you and your army to bits!"

Jay felt Perl and Sakona waiver, but he stood strong, "That's the best you've got?"

"What?!" croaked Erlek.

"You're lying. I take it you're not the Kan'zi Superior of Lies, since that was pretty lame." Erlek laughed, but it sounded forced. "You're trying to scare us, but I see through you. Tough luck."

Erlek stepped off her throne. She waved her claws, casting aside her shroud. Jay, Perl, and Sakona stared at the terrifying creature: her back arched, hanging low like a hook. Her yellow teeth glittered in the room's red light. Her triangular green eyes locked on Jay. She snarled.

"Maybe so, but there is a real thing that you fear. It's something all Arlish fear. Death!"

She cast a red bolt at Jay. He leapt aside, dodging her Vitex just in time. He, Perl, and Sakona took cover behind a large altar.

Erlek shrieked, "Seize them!"

Her minions crawled toward their prey. But Perl leapt atop the altar, summoned a heap of Vitex, and blasted it at the charging Kan'zi. Her power smashed five into the air. She slipped back down, behind the altar.

"Five down… I think. But I'm almost out of fuel."

"I've got some," said Jay. "Sakona, take down those minions. Perl and I will take Erlek."

At Jay's command, they dashed out of cover. Sakona ran with her sword and shield drawn. She charged into the mob of minions and slashed with speed. Jay and Perl tucked behind the room's columns. Perl drew Vitex from the rest of her vine and hurled it at Erlek.

But the creature cast out her own power to meet Perl's. The energy met and exploded. Erlek cackled.

"That's all I've got," said Perl.

"Take some of mine!"

Jay ripped his vine in half and tossed it to Perl. But Sakona was overwhelmed. She slayed two, but the other three circled her.

Jay drew the rest of his Vitex. It was only a handful, but he hurled it at the minions with all his might. It struck one, blasting him into a column. Jay ran to Sakona's aid and struck another Kan'zi with his lance. Together, they battled the last monster and won.

"Help!" called Perl.

Jay saw Erlek fire another bolt. Perl used her last vine to cast out a shield, saving her life. But Erlek readied another strike. Perl had no cover and Jay had no fuel. Perl put her hands over her eyes, submitting to a horrifying fate.

Jay knew there was only one way to save Perl. He thought of Captain Zye and Wald. He trembled. He knew it would hurt. He thought of Sakona. He wavered. He knew it would hurt *her*.

He wanted to save Perl, but he couldn't move. His body froze in terror, afraid of pain, afraid of death. But he thought of Perl again. The moment he stopped thinking of himself and started thinking of Perl, his body was freed.

With incredible courage, he put his fingers to his chest. Sweat dripped down his face, passing his eyes like tears.

Seeing him, Sakona shouted, "Jay, no!"

Jay pushed his shaking hands forward and pointed at Erlek. He felt a fiery sting, shocking from his chest. It was hotter than anything he had ever felt. The burn swelled and coursed into his hands. His Vitex was leaving his body.

The Vitex blinded Jay. He saw only a glare, but he could feel the power race out of his fingertips. Suddenly, he felt cold. Then he felt nothing at all.

Chapter XXIX

THE POWER OF VITEX

The room lit up with Jay's energy. It zapped across the stone floor and struck Erlek. She shrieked in pain. She floundered, shouting and wailing. Stumbling back and forth, she fought for her life. She gasped her last breath of air, falling to the black stone floor. Erlek was dead.

Jay collapsed. His eyes closed and his face went blue.

Sakona and Perl rushed to him. Sakona held his body and put her hand on his chest. She searched for his heartbeat, but felt nothing.

"There must be something we can do! Perl, what can we do?"

But Perl stared at Jay in utter shock.

"I can't lose anyone else. Jay, please!" Sakona held Jay's head, begging him to come back. But he didn't move. Jay was gone.

Sakona burst into tears while Perl sat beside her with a blank stare. They hardly noticed Nul enter the room with the army. They won the battle, but when they saw Jay, they kneeled in respect. Loosha waddled up and sulked. Her stump tail sagged as she rested her fat chin on Jay's belly.

A single spark of Vitex floated out of Nul's wooden armor. It drifted across the room and hovered above Jay. A spark left

Bobo's armor and joined Nul's.

"Who's doing that?" sniffled Sakona.

"No one," said Nul. "I've never seen anything like this."

Vitex flaked from all over the room—out of armor and weapons. Soon, a shining golden orb formed. It hung in the air, glowing more and more radiant. When it was nearly too bright to bear, it splashed onto Jay. The Vitex sank into his body. Perl, Sakona, and the army stared. The silent room held its breath.

Jay's eyes opened. The warm Vitex flowed from his chest to the rest of his cold body. He felt each limb coming to life again. He twitched his shoulders, then, arms, then hands, then fingers. He felt better and stronger than ever before, like the first time he drank water. He sat up and took in a deep breath of life. The army cheered as Sakona and Perl wrapped him in a hug.

"What happened?" asked Jay.

"You saved my life and killed Erlek!" said Perl.

"Did I… was I gone?"

Sakona nodded; she couldn't choke out any words. She was still crying—her tears turning from sadness to joy.

"Then, how am I still here?"

"Hold that question," said Nul, stepping forward. "We've still got to destroy this place."

"Yes," said Jay, rising to his feet. "Bobo, lend me some fuel."

"Wait, are you okay to do that?" asked Perl.

"Yeah. Actually, I feel great. Really great!"

"Excellent, excellent," said Bobo, leaning forward. "Take what you need."

Jay stretched his legs into a combat stance. He aimed his pointer and middle fingers to Bobo's armor. Next, he lifted his palms up toward the ceiling. Out of Bobo's armor flowed a stream of Vitex—greater than he had ever summoned before. Sakona and Perl gasped as Jay composed the Vitex into a masterful strike which shattered the factory.

With the temple destroyed, Jay, his friends, and his army rose out of the Black Fissure and returned to Fallengard. They came to the imperial harbor, which lay in the twilight of the Bright District. Airships by the hundreds, of all shapes and sizes, narrowly lined the dark wooden dock. Gardish sailors watched as Jay and his victorious force marched down the pier. The Gardish had no idea that the rag-tag gathering of men and women before them had saved their city and their lives.

Jay wanted them to know. He wanted to shake their souls awake with the thrilling details of the war he waged for their sakes. But, he knew that Rellen would soon share the truth with the whole country.

They came at last to the Noble Rogue. Her thick brown hull and brilliant blue sails warmed Jay's heart. But he also felt sad, for he would now part ways with a few dear friends.

Rellen drew forward to say her goodbye first. "Jay, you've done a great thing. You and your friends saved the Blue Sea! We are in your debt."

"Thanks, Rellen. You fought pretty well for an old lady."

"And you, for a young boy."

As the mystic bowed and walked away, Elder Nul came next. "I'll stay here for a time. I'll work with Rellen and the Sanctum of Lords to ensure the civil war ends and Fallengard learns to trust each other again."

"Wait a minute—you want me to explain this to Metrarch by myself?"

Elder Nul smiled and said, "I don't think it will be quite so challenging as you think. Tell him that I'll come as soon as I'm able. Also, I think I'll invite the Mystics to join the League. They're strong fighters and we have a lot in common. What do you think?"

"That's a great idea."

"I must admit, Jay," said Nul, "I had many doubts about you. But today, you proved yourself a true member of the League."

Finally, Padea shyly came forward. "Oh, Jay. We lost a few good farmers."

Jay frowned with Padea. "I'm sorry to hear that."

"Don't be. When we first met you, you taught us how to fight with honor. Today we learned how to die with honor." She curtsied and said, "I'm so proud to know you. You've changed my life more than once."

Jay, Perl, and Sakona waved farewell to their friends. They boarded the Rogue, followed by Bobo, a handful of League members, Mackie Slook, and his democratic crew. Sakona ordered the engines warmed. The propellors churned, the vessel lifted off the dock, and the Noble Rogue sailed out of Fallengard's domed wall.

Leaving behind the dark and chilled city, they were bathed in a wave of heat and sunshine. Most retreated below deck to keep cool, but Jay stayed above, gazing out at the blue sandstorm swirling below.

The Blue Sea had already begun to sink. Jay imagined that soon, the sand of all the southern world would fade. Trees and forests and grassy hills would return.

The voyage to High Alacon was to be short since they caught favorable winds. But Jay wished in vain for the winds to change direction or cease altogether. For one, he feared Metrarch. They blatantly disobeyed him—how would he apologize? Should he apologize? And two, he noticed that Sakona barely left his side. That was a welcome surprise, but he worried that once they arrived, she would, for some unknown reason, grow disinterested with him again.

When evening came, Mackie Slook cooked a steaming stew,

served with hickelberry bread. When they received their helping, Jay, Perl, and Sakona moseyed up to the bow.

"Jay," started Perl, "What was it like? Shooting out your own Vitex, and well… you know."

"It was rough. It hurt a lot. But it all happened so fast, I don't remember much. Just a flash of light." Jay rubbed his chest. It still pained him a bit.

"Was it a hard choice to make?"

"To be honest, yeah—at first. But you were in trouble, and that made it easy."

Perl smiled, "Thanks."

"Before this," said Sakona, "I thought that sacrifice was stupid. And even in the temple, when you were gone and I was holding you, I still felt that way. But I understand it now. I don't like it, but I get it."

The next day they came to High Alacon. They landed the Rogue atop the castle's widest tower. Immediately, a team of armored knights emerged from below. They wore swords, shields and stone-cold faces. They escorted Jay and his followers through the castle, into the cavern. Metrarch was waiting for them.

The rest of the League gathered around to hear Jay's testimony. Jay did his best to relay the events, but it was all serious business. He stumbled and fumbled a few times, but he made it through all right. It didn't help that Metrarch was so silent and stern.

Jay concluded, "We fought Erlek and I used my own Vitex to slay her. I was… gone. But then, somehow, I came back."

Bobo stepped up, "It was amazing, amazing! Vitex flowed out of our armor on its own. It rushed into Jay and revived him."

Metrarch scratched his chin.

"Do you know how that happened?" asked Perl.

The League Master silently shook his head. He hadn't spoken aloud since they arrived.

"So," continued Jay, "we destroyed the temple and defeated Erlek—which is pretty great and all. But we're sorry we disobeyed you."

"No, I'm sorry," said Metrarch in a low voice. "I should have had more courage." After a long sigh and a few paces this way and that, Metrarch said, "Lor Emai spoke to you?"

Jay nodded.

Metrarch sighed, "I should have believed you. I should have rejoiced that he spoke to anyone at all, not envied the fact he didn't choose me. I thought he gave up on us. I lost my faith, but you restored it, Jay." Metrarch faced the rest of the League. "We must celebrate this victory and these heroes! Thanks to them, we can hope again."

That night, the League hosted a great feast. They cleaned and themed every corner of the castle. Illustrious green banners dangled in each hall. Scarlet streamers fluttered across wooden beams. Glistening torches bathed the stone in gold. Music and dancing feet echoed from the cavern to the tallest tower. High Alacon had not seen a feast as grand since the King on High sat on his throne.

Jay, Perl, Sakona, and Loosha ate in the throne room, but midway through their meal, Jay saw Metrarch climb the winding stairs of the tallest tower. He followed the League Master and found him on the roof, gazing out at the waning ocean. Jay joined him in silence for a time.

"So, what do you think? About Elska helping us?"

Metrarch sighed. "I'm as confused by it as you. It could mean anything. At best, she's turning back to good. At worst... perhaps she only hated Erlek and wanted us to destroy her."

"They might have hated each other?"

"Evil is like that—they're divided and cruel. Good is united and whole, but evil is fractured and torn by hate and deceit. It's possible she wanted Erlek out of the way for some other scheme of hers."

Jay nodded and thought for a while longer. He asked, "Metrarch, why am I alive? Why did that Vitex revive me?"

"Now there's a mystery." Metrarch took long strides back and forth while scratching his chin. "Nature will only grant herself to those who prove to be her friend. I suppose your sacrifice showed that your heart was pure. And now, it seems, you can bend more Vitex."

"But that didn't happen when Wald died. Do you think it might ever happen again?"

"That's a fair thought. No, I don't think so. I would caution you from trying it again! Remember, nature isn't in our control. We can't fully understand her." Metrarch noticed a black scorch on Jay's upper torso and forearms. "Who was with you when you drew your Vitex?"

"Perl and Sakona. Perl's eyes were covered."

"Hmm. I should like to speak with Sakona soon. She witnessed a scary thing." But changing the subject, Metrarch quickly added, "And dare I say, she seems fond of you!"

Jay blushed, but covered his mouth to keep cool. He pretended to be wiping something from his cheeks. "You think so?"

"Oh, I think so. Be honest and good. Then, what is meant to be will work itself out. It also can't hurt that you're so special."

"Well, feel free to keep talking me up when she's around."

Metrarch laughed. He set his eyes to the horizon again. "Hope is restored. The southern sandstorm sea is fading and with it, the enemy's power. Then the Arlish will rise again."

A few moments later, Perl, Sakona, and Loosha joined them atop the tower. Together, they watched waves crash against the castle, sounding a round of applause. They stared until the wide sky deepened from blue to purple.

They spoke of their adventure thus far: of pirate coves, of secret worlds, of raging yavyu and kruski, of magic, of Kan'zi and Mystics. Jay remembered his home and life on Onaga, but strangely enough, he couldn't recognize either. Not that he couldn't recall those things, but he couldn't recall *himself* in those things. Home felt so distant and his mind was set on the future.

Only a few weeks ago, Jay longed to be free, roaming the seas and seeing the world. Now he had his very own adventure. Though the journey was different than what he expected, he wouldn't have traded it for the world. Plus, the adventure was far from over. There were still five temples to find and a war to wage.

Far off, sprouting on the horizon, hills and branches peeked out of the ocean. The sand had already sank so much that the lands of old were starting to appear again. Jay and his friends spoke of their next adventure. They dreamed of a wider world filled with greens and blues, woods and lakes, hills and seas.

Metrarch moved to the stairwell, ready to return to the feast. But, Perl stopped him and said, "Metrarch, I've been thinking… Lots of special things have happened to Jay lately. Could this all somehow mean that Lor Emai has chosen Jay to be the next Hero of Arland? Could it be that Jay is the Arlo Kai?"

After a long pause, Metrarch sighed and said, "No. The Arlo Kai is Elska."